ALLY SHERRICK

VITA AND THE GLADIATOR

Chicken House

2 PALMER STREET, FROME,
SOMERSET BA11 1DS

Text © Ally Sherrick 2023
Illustration © Nan Lawson 2023

First published in Great Britain in 2023
Chicken House
2 Palmer Street
Frome, Somerset BA11 1DS
United Kingdom
www.chickenhousebooks.com

Chicken House/Scholastic Ireland, 89E Lagan Road, Dublin Industrial Estate, Glasnevin, Dublin D11 HP5F, Republic of Ireland

Cover design and interior design by Steve Wells
Typeset by Dorchester Typesetting Group Ltd
Printed and bound in Great Britain by CPI Group (UK) Ltd, Croydon, CR0 4YY

FSC
www.fsc.org
MIX
Paper | Supporting
responsible forestry
FSC® C171272

1 3 5 7 9 10 8 6 4 2

British Library Cataloguing in Publication data available.

ISBN 978-1-913696-53-5
eISBN 978-1-915026-26-2

For Brendan and Kieran
Kia kaha, Kia māia, Kia manawanui

'SOMEONE, I TELL YOU, IN ANOTHER
TIME WILL REMEMBER US.'

SAPPHO

I

Londinium, Roman Province of Britannia, 125 CE

Vita stood proud in her battle chariot as it thundered towards the Roman lines. She and her army of blue-faced warriors were seriously outnumbered, but she wouldn't yield – not without a fight. She raised her spear and prepared to lead the charge . . .

BANG!

She started and looked up from her desk. The front door – which meant Mother and Lucius had gone at last! A flutter of excitement rippled through her. It was nearly time.

But first, she couldn't resist one final read-through of her poem. As she scanned the neat lines of verse that sloped across the papyrus's creamy-yellow surface, her chest filled with a warm glow of pride. She drew in a breath and read the title out loud:

'*The defeat of Boudicca, the fearsome ruler of the Iceni who burnt Londinium to the ground.*'

It sounded good. Queen Boudicca had been the arch-enemy of the Empire, but still, Vita couldn't help admiring her courage – standing up to the might of the Roman army like that. Taking charge of her own destiny. And Father had said she fought bravely too . . .

She felt a sudden rush of affection. Dear Father! He was the only one in the family who really understood her – her love for reading and telling stories.

A thought flashed into her head. Why not slip into his study and leave her poem as a surprise for when he got back from his meeting at the Forum? Then, if he liked it, she could read it out loud at her feast-day meal tonight. She rolled up the scroll and tied it with her favourite red hair ribbon, then poked her head out into the passageway. The only movement came from the shadows cast by a pair of flickering candles at the shrine of the household gods in the alcove opposite. The gods would approve of her actions, she was certain. She tiptoed past it and up to the study door.

She knocked once and waited, but there was no reply. Taking a deep breath, she pushed the door open and stepped inside. Her nose pricked at the familiar smell of dried papyrus and old leather. She loved this place. It was where Father worked when he wasn't at his office at the basilica in town. His books on law and justice were here, written on neatly rolled scrolls stored on the specially built shelves. Most precious of all was his collection of poetry and plays, which he let Vita borrow from if her tutor gave good reports of her studies.

She was so busy pondering what she might read next, she didn't hear the approach of limping footsteps until it was too late.

'Vita?'

She spun round, cheeks flushing.

'What are you doing in here?' Her father stood frowning in the doorway.

'I-I'm sorry, Father. I just wanted to leave this for you. It's a poem.' Vita held out the scroll. 'I was hoping to read it to you at my birthday feast.'

He took it from her, his mouth forced into a tired-looking smile. Vita's heart squeezed. Father had seemed restless and ill at ease these past few days. He worked too hard. That's what Mother said; though of course she never complained about the fine jewels and clothes that came with being a senior magistrate's wife.

'So this is what you have been spending your morning doing? Your mother won't be pleased, you know. You were meant to be doing your needlework.'

Vita's stomach clutched. He was talking about her wedding gown. Mother had been on at her for days to finish it. She was fourteen now, but it was still hard to believe that in a few short weeks, she'd be the wife of Father's old army comrade, Gaius Cassius Agrippa. The thought of spending the rest of her life a Roman matron like Mother, stitching robes, designing menus and making sure the slaves carried out their chores, filled her with dread.

At least she had her writing – provided Agrippa would let her carry on with it. She prayed to the gods he would. It was what she wanted most in the world. To write poems and plays and have them performed across the Empire.

Her father's sigh brought her back to the room with a jolt. 'I'm sorry, Little Owl. I did not mean to speak harshly.' He touched a hand to Vita's hair.

Her heart fluttered at his use of her special pet name. The owl was sacred to her favourite goddess, Minerva – the goddess of wisdom, poetry and justice.

A rat-tat sounded on the study door.

Her father tensed and dropped his hand to his side. 'Come!'

The door swung open to reveal the stocky, dark-haired figure of their house steward.

'Felix. You're back.' Her father's frown deepened. 'Did

you deliver the message as I asked?'

'Yes, master.' The slave pressed his hands together and gave a quick bow. As he raised them, Vita's eye was drawn again to the purple scar that ripped like a lightning bolt from his right elbow to the base of his hand. A gift from his former master, or so their nursemaid, Festa, had told her.

Father was a just master and would never dream of doing such a thing. But there were others who didn't think twice about it, Vita knew. She shivered and looked away.

Her father gave the steward a grim-faced nod. 'Good, then you may go. I will call if I need you.'

'Very good, master.' Felix bowed and left them.

Her father stood there for a moment looking into the empty space, then, heaving another sigh, turned back to face her. 'You must leave me now, Daughter. I have work to do.' Giving her shoulder a quick squeeze, he limped past her towards the big oak desk.

'But ... my poem?'

'What?' He glanced at the scroll still clutched in his right hand. 'Oh yes, I will try and look at it later.' He dropped it on the desk-top and sank down into his high-backed chair. Then, picking up a sheet of papyrus from the pile in front of him, he raked a hand through his greying hair and began to read.

Fighting down her disappointment, Vita slipped out of the room. Something was wrong, she was convinced of it. Father had been so distracted he hadn't even wished her a happy feast-day. Perhaps there'd been trouble at the Council this morning? A disagreement with one of the other magistrates? Well, whatever it was, she didn't have time to worry about it now.

Thank goodness Mother had taken Lucius with her on the visit to her friend's. Vita felt a quick pang of pity for her little brother. He'd be bored silly having to sit there and listen to them complaining about how expensive olive oil was these days. But if he'd stayed behind, it would have made the job of sneaking out without being noticed a whole lot harder.

She darted into his room and felt beneath the low mattress Festa slept on for the maid's spare tunic and hooded cloak, then hurried back to her own room to change. A few moments later and the transformation was complete. Vita, daughter of brave legionary commander, councillor and magistrate Marcus Tullius Verus, had become Vita the slave-girl.

As she stepped into the light, the hubbub of street sounds swelled up around her – the cries of wandering pedlars, the rattle and bang of traders pulling down their shop counters and the clitter-clatter of hobnails as people hurried past.

An assortment of smells tickled her nose. The sweet, yeasty fragrance of fresh bread coming from the baker's a few doors down. A tongue-tingling waft of grilled sausage from the tray of a passing street-seller. And beneath it all, a faint whiff of mud and saltiness blowing uphill from the river. If she weren't in such a hurry, she'd have stopped to savour it all. Her new-found freedom too. But the sun was already high in the sky. Casting a quick glance about her, she tugged the hood down over her forehead and set off at a brisk walk along the dusty, gravel-covered road that led to the Forum.

At first she revelled in being out in the street on her own. But as she walked on, a niggle of irritation began to take hold. Normally, if she'd been with Mother, the more well-to-do citizens would have nodded their heads in recognition, while the freedmen and women and slaves would have given way to them. Now the common folk barged past her while the richer-looking ones didn't seem to notice her at all. Still, at least it meant the disguise was working.

She didn't see the man until it was too late.

'*Ouf!* Careful, girl!'

Her stomach clawed at the sound of his voice. Cassius Agrippa, her future husband! But as she ducked sideways to avoid him, a sudden breeze caught her hood, pulling it back from her head.

A hand shot out and gripped hold of her chin, turning her face into the light. Agrippa's grey eyes locked with hers, then widened in surprise. 'Vita?'

She gave a silent groan. She was done for now.

II

Agrippa loosened his grip and, cocking a pale eyebrow, scanned Vita up and down. 'Where are you going in such a hurry? And all wrapped up in this . . .' He fingered the rough wool of her cloak and pulled a face. 'This slave-girl's disguise?'

Her face flooded with hot shame. This was awful! He'd be bound to report her to Father. And once Mother found out she'd never hear the end of it. She bit down on her lip, racking her brains for a convincing excuse – but nothing came.

Her only chance was to confess the truth and throw herself on his mercy. She sucked in a breath. 'I'm sorry! It's just that there's . . . well, there's this play at the Forum, and as it's my feast-day, I thought—'

'You thought you would sneak out when your parents weren't looking and go along to see it?'

Vita flushed again. 'Yes. But . . . but if you let me go, I'll turn round and head straight home and they need never know.'

Agrippa pulled back his shoulders and cleared his throat. 'I am on my way to see your father now, as it happens.'

Her stomach gave a quick somersault. 'Please, don't say anything to him, I beg of you.' As she clutched the edge of his toga, she caught a faint waft of the familiar lemon-pine scent of the frankincense oil he liked to wear.

He heaved a sigh and, looking down, began to twist the gold ring on the little finger of his right hand – the one with the dark red stone and the leaping bull carved into it.

Vita's throat tightened. He was going to tell on her, she was sure of it. If he did, her feast-day would be all but ruined. But when he looked up again, instead of the expected frown, Agrippa's face wore a look of amused mischief.

'I like your spirit! And rules are meant to be broken after all. Go and see your play and I promise, legionary's honour, your little expedition will be our secret.'

Vita started in amazement. 'Really?'

'Yes, really. I would join you myself . . .' He gave another small sigh and looked away up the street. 'But alas, your father's request to see me sounded urgent.'

A wave of relief flooded through her. 'Thank you, sir.' She dipped down into a grateful curtsey.

Agrippa batted his hand. 'There is no need for that. It is against my better judgement, but . . . well, go and enjoy yourself. Just remember not to speak to anyone. And make sure to hurry back as soon as the play ends. I would never forgive myself if anything ill befell you.' He touched a finger to her cheek. 'And if your father found out, he would not forgive me either.'

Before he could change his mind, Vita pulled the hood back over her head and, with another quick curtsey, darted off into the crowd. She'd had a lucky escape. She wasn't keen on the idea of being someone's wife, but she had to admit there were worse choices than Agrippa.

He and her father had served in the same legion – the Ninth Hispana – up in the wild northlands, beyond where Emperor Hadrian was now building his wall. According to Mother, Agrippa had joined her father's unit as little more than a boy. Father, a seasoned soldier by then, had taken him under his wing and taught him everything he knew, and the younger man had looked up to him in return. The bond forged between them had become stronger still when, in a battle with a band of fearsome Caledonian tribesmen, Agrippa had rescued Father from certain death.

Father had been invalided out of the army shortly after, but Agrippa had been decorated as a war hero and given his own command. Then, after his service was finally up two years ago, he'd come to Londinium with the aim of following Father into the magistracy.

There was no doubting he was proud of his record as a soldier. Ambitious for the future too. A good thing in a husband, Mother said. But Agrippa had never really shown his serious side with Vita. Instead, he spent the time when they were together entertaining her with impressions of his fellow junior magistrates, or else rolling his eyes behind Mother's back when she scolded Vita for some small fault or other. She supposed it was that part of him that had let her go now.

As she arrived at the red-roofed gateway that led into the Forum's enormous square, a pair of advertisements daubed in black paint on the wall outside caught her eye. A faded one announcing that the famed warrior, Cronos, would fight visiting champion gladiator, Ajax, at the town arena on the Ides of April, and another in fresher-looking paint saying that Lupa would hunt an array of savage beasts on the Nones of July. Vita shuddered at the thought. But she didn't have time to linger.

Lifting her cloak above her ankles, she darted beneath the arch and into the marketplace beyond. It was bustling with people speaking in a babble of tongues – some in

Latin, others the native British, and yet more in languages she had no hope of understanding. She scooted past the clusters of chattering matrons browsing at the market stalls and gave a wide berth to a group of men dressed in the same style of flowing, purple-edged magistrate's toga her father wore, in case his friends were among them.

When she reached the bronze statue of the Emperor in the middle of the square, she pulled up and cast about her. There was no sign of the actors yet. A sharp crack followed by a groan made her start. A gang of slaves in sweat-stained tunics were hard at work making repairs to the wall of a shrine in the shadow of the great basilica. A mean-faced man she guessed must be the overseer stood over one of them, whip in hand. Vita swallowed and turned away before he could deal the slave another blow.

At the same moment a burst of flute music sounded behind her. She twisted round. A small ragtag band of musicians and people in costume were marching up to a wooden platform set against a temple wall opposite the Forum entrance. A fresh thrill of excitement gripped her.

As she hurried back across the square and out on to the street again, a slow drumbeat started up. The crowd now gathered in front of the makeshift stage set up a cheer and began to clap and stamp in time. Vita hesitated for a moment, then, holding her breath, dived in amongst the heaving mass.

She'd almost reached the front when the drumming fell silent. The clapping and stamping ebbed away and an athletic-looking man wearing a bronze-coloured helmet and patched red tunic stepped out on to the stage and struck the pose of a hero, legs straddled, right hand clamped on the hilt of a rusty-looking sword. A mousy-haired woman holding a wooden flute, and a freckle-faced drummer-boy followed in his wake. Determined to get a good view, Vita stuck out her elbows and shoved her way to the front.

A shiver pulsed through her as she peered up at the stage. This was it, the moment she'd been waiting for. She closed her eyes and prepared herself to be carried away to a land of heroes and monsters by the magic of the words.

III

The actor in the bronze helmet drew his sword from its scabbard and held it aloft.

'I am Theseus, Prince of Athens. I have voyaged to this fair island of Crete to do battle with the dreaded Minotaur, to slay it and put a stop to its reign of chaos and fear.'

Vita's heart bumped against her ribs. The story of Theseus and the Minotaur – one of her favourites! As the crowd gave a rousing cheer in reply, she glanced about her. Dare she join in? If Lucius were here, he would. It was all right for boys. They could do that sort of thing. But why not? There was no one here to stop her after all. She took a quick swallow then called out the hero's name – quietly at first, then louder, and louder still, until soon she was yelling it with the best of them.

The actor glanced about him, smiling, then threw up his hand for silence. 'Thank you, my friends. Thank you! But I cannot meet this challenge on my own. To help me find my way back out of the maze of tunnels where the monster dwells, I need the help of a beautiful maiden – the Princess Ariadne.' Hand angled against his forehead, he swept the faces of the crowd. 'And by the greatness of Jupiter . . .' His eyes came to rest on Vita as he spoke the words. 'I think I have found her!' He winked and gave a small bow.

Vita's stomach lurched. What was he talking about? She took a step back, but the man behind blocked her way. To roars of approval, he circled a hairy great arm round her waist. Then, sweeping her up off her feet, he hoisted her over his shoulder and swung her up to join Theseus on the stage.

'Thank you, good sir.' The actor tipped him a nod and seized Vita by the hand. 'Now, my fair princess, don't be shy.' He flashed her a dazzling smile then yanked back her hood and spun her round to face the audience. 'Friends, I give you the Princess Ariadne!'

Vita's eyes swam with a sudden blur of faces and a loud rushing sound filled her ears. She swayed, on the verge of falling, but checked herself and gulped in a breath. Slowly the faces came back into focus. But now they had eyes –

eyes she might know; that might know her too. Wasn't that one of the magistrates from the Forum frowning back at her? And in front of him a bunch of the matrons who'd been shopping at the stalls. If her mother's friends were among them . . . Heart bumping, she made to pull up her hood again, but the actor snatched her hands and pinned them to her sides. Her skin pricked with sweat. She had to get down from here before she was recognized.

As if reading her thoughts, the actor tightened his grip and signalled to the woman with the flute. 'Give her the twine!' The woman drew a ball of rough string from beneath her robe and shoved it at Vita.

'But . . . but I just want to watch.'

'Come now. The noble classes might consider us actors little better than beasts, but surely a poor slave-girl like you would give anything to be a princess for a day?'

Guffaws of laughter rippled through the audience. Vita's cheeks flushed with a mix of anger and shame, but before she could protest again, the actor cupped a hand to his ear.

'Hark! The monster comes!'

Amid gasps and shrieks from the crowd, the boy with the drum started up a slow, menacing beat. As it gathered pace, a bellowing roar ripped through the air. Vita started and whipped round in time to see a creature, half-man, half-bull, spring on to the stage from the temple steps above. The beast pawed the wooden boards with a hobnailed black boot and tossed its shaggy brown head. Then, with a loud snort, it pulled into a crouch and pointed its blood-tipped horns straight at her.

Vita knew it wasn't real, but for a moment a bolt of blood-freezing terror rooted her to the spot. Then as the crowd yelled and stamped their feet, she jolted back to life – she had to get off the stage. Now!

She flicked a glance at the actor's sandalled toes. It was her only chance. Lifting her right knee she stamped her foot down hard on top of them. With a cry of pain he released her and hopped backwards into the musicians, sending them toppling to the ground. The crowd exploded into mocking whoops and howls.

Vita took a running jump. She fell awkwardly but managed to right herself and, head down, made for a gap in the spectators. Jeers and catcalls sounded all around, but she kept going until at last, after a final desperate surge, she burst free.

Dragging her hood up, she dashed back inside the Forum gate and scanned about her desperately seeking a place to hide. Her eyes snagged on a pile of wooden crates stacked beside the shrine where the slaves were working. Heart pounding, she sprinted over and dropped down behind them. She counted to ten, then murmuring a quick prayer to the goddess Fortuna, dared herself to peer back across the square towards the gate.

There was no sign of anyone coming after her. A few moments later, the actor's voice struck up again in the street outside, bewailing the loss of 'my fair Ariadne' and declaring he would have to fight the beast on his own. In spite of everything, Vita's heart clenched. She was going to miss the best bit. The final grisly scene when Theseus struck off the Minotaur's head and followed Ariadne's thread out of the labyrinth to safety.

A sudden shadow loomed over her. 'What are you doing hiding behind there? Answer me now, slave, or I'll give you a beating you'll never forget.'

A hand reached down and dragged her out into the light.

Vita's stomach gripped. It was the mean-faced overseer from earlier, the one she'd seen beating the slave.

'Well?' The man narrowed his eyes and dug the leather butt of his whip in to her ribs.

A spurt of anger spiralled up inside her. Glancing around to make sure there was no one who might recognize her, Vita threw back her hood and – staring him square in the eye – spoke in her best Latin.

'I am the daughter of Marcus Tullius Verus, senior magistrate and brave soldier of the Ninth Legion of Hispana. And if you don't unhand me at once, I . . . I shall report you to my father and have *you* whipped.'

The overseer's bushy black eyebrows shot up his weather-beaten forehead. But instead of bowing and asking her forgiveness, he dug the whip in harder, forcing her back against the crates. 'And I'm the Emperor Hadrian! Don't mess with me, girl. I meant what I said.' His expression took on a look of sudden cunning. 'You know what I think? That you're a runaway. And if your master doesn't know where you are, why then' – his lips curled into an unpleasant smirk – 'you're fair game, aren't you, my little dove?' He dropped his free hand to a set of iron manacles dangling from his belt and fingered them menacingly.

Vita's mouth dried. 'Look, I told you I'm not a slave. I am—'

'Excuse me, sir!'

'What?' The man swung round, making sure to keep the whip pressed hard against Vita's ribs.

It was a boy. Not much older than herself she guessed, with dark brown eyes and curly black hair.

'My master. He would like to speak to you.' He spoke the native tongue but with a mouth full of clicks and whirrs.

'Your master? And who might that be?' The overseer's voice was tight and full of suspicion.

'Over there!' The boy pointed across the marketplace to where a grand-looking man dressed in the robes of a senior magistrate stood.

'What does he want?'

'He is looking for someone to build a new bath-house for his villa on the other side of the river. It will be worth plenty *denarii*.'

The overseer's eyes lit up at the mention of money. 'Wait here and make sure this one doesn't go anywhere.' He jerked his head at Vita, then drew a small copper coin from his waist-pouch and held it out to the boy.

He pulled a face. 'Make it a *sestertius*, master, and I'll do it.'

The man gave an impatient-sounding growl then fished out a larger, gold-coloured coin and threw it at the boy's feet. He scooped it up and positioned himself in front of Vita, arms rammed across his chest, legs apart.

As the overseer lumbered away, Vita eyed the boy warily. He was slender and long-limbed. If she dodged him and ran, he'd be bound to catch her. Still, it was worth a try. But before she could make her move, the boy snatched her hand.

'Come with me. Quick!' He tugged her off through the crowds, ducking and weaving between the busy market stalls. As they reached the Forum gate, he jerked to a stop and darted a look back over his shoulder. Vita did the same. The overseer had reached the magistrate now and was clearly doing his best to explain himself, jabbing his whip to the empty space where she and the boy had been standing moments before.

Her eyes widened. 'You lied about that man wanting to see him, didn't you?'

The boy shrugged and flashed her a smile, then pulled her after him, out through the gate, down a side street and into the doorway of a closed-down shop.

'We will be safe here.' He put his hands on his hips and sucked in a breath, then shot her a look of concern. 'Are you all right? He did not hurt you?'

She blushed, flustered by his sudden gentleness, then turned away, cross with herself for letting him see how scared she felt.

'I saw you earlier with the actors. You would have made a good Ariadne.'

Was he teasing her? She spun round frowning. But his expression looked innocent enough.

'Who are you?'

'The man I was sold to called me Leander, but my real name is—' He hesitated, then bit down quickly on his lip. 'It doesn't matter.'

'Won't he – the magistrate – be angry with you for running away like that?'

He threw her a puzzled look then burst into laughter. 'He isn't my master! No one is.'

'But I thought you said he was?'

He rolled his eyes. 'You're a green one, aren't you?'

'I'm not!' Vita flushed again and stepped back from him. Whoever this boy belonged – or didn't belong – to, she'd had enough of his cheek. Besides, she was wasting valuable time. She needed to get home before she was missed. She went to step out into the street.

'Hey, wait!' The boy grabbed her arm. 'What's your name?'

She twisted free. 'Why should I tell you? You didn't tell me yours.'

He held up his hands. 'All right. Look, I understand if you'd rather keep it a secret. But why not come and join us? You would be safe then.'

She frowned. 'Us?'

'Yes, me and the others like me. We live out in the marshes, to the north of town. Beyond the place of the dead.'

She gave a quick shudder. 'No thank you. I shall be perfectly safe on my own.'

He threw her a sly look. 'Just like you were before I rescued you?'

Vita drew back her shoulders and lifted her chin as high as it would go. 'I don't need rescuing. I'm grateful for what you did back there, but actually I'm quite capable of looking after myself. Now, let me pass.' She gave a loud sniff and with a swish of her cloak, made to push past him.

His lips twitched, but he did as she'd asked without

another word. She set off at a determined march, but she hadn't gone far when a voice called out after her.

'Goodbye, Ariadne. And don't forget, if you change your mind, you know where to find us. We need more like you for what is to come.'

'What do you mean?' She whirled about, but the doorway – and the street – were empty.

As Vita reached the house, she pulled to a stop and glanced up at the windows, their blinds half drawn to keep the dust from blowing in off the road. Were Mother and Lucius back yet? She hoped not. But all she had to do was get back inside and change and no one would be any the wiser about her little expedition – except Agrippa. Praying to the gods he'd kept his promise not to tell on her, she pushed the door open and, holding her breath, stepped into the shadow-filled passageway.

Save for a distant rattle and bang of pots, all was quiet. As she crept forward, a delicious smell of spices and roasting meat wafted towards her. Her mouth watering, she scurried along the passageway towards her room. But as she passed the study door, low voices sounded from the other side. Mother's first, then Father's.

'She needs to be told.'

'I will speak with her, dearest, but let her enjoy the rest of her feast-day first.'

'But, Husband—'

'Hush, Metella. It can wait a little longer.'

Vita's heart sank. Had Agrippa told Father about seeing her after all?

A patter of footsteps sounded on the flagstones behind her. She turned to see Lucius running towards her, his right hand gripping a short wooden sword, his left arm hooked through a shield painted with the symbol of the Imperial eagle.

'Vita! You'll never guess what! Mother's friend has got a new puppy. He's called Brutus and he's eight weeks old and if I'm good, her friend says I can go back and play with him next week.'

She rolled her eyes. This was the last thing she needed. 'Not now, Lucius!' But then, as she pushed past him, he slipped and fell, clattering to the ground. There was a moment's silence followed by an ear-splitting wail.

Vita's chest cramped. 'I'm sorry, little brother!' She dropped down and pulled him into a hug.

She didn't hear the creak of the door until it was too late.

'Vita? What in divine Juno's name is going on?'

IV

Once she'd checked Lucius over and sent him off to the kitchen for milk and honey-cakes, Vita's mother drew herself to her full height and fixed Vita with a suspicious-looking stare. 'Where were you going in such a hurry, Daughter, and why' – she arched her tweezered eyebrows – 'are you dressed like that?'

Before Vita could think of a convincing reply her father appeared frowning at the study door. The frown deepened as he took in her disguise. 'Let us discuss this in private.' He gestured for them both to follow him inside.

Vita's stomach tightened. She would be punished now for sure – feast-day or no feast-day.

As she waited for her parents to take their places – her

father behind his desk, her mother on the low padded couch beneath the window – she spotted her poem on top of a pile of papyrus scrolls, the ribbon still tied neatly in place. A pang of disappointment gripped her. Father hadn't read it yet. And now there'd be no chance of reading it out at her feast later – if it even went ahead. Her eyes pricked with sudden tears. She blinked them back and waited for him to speak.

He shot her another dark look and shook his head. 'Why are you wearing Festa's things?'

Agrippa hadn't told them then.

Vita bit her lip.

'Answer me, Daughter.'

It was no use. She couldn't lie to him. Taking a deep breath in, she let the whole sorry tale spill out, though she avoided the bit about being forced up on stage, or what had happened after in the Forum. The shame of that would be too much for a proud woman like Mother to bear.

At the mention of her encounter with Agrippa, her father's expression darkened even further, and for a moment he looked away. Meanwhile, Mother's face grew paler and paler, her fingers twisting the coral necklace at her throat so tight Vita thought the cord might snap and scatter the beads across the floor.

When Vita had finished, her mother leant forward as if to speak. But Vita's father shook his head and she sat back again in silence. Steepling his fingers, he stared down at the desk-top, then drew in a breath and looked up again.

'Thank you for being honest with us, Vita. Now, please apologize to your mother. Then you and I must talk alone.'

Vita's heart shrank up inside her. She'd disappointed him. She could see it in his eyes. Whatever other punishment might lie in store, nothing could be worse than that.

She cleared her throat and forced herself to meet her mother's gaze. 'I'm sorry, Mother. I shouldn't have dishonoured you.' She bowed her head.

'Oh, Daughter!' With a choked sob, her mother rose from the couch and pulled Vita into an awkward hug. Then, dabbing her cheeks with the end of her stole, she shot an anguished glance at Vita's father and glided from the room without another word.

Vita threw a puzzled glance after her. She'd expected Mother to be angry. But not upset like this . . . Was something else going on?

She turned back to her father. His face still wore the same unhappy frown from before. He gave a deep sigh, then gripped the edge of the desk and pulled himself up out of his chair.

Vita's chest tightened again. He would tell her off properly now for sure. She hung her head in readiness. But when his words came, they weren't what she was expecting.

'I have something for you, Little Owl.'

She blinked and raised her head. 'You . . . you do?'

He nodded. 'I was going to give it to you at your feast later. But, you might as well have it now . . .' He twisted round and lifted a large oblong box from the shelf behind him. 'Here.' As he handed it to her, its polished surface glowed in the afternoon light.

Vita's breath caught in her throat. 'Thank you, Father.' She stroked her fingers over the silky-smooth, chestnut-coloured wood and looked back at him in wonder. 'It's beautiful!'

A smile fluttered across his face. 'There is something inside too. But you will need this to find out what.' He uncurled his right hand to reveal a length of leather cord and threaded on to it, what looked like a small pendant.

Putting the box down carefully on the desk, Vita took it from him. But she was wrong – it wasn't a pendant, it was a key. Made of bronze and fashioned in the shape of an owl's head with two glittering black stones for eyes.

'Aren't you going to unlock it?'

Fingers tingling with excitement, she slid the key into the lock and turned it. As she lifted the lid, she let out a loud gasp. For there, each slotted into its own compart-ment, was a folded wax tablet and stylus, a bottle of dark black ink and three reed pens, and, most precious of all, a scroll of the finest creamy-coloured papyrus she had ever seen.

'So what do you think?'

She looked up at him, heart brimming. 'I love it, Father! It's the best feast-day gift I've ever had.'

He smiled again, more broadly this time. 'I am glad. You have a talent for words, Little Owl.' He picked up the scroll she'd given him earlier and held it out to her.

Her heart skipped a beat. So he *had* read her poem after all!

'You must be sure not to waste it, whatever Fortuna may have in store for you.' His eyes clouded for a moment, then brightened again. 'Now off you go. And make sure to change out of those things before your mother sees you again, or neither of us will hear the last of it.'

'Yes, Father. And thank you again!' Dropping him a quick curtsey, Vita tucked the scroll under her arm and, cradling the box to her chest, hurried off back to her room.

As she set the box down on her desk and lifted the lid again, a fresh wave of love rushed through her. Father had always encouraged her to think for herself. To be the best person she could be. And now he'd as good as told her he thought she should be a writer too. He'd speak to Agrippa about allowing her to carry on with her writing once they were married, she was sure. She just hoped she hadn't got Agrippa into trouble by telling her parents he'd let her go off to see the play.

She glanced down at her tunic. She needed to change,

but the adventures of the day had tired her out. There was time for a quick nap first. Dropping her poem on the desk, she locked the box and stowed it safely under her bed. Then, tying the owl-key pendant round her neck, she kicked off her sandals and flopped down on to the mattress.

As she closed her eyes, a vague, nagging thought flitted into her head. Something to do with the conversation she'd overheard her parents having when she arrived home and then, how tearful Mother had been. But before she could think any more about it, sleep stole in and spirited her away.

A loud crash jerked her awake. She snapped her eyes open and sat up. The room was in near darkness, a thin wedge of moonlight slanting in beneath the window blind. So late? Why had no one come to wake her? She held her breath and listened. Silence. A shiver rippled through her. Something wasn't right – she could feel it.

Untangling herself from the blanket, she slid from the bed, her skin prickling anew against the feel of Festa's rough-spun clothes. As she reached the door, a blood-chilling scream pierced the air. It was followed moments later by the strangled cry of 'Marcus!', then her brother's voice, high and terror-filled.

And now another voice too. A man's, but one she didn't

recognize. Where was Father? A bolt of cold panic tore through her. Steeling herself, she made to lift the latch. At the same moment the door swung inwards and a figure dashed inside.

'You have to come now, young mistress. Please!'

'Festa! What's happening?'

The maid shook her head and pressed a finger to her lips, then seized her by the hand.

'But I heard screaming.' Vita struggled against her, but Festa's grip only tightened.

'Hurry!' With a quick look behind, she bundled Vita along the passage, through the front door and into the moonlit street beyond.

As they reached the safety of a narrow alleyway, Vita made to wrench free again, but Festa pulled her close.

'You cannot go back there, mistress. It is too dangerous!'

'Why? What's happened?'

The maid bit her lip and turned away.

'Tell me!'

She shivered and looked back at Vita again. 'Bad men have come.'

'Bad men? Who?'

'I-I don't know. They kept their faces hidden, but there were two. They slipped in through the garden while we were readying things for your feast.'

A fresh tide of panic surged up Vita's chest. 'What? But

why didn't Felix stop them?'

Festa shook her head again. 'He was out on an errand for the Master and not yet returned . . . The men . . . they killed Cottia. Rosia too.'

Cottia and Rosia, the family's loyal servants, dead? How was it possible? But the scream she'd heard had been Mother's. A ball of sour liquid shot up the back of Vita's throat. Her family was in danger. She had to do something before it was too late.

Determined not to let Festa stop her a second time, she yanked herself free and sprinted across the street to the open door. She hesitated for a moment, eyes sieving the candlelit gloom. No sign of movement inside. No sounds either. Counting to three, she crept across the threshold and into the shadows beyond.

As she neared the dining room, her foot clipped something lying on the ground. She reached down and picked it up. It looked like the leather bracelet she'd seen Felix wearing, but it was covered in something sticky. She held it to her nose and took a quick sniff. Blood! She flung it down and, heart pounding, edged towards the half-open door. When she reached it, she held her breath and listened again. Silence. Balling her fingers into fists, she pushed the door open and stepped inside.

The room was in darkness except for the glow from a single oil lamp in the centre of the table. But it was enough to make out the wreckage that lay all around – the shattered plates and glasses; the overturned dining couches; and Mother's favourite statue of a boy playing a flute toppled from its plinth and smashed in pieces.

There was no sign of her parents; Lucius either. Gods be thanked! They must have managed to get away. She was about to turn back when her eye snagged on something poking out from behind one of the couches. The tip of a man's leather boot.

She blinked, willing it to be a trick of the light.

But it wasn't.

Bracing herself, she snatched up a knife from the table and inched slowly forwards. When she reached the couch, she took a deep breath and peered over the top.

Her stomach twisted at the sight that met her eyes.

'Father!'

He was lying face down on the tiles, a dark stain spreading from the hilt of a sword – his own army-issue *gladius* – embedded in his back. Hurling herself round the couch, Vita dropped down beside him.

Please let him be alive. Please. She reached out and shook him gently by the shoulder.

'Father. It's me, Vita!'

She shook him again – harder this time. His head lolled to one side, and then, staring down into his dark, blank eyes, she knew the awful truth.

She gave a choked cry and threw her arms about him, willing the gods to bring him back to life.

A crunch of glass sounded behind her.

'Isn't that touching? A loyal slave weeping over her dead master's body.' It was a man's voice, harsh and rasping.

She spun round, eyes swimming with tears. A dark cloaked figure stood over her, the blade of a dagger glinting in his left hand. She opened her mouth to scream, but a sharp blow to the head stopped her and then everything went black.

V

At first, when Vita came to the only thing she knew was a rough, cold hardness beneath her and the endless pounding of a drum inside her head. And then a new sound – a woman's scream, growing louder and more piercing with every beat. She twisted her head away, but the scream grew even louder. And now, though her eyes were still closed, she could see things too. Terrible things. A room in ruins, a hooded figure in the shadows and a man lying in a pool of his own dark red blood.

Father!

A band of white-hot pain clamped round her chest. She snapped her eyes open and made to cry out, but her mouth was blocked with a greasy, foul-tasting thing and now all she could see was a swathe of black fog broken only by a faint, pulsing pinprick of light.

She tried to sit up, but her arms and legs were heavy as lead and she couldn't seem to pull them apart. She froze. What if she was dead too and in the Underworld?

A loud bang made her start. And footsteps – coming towards her! She kicked herself backwards, heart pounding.

A shadow loomed over her. 'Let's take a proper look at you then.' A hand seized her by the tunic and dragged her upright. There was a sharp tug at the back of her head followed by the rough scrape of what felt like sackcloth against her cheeks and a rush of cool air on her skin.

She swallowed and looked up blinking. A heavy-set man in a brown leather tunic and leggings stood over her, a patched flour sack swinging from his right hand.

One of the killers. It must be! She tried to scream for help, but the thing in her mouth was in the way. And her hands and feet were bound too.

'Easy now!' The man threw down the sack and held up his hands. Vita shrank back at the sight of a purple stump on the left one in place of where his little finger should be. But he didn't seem to notice. Instead, swiping an oil lamp from the wall niche opposite, he dropped down on his haunches and held the flame up to her face. She jerked her head away, but he seized her chin and pulled it back round.

'No need to be shy.'

She gagged at the wave of hot meaty breath. Her captor looked her up and down and gave an approving nod. 'You're a pretty one. Not that looks count for much in this place.' He snorted, then lifted to his feet and shoved the lamp back where he'd got it from.

The knot in Vita's stomach tightened. He wasn't the man who'd hit her. She'd recognize that rasping voice anywhere. He must be his accomplice. But who were they? And what had they done with Mother and Lucius?

The man squatted down again and made a grab for her hands. She snatched them away and kicked out at him with her feet.

He growled and fixed her with a black-eyed stare. 'You runaways are all the same. I paid that ruffian good money for you, but I'm regretting it already.'

Vita stiffened. Runaway? Paid? What was he talking about?

The words of Father's killer snaked back into her ears. *A loyal slave weeping over her dead master's body.* As she stared down at her patched tunic – Festa's tunic – her heart gave a sickening jolt. Of course! The man hadn't killed her because he'd thought she was just a house-slave: something he could sell on. But what did that mean for Mother and Lucius? She shook her head. She couldn't think about it now. She had to get this man – whoever he was – to let her go. Then she'd go straight to Agrippa's house and raise the alarm.

She made a groaning sound and gestured at the gag.

The man frowned. 'You're not going to cause me any trouble, are you?'

She shook her head.

He shot her a warning look then reached out and fished the length of cloth from her mouth. Vita spat the final bit free and sucked in a breath.

'Please. The man who brought me here. He was lying. I'm not a slave.'

Her captor flared his nostrils and gave another bullish snort. 'That's what they all say.'

'But . . . But it's true! I—'

'Quiet!' He dragged her back by the hair. 'Or I'll throw you to the next lot of bears we get in. Though they'll make quick work of a twiggy thing like you.'

Vita's throat tightened. Bears? What bears? She tried to twist free, but he held her fast.

'A spoilt house-slave from the look of that creamy soft skin.' He trailed the stump of his missing finger across her cheek. 'Well, you'll find no creature comforts here. At least, not the sort you've been used to.' He gave a mocking laugh and, sliding his hand to his belt, whipped out a short-bladed knife.

'No, please!' Vita jerked up her arms.

'I'm not going to hurt you. Not if you do what I tell you to.' Grabbing hold of her ankles, he sliced through the rope and hauled her up on her feet. As she swayed about trying to get her balance, he turned and marched to the door. 'Janus!'

There was a pitter-patter of feet and a small dark-haired man dressed in a black tunic scurried into the room. 'Yes, Master Otho.' As the man gave a bow, a twist of copper flashed at his neck.

'We've got a new girl to settle in. Who shall we give her to?'

The dark-haired man – Janus – darted Vita a quick glance. He reminded her of the sharp-faced weasel she'd once seen steal an entire clutch of eggs from a blackbird's nest in their garden – carrying them away one by one in its needle-like teeth. And now . . . now her home was like the nest too – cold and dead and empty. She scrunched her eyes shut in a bid to blot out the gut-wrenching memory, but the slave's wheedling reply forced her to open them again.

'We could put her with Cronos, master. After the unfortunate incident with the boy last week, he needs a fresh servant.' He raised a hand and stroked what she saw now was a copper-wire necklet at his throat.

Vita frowned. That name – Cronos. She'd heard it before somewhere, she was sure . . .

The other man – Otho – grunted. 'The Skull-Crusher? He'd have her for breakfast! No, we'll find him some other poor soul to torment.' He thrust Vita towards the slave. 'Give her to the She-Wolf. At least then she'll stand a fighting chance.'

Janus gave a high, braying laugh then dropped into another bow. 'Very good, master.'

Vita's stomach gripped. Skull-crushers? She-wolves? What was this place? She snatched at Otho's sleeve.

'You have to listen to me! The man who brought me here killed my fa—'

Otho's eyes flashed with fresh anger. 'What did I say?' He raised a hand as if to strike her.

She flinched but the blow didn't come.

'Take her away, before I change my mind and let Cronos suck on her bones after all.'

'At once, master!' The slave snatched up the length of rope dangling from Vita's bound hands.

'And give her something to eat and drink or she'll be fit for nothing in the morning.'

'Yes, Master Otho.'

As Janus yanked her towards the door, Vita was overcome by a dragging heaviness. She had done her best to explain things to this Otho, but he didn't want to listen, and she didn't have the energy to fight any more. Father was dead. And as for poor Mother and Lucius . . . Tears spiked her eyes and spilt down her cheeks. With a juddering sigh she hung her head and let herself be hauled into the passageway outside.

What little light there was came from a row of flaming wicks floating in oil-filled basins dug into the passage walls. There were doors set into the walls too. Wooden ones, each with the same heavy-looking bar fixed across it and a pair of wooden bowls and two beakers set on the ground in front. Most of the bowls were empty, but there were dried crusts of bread in one and a brown dollop of what looked like cold beans in another.

Janus scooped up the crusts as they passed and thrust them at Vita with a spiteful-sounding chuckle. 'Supper?'

She was ravenous, but if he thought she was going to eat someone's leftovers . . . She turned her face away.

'Not good enough for you, eh? Well, if you don't want it . . .' As he made to whip the crusts away again, the grim thought struck Vita that she'd probably not get anything better until morning. Snatching them off him, she forced herself to take a bite. He gave another laugh, then picked up a beaker and shoved it at her. 'Here. Something to wash it down with.'

As she gulped down the muddy-tasting contents, a muffled groan sounded from the other side of the door. She leapt back in fear, flinging the beaker to the ground.

'Wh-where are we?'

'You'll find out soon enough.' Janus yanked on the rope and picked up his pace, forcing her into a trot behind.

They turned a corner into another passage, narrower, worse-lit and with only a single door at the far end. Pulling up before it, Janus slid open a small hatch set into the wood then turned back to Vita with a thin-lipped smile.

'She's sleeping. But one sniff of you and she'll be wide awake.' Untying Vita's hands, he heaved the wooden bar from its cradles, pushed the door open and shoved her into the black space beyond.

'Some company for you, She-Wolf! Don't eat her all at once!' He slammed the door shut with another hee-hawing laugh.

'No! Wait!' As Vita twisted round there was a loud thunk followed by a pair of footsteps scurrying away. She gave a dry swallow and turned back slowly into the room.

A slice of moonlight slanted in through a high, barred window, casting a pale grey glow across the straw-covered floor. Beyond it, the room was in total darkness. It pressed in on her, dank and sour-smelling. But there was something else. A thing watching her from the shadows. She could sense it. Hear it too. A soft panting. And now a light patter of feet. Heart pounding, she backed up against the door.

The pattering drew closer then stopped. Something cold and wet nudged her right ankle. She jerked it away with a cry. A low growl sounded and a pair of yellow-gold eyes glittered back at her. She made to scream, but all that came out was a choked whisper. The beast growled again. She spun round, but there was nowhere left to go. Jerking her arms up, she prayed to the gods for a quick end and braced herself for the attack.

'Col! Leave!'

The creature gave a sharp bark.

'I said, leave!'

There was a disappointed-sounding yip and the quick pad of retreating paws.

Trembling, Vita lowered her arms and peered into the darkness. A figure sat squatting on the floor a man's stride away from her. She sucked in a breath.

'Th-thank you.'

'Why thank me?' The voice was low but impatient-sounding, speaking a strange guttural form of the native British tongue that made it hard to tell if it belonged to a man or a woman.

'B-but your . . . your beast. It was going to attack.'

'Not unless I told him to. And why risk the anger of the Horned One with such a poorly matched kill?'

Vita's stomach clenched. 'The horned one?'

'The god of the hunt. But I can tell already it would be a waste of good air to talk of him with you. Enough of your questions. My friend and I need our sleep, and you have broken it.'

The figure slid down with a loud huffing sound and lengthened itself along the ground.

'But . . . but who are you? And what is this place?'

'Did you not hear me the first time? Perhaps I should set my wolf on you after all? What do you say, Col?'

The animal replied with a high-pitched whine.

Vita shivered and shrank back into the corner. Why had they thrown her in here with this wild pair? And what would they do to her if she dropped her guard? She shuddered and clutched her arms about her. It didn't bear thinking of. But if she made it through the night, she'd insist on seeing the one called Otho again. Tell him what had happened; who she really was. The sooner she made him realize the truth, the sooner she could get out of here and go for help.

And then, as the awfulness of what had happened crashed over her again like an ice-cold wave, she was gripped by a sudden, dizzying sickness. She bent over and retched loudly. But if the sharp-tongued stranger or the wolf heard, they gave no sign.

Wiping her mouth with the back of her hand, she sank to the ground and, curling herself in a ball, fumbled for the owl-key round her neck. Still there, thank Minerva! She'd been so happy when Father gave it to her. But now . . . now everything had changed.

Choking back a fresh wave of tears, she pressed the

warm metal to her lips and whispered a stuttering prayer for his soul; for Mother and Lucius too. As she spoke the last words, her eyes fluttered shut. She forced them open, but it was no use. The urge to sleep was too strong. She closed them again and gave up the fight.

VI

Vita woke to find a face pressed to the bars of the door-hatch. It wasn't Janus but another, bristle-cheeked man, with a filthy-looking patch of cloth tied over his left eye. Throwing a nervous glance behind, she jumped to her feet and forced herself to meet his gaze.

'Take me to your master. I . . . I have to speak to him at once.'

The man raised a straggly eyebrow then shook his head. 'I'm afraid I can't do that, girly. The Master's busy right now. You're to come with me, the pair of you.' The man threw a quick look past her into the shadows then disappeared from view. Moments later there was a scraping sound and the door creaked open to reveal his bulky figure filling the frame.

'Come on. Out with you.' The man jerked a stubby thumb at Vita, then bellowed over the top of her head. 'You too, She-Wolf. Unless you want old Cronos to have your share of the slop?'

A snarling bark sounded from somewhere behind. Vita twisted round in time to see a silver-grey wolf spring towards her. She screamed and flung herself against the nearest wall. But the creature had its sights set on a different prey. Bounding past her, it pulled back its jaws and baring two rows of sharp, white teeth, gave the man a threatening growl.

'Get away, brute!' The man whipped a stick from his belt. As he jabbed at the wolf, forcing it back, a voice rang out in the same harsh tones as the night before.

'Touch him, Argus, and the breath you take after will be your last.'

A hand gripped Vita's arm, yanking her aside, and a tall figure in a grey woollen tunic and breeches shoved in between the wolf and the man, hands on hips, legs apart.

The man – Argus, who'd surely been named after the many-eyed guardian of Greek myth in jest – held up a hand. 'All right! All right! Keep your blue-faced thatch on. But that animal stays here.' He thrust the stick at the wolf again. 'And don't forget, it's the Emperor's Latin we speak in here, unless you want a day in the lock-up?' He slammed the door shut with a grunt and pounded off down the passage, pulling Vita behind him.

She thought about resisting, but she didn't have the strength for it. And now all the dark and terrible memories came flooding back again. The ear-splitting scream, Father lying there dead, the blow to the back of her head . . . And what of Mother and Lucius? They were surely dead too.

She swallowed hard and in a bid to distract herself, glanced back at the one they called the She-Wolf. She was loping at a distance behind them, head held high, eyes – a bright moss-green – unblinking and fixed on a point above their heads. Vita gave a quick shiver. The wolf-woman looked every bit as wild as she'd imagined Queen Boudicca and her barbarian warriors to be. But instead of the painted blue face, where it showed through the layer of grey grime, her skin was pale. And in place of a mane of flaming red hair, a bunch of long dirty-blonde locks sprang from a topknot on the crown of her head.

How old was she? It was hard to tell. Feeling bolder now she was without her wolf, Vita tried to catch her eye. But the wolf-woman refused to meet it, as if Vita didn't exist. Her manners hadn't improved overnight, that was for sure. Vita puffed out a breath and switched her gaze to the passage they'd turned into. It was the same one the weaselly-faced slave, Janus, had brought her down last night. The lamps were out now though and the doors stood wide open, revealing a pair of simple wooden truckle-beds, a table and two roughly made stools in each room. She chewed on her lip. It looked like some sort of army barracks.

'Where are they? The soldiers?'

Argus exploded into a loud guffaw. 'Soldiers? Criminals, more like! Though we've got a fair few slaves and enemy prisoners too. And then there's the odd debt-dodger or glory-seeking madman that's volunteered. 'Course, some in here like to think they're a cut above the rest.' He threw a glance over his shoulder. 'Ain't that right, She-Wolf?'

The wolf-woman's shoulders stiffened, but her gaze remained fixed in the distance as though she hadn't heard.

Vita frowned. So it was a prison? But if so, why would someone volunteer to live here? She threw another glance at the wolf-woman. She certainly didn't look like she'd asked to be in this place. Which meant she was either a slave, a prisoner-of-war – or worse still, she'd committed some sort of dreadful crime. Her stomach gripped with a wave of fresh fear.

Argus shook his head. 'She's a rebel, that one. Needs more taming, if you ask me. But she brings in the money, and that's what old Otho cares about.' He pulled to a stop in front of a large wooden door. A rise and fall of voices and the scrape and clatter of what sounded like people eating came from the other side.

What did he mean, bring in the money? Before she had the chance to ask, the slave flung the door open and pushed her inside.

Vita scanned nervously about her. She was standing in a low-ceilinged room lit by a row of high windows set at intervals along its length. In the centre of the room stood two trestle tables. They were flanked on either side by a line of wooden benches occupied by a bunch of rough-looking men dressed in worn leather tunics. Some, heads bent low, were shovelling spoonfuls of what appeared to be lumpy grey mud into their mouths. Others were busy yelling to each other over their neighbours' heads, or banging the table-top until one of a pair of whey-faced girls slopped yet more of the steaming grey mixture from the iron pots they were hauling into their bowls.

Vita shuddered. So this was what criminals looked like. She didn't dare to imagine all the terrible things they'd done. She had to get out of here. Find Otho and make him release her – now! She made to turn round, but the man with the eyepatch blocked her way.

'Steady now, girly. We can't let the prize bulls go hungry!' He jerked his head at the men and nudged her forward.

A cry went up from the end of the nearest table. 'Will you look at what old Argus has brought us, lads! A pretty new kitchen maid. And just in time for breakfast too!'

The voices and clatter died away as what felt like a hundred pairs of eyes turned to look at her. Even the serving-girls stopped what they were doing to stare. Vita's cheeks flushed with sudden heat. She stumbled backwards, but a man with a mangled left ear reached out and grabbed her arm.

'Come on, sweetness. We won't bite!' He turned and winked at his comrades, who burst into gales of rough laughter.

'Leave her be!' It was the wolf-woman. In one swift movement she wrenched Vita free and positioned herself alongside her, arms jammed across her chest, face pulled into a dark frown.

'Whoa! I'm scared!' The man with the mangled ear drew back in mock horror, though his eyes carried in them a flicker of genuine fear.

'Hey, Lupa!' A thunderous voice bellowed from the far end of the room. 'Go catch us a boar, will you? This porridge tastes worse than a pile of your mangy dog's dung!'

Vita frowned. That name . . . Lupa. It sounded familiar.

The wolf-woman took a step forward, fingers knuckled into fists.

'You want to fight?' The speaker – a colossus of a man – had risen from his seat at the head of the table furthest from the door. He was easily half as tall again as Lupa, his great barrel-shaped chest and arm muscles straining against the black leather tunic he wore as if, any moment, about to burst free. But more fearsome still was his closely shaved, boulder-like head and the long yellow beard twisted in two forked plaits which reached to the bronze-buckled belt at his waist.

As he stepped out into the room and pulled himself up to his full, awful height, the men sitting with him banged the table with their fists and chanted together in a harsh tongue Vita didn't understand. She swallowed and threw a hurried glance back at Lupa. The muscles in the wolf-woman's jaw twitched, but she showed no other sign of moving. Why didn't she run?

The giant advanced slowly towards them, cracking his hair-covered knuckles as he went. The roar of voices grew even louder as the rest of the men in the room joined in. This time it was a single word they shouted:

Cronos! Cronos! Cronos!

Vita's skin prickled. It suited him. He looked just how she imagined the great Titan god Cronos would look, as he feasted on his own newborn children to stop the prophecy that said they would one day overthrow him from coming true.

And then it dawned on her where she'd recognized the name from the night before. Lupa's too. They'd been on the posters at the Forum – the ones advertising the arena shows. But that could mean only one thing. A fresh spike of fear clawed her chest. They were gladiators, the lot of them. And this . . . Her mouth gaped as she scanned the roomful of jeering faces. This must be their training school.

She swallowed and flicked a look back at the giant. He was close enough now for Vita to see the angry fire smouldering in his bloodshot eyes, and the puckered purple line of a scar running from the base of his chin to the neckline of his tunic.

She threw Lupa another glance. She was standing firm, but surely, however wild she was, she was no match for this . . . this 'Skull-Crusher'.

The giant was almost upon them now. The men were up on their feet, yelling at the tops of their voices, urging him on. He was so close she could smell his sour sweat. Feel his hot breath on her face. And now . . . Vita's stomach balled up inside her. Now he was raising his fist. Getting ready to strike.

Still the wolf-woman stood her ground, though a bead of shining sweat had begun to track down her left cheek.

Vita licked her lips. The wolf-woman had defended her; she had to return the favour. As she cast about her, looking for something – anything – her eye snagged on a discarded porridge pot, the ladle poking from the remains of the gloopy mess inside.

Dashing over, she scooped up a dripping mound of the stuff and taking quick aim, launched it at the Skull-Crusher's head. It landed with a slippery wet smack right between his eyes. For an instant he froze, then with a savage cry he swiped furiously at the steaming grey lumps now sticking his eyelids together and sliding down his yellow-bristled cheeks.

The room fell deathly silent. The wolf-woman swung about and stared at Vita in wide-eyed surprise. She opened her mouth, but her words were drowned out by an ear-splitting roar.

'I'll pulp your brains to mush. Both of you!' The Skull-Crusher leapt towards them, nostrils flaring, hands clawed. Quicker than lightning, the wolf-woman snatched up the pot and lifted it high above her head.

At the same moment the door behind them banged open and a voice thundered out in fury, 'What is the meaning of this? Unarm her at once!' Otho strode into the centre of the room.

A pair of men at the nearest table lunged at the wolf-woman. One grabbed her about the middle while another wrestled the porridge pot from her and locked a heavily muscled arm round her neck.

'Out of my way, girl!' Otho pushed past Vita and thrust himself between the wolf-woman and Cronos. 'I will not have fighting in my school unless it's authorized by me, d'you hear?' He glared at the Skull-Crusher. The giant shot him a scowling look as if he would strike him down too, then slowly lowered his arms.

'As for you, She-Wolf . . .' Otho turned to face the wolf-woman. 'You should stick to baiting boars and bears, not picking quarrels with my prize-fighter.' She stared back at him, unblinking, her jaw set like stone.

Otho gave a loud snort then jerked his head at the two men holding her. 'Take her away and throw her in the punishment-cell. We'll see what a bit of time in the dark with the slugs and cockroaches does to damp down her fire. Cronos . . .' He turned to the Skull-Crusher. 'Go and get cleaned up. As for the rest of you' – he threw an impatient glance around the room – 'do what business you have to in the latrines and then out to the training ground. And jump to it, we've wasted enough of the day already!'

Vita's chest tightened as she watched the two men force-march the wolf-woman out through the door. It wasn't fair. She might be an ill-mannered barbarian, but she'd stood up for Vita. She darted over to Otho. 'But . . . but she didn't start things.'

His eyebrows forked in angry-looking surprise. 'What?'

'She wasn't the one that picked the fight. It was him. The one called Cronos.' She pointed at the giant as he lumbered out through the door.

Otho's eyes narrowed into two black points. 'Did I ask

for your opinion?'

'No, but—'

'Well then. Clear up this mess.' He jabbed a thumb at the splatters of porridge plastered across the floor and tables. 'And then go and help the other slave-girls clean out the men's rooms.'

Snatching her chance, Vita pulled back her shoulders and forced herself to look him in the eye. 'But I am not a slave. I tried to tell you last night. I'm—'

Otho glowered down at her. 'Enough! Unless you want a thrashing?' His damaged hand dropped to a leather-covered whip at his belt.

Trembling, Vita shook her head and backed away.

'Good! What's your name?'

'Vita.'

'Hmmm. It suits you.' He turned to Janus, who had appeared as if from thin air at his side. 'Make sure *Vita* here does as she's told. And if not, you have my permission to beat her.'

'Yes, master.' The weasel-faced slave gave a quick bow.

'Oh, and put her on half-rations for a couple of days. She needs to learn who's master around here.' He threw Vita another frowning glance. 'Damn runaways! More trouble than they're worth, and that's Jupiter's honest truth.' Hooking his thumbs into his belt, he turned on his heel and stomped back out through the door.

A burst of anger shot through Vita. She wanted to cry after him that he wouldn't dare beat her if he knew who her parents were. And if he didn't let her go, then . . .

Then what? She might be the daughter of respected Roman citizens, but unless she could persuade Otho of the truth, as his slave she was powerless. She heaved a sigh, but before she had the chance to think anything more, Janus thrust a wooden bucket and a length of grubby-looking cloth at her.

'You heard what he said, girl. Now get mopping!'

VII ~

Vita scrubbed mechanically at the floor of the small, dank-smelling room, head still spinning at the knowledge of what this place really was – a school for gladiators. Her parents' house was only a few streets from the arena where the fighting shows took place. But it might as well have been the distance between Mount Olympus and Hades. She and Lucius had never been to the arena. Father would not allow it. He'd disapproved of pitting men against each other in mortal combat. Even if, as the one called Argus had said, most were common criminals, prisoners-of-war or slaves.

She knew what sort of things went on there though. She'd overheard Agrippa and some of Father's other friends speaking of it once when they'd dined at their house. And besides the posters advertising the spectacles, as they called them, she'd seen images of the different kinds of gladiators on souvenir pottery sold in the market.

She shivered. But the feeling was quickly overpowered by a deep, grinding ache in her chest as thoughts of what had happened to her family came flooding in again.

She shook her head. She couldn't let herself give up. She had to get out of here, find Cassius Agrippa and tell him what she knew so the ones responsible could be caught and brought to justice. She owed it to Father. To all of them. Leaning back on her heels, she clasped her hands together and prayed to Minerva to help her find a way of escape.

Footsteps thudded along the passageway outside. Her stomach clenched. If they found her shirking she'd be whipped. She dropped back on to her hands and knees and set about scrubbing again, doing her best to ignore the sting of the blisters which had already begun to bloom on the soft skin of her palms.

'Out of the way!'

She started and jumped to her feet. Three men in sweat-stained leather tunics stood in the open doorway. The tallest one – the man with the damaged ear from earlier – and a shorter, bearded one, both supporting a third much younger man, head drooping, between them.

She pulled to one side and watched as the pair swung

their comrade down on the truckle-bed. His head lolled back to reveal a large ugly-looking gash on his forehead, blood still pumping from the wound. Deep, crimson blood. Like Father's . . . The walls began to swim up around her.

'Well, don't just stand there, girl! Go and fetch more water.'

Sucking in a breath, Vita snatched up the bucket and hurried off in the direction of the courtyard. As she approached it, she heard a man's voice barking orders and the cries of other men mixed with what sounded like the clash of sticks.

When Janus had taken her to fetch water from the well earlier, the place had been empty. But now, as she stepped out from the shadow of the thatched porch, a different sight met her eyes. The large sand-covered square was full of men, some dressed in their leather tunics and breeches, others stripped to the waist, their chests and arms glistening with sweat. There were several working in pairs, armed with a short wooden sword in one hand and a round shield in the other. As they squared up to each other, a man watching from the sidelines jumped in now and then to correct a position or demonstrate a better way to wrong-foot an opponent or parry a blow.

Other men worked on their own, jabbing with long poles at what looked like a row of turnips set on posts at head height, while sweeping the dusty ground with netted ropes as they advanced. Yet more were stretching and bending, or thumping cloth-bound fists into full grain sacks suspended from beams fixed to the wall.

And then Vita's heart did a quick flip. Because there in the centre of it all stood Otho, and dwarfing him, the hulking figure of Cronos. From the way he was waving his hands and talking excitedly at the giant, the gladiator-master was clearly upset, though she was too far away to hear his words. As for the Skull-Crusher, he stood there with a bored look on his face, calmly wiping the edge of his wooden sword on his tunic with slow, careful strokes. Dipping her head down, she ran to the well, refilled the bucket and hurried back inside.

When she reached the room, the injured man had come to and was groaning loudly and clutching at his forehead.

'Here! Give me that!' The man with the mangled ear snatched the cloth from her.

'But . . . but it's not clean.'

'A bit of dirt's not going to kill him.' He dunked the cloth in the water and pressed it to the wound. The injured man gave a yelp of pain. 'Don't be such a baby, Decimus. It's only a scratch.'

The bearded man frowned at their wounded friend, then spoke in the British tongue. 'What was he thinking of, tangling with the Skull-Crusher like that? Volunteers! Always chasing the glory, eh?'

His comrade gave a loud snort and replied in the same tongue. 'He's lucky it was only a training weapon. If they'd been in the arena . . .' He shook his head and drew in a whistling breath.

The bearded one nodded. 'You're right. Mind you, Cronos's blood was up after that business at breakfast with Lupa. She's a wild one. I don't know why Otho puts up with her.'

'Yes you do. She brings in the punters. A girl-hunter who never misses her mark and fills the coffers with silver into the bargain. What's not to love?'

'Well, that's as may be, but one of these days she'll over-step herself. Cronos has been used to being top dog since he got dragged here from the forests of Germania with the rest of those barbarian friends of his. He doesn't like anyone else trying to steal his spot – least of all a Blue-face who's not even a proper gladiator. And a female too.'

The man with the mangled ear grunted his agreement. 'She might be a native, but she's not like us. Those north-erners live like animals, hiding out in caves, eating their meat raw.' He squeezed out the bloody cloth and, ignoring the wounded man's groans, swabbed at the gash again. 'Rabble-rousers, the lot of 'em. No wonder the Emperor's got his army busy building a wall to keep 'em out.'

The bearded one nodded again then gripped his friend's arm. 'Talking of soldiers, did you hear the news the kitchen delivery boy brought in about that magistrate bigwig? Blerus? Terus? Something like that. Found dead as a doornail in a pool of his own blood.'

Father! Vita gave a choked cry and stumbled against the side of the bed.

The man with the mangled ear swung round. 'What's wrong with you?'

'Nothing, I—' She took a quick breath and pulled back into the shadows.

The wounded man let out another groan, then leant his head over the side of the bed and threw up.

The bearded man shook his head. 'He needs a proper patch-up. You, girl. Go and tell that louse Janus to bring the doctor quick!'

Pressing her nose to her sleeve, Vita stepped back outside. So they'd discovered Father's body. But what about Mother and Lucius? And the murderers – had they been caught yet? She hovered in the shadows desperate to learn more. But the pair had switched back to talking about the injured man.

She'd have to try and find out some other way. Heart cramping, she set off in search of Otho's oily assistant.

A chance came when Janus ordered Vita to help dish up the men their midday meal. But the two serving-girls backed away like a pair of frightened mice when she asked them for news. And the red-faced cook who thrust a serving-pot full of steaming stew through the kitchen hatch at her was in no mood for questions either.

In spite of how awful she felt, Vita couldn't help her stomach from grumbling at the rich, herby smell. It had been so long since she'd eaten a proper meal. As the men filed into the dining hall, she snatched up the ladle and took a small mouthful. It was good. She scooped up another, and giving it a quick blow, shovelled it down. She was about to steal a third, when a voice squawked through the hatch.

'Hey, new girl! Stop your thieving and get to work.' The cook clattered down her knife and came bustling out of the kitchen, face scrunched into an angry-looking frown.

Cheeks burning, Vita plunged the ladle back in the pot, and swinging it up with both hands, lugged it off to the table furthest from Cronos and his gang.

In spite of doing her best to eavesdrop on the men's conversations, she could glean nothing else, and after dropping more stew into laps than bowls, the cook shrieked for Janus, who sent her off to clean out the rest of the men's sleeping quarters instead.

By the time she'd finished and then helped with the supper-time meal – to more chiding from Cook when she threw a whole jar-load of fish sauce into the broth – Vita was exhausted. She'd never worked so hard in all her life.

No wonder Festa and the other house-slaves had looked so worn out at the end of each day.

It was only as Argus marched her up to the door of the sleeping-cell that Vita's thoughts turned guiltily back to the wolf-woman. Had they let her out of the punishment-cell yet? And what about her wolf?

A growling bark sounded as if in answer.

She backed away, arms clutched tight against her chest.

'Don't worry about old Wolfie. His bark's worse than his bite.' The slave shot her a gap-toothed grin. Then, opening the door, he shoved her through it and before she could protest, slammed it shut behind her.

∝∝∝ VIII ∝∝∝

As Vita peered into the gloom, a four-legged shape sloped out of the shadows towards her, gold eyes gleaming. She froze, willing the wolf-woman to call the creature off. But the call didn't come. Her scalp pricked. If it was hungry, she was done for.

But wait! She still had the bread she'd saved from supper. She slid it from her tunic sleeve and, with trembling fingers, tore off a hunk and threw it to the ground. The wolf jerked to a stop, gave the bread a quick sniff and gulped it down in one mouthful.

Heart racing, Vita broke off another piece, and daring herself to kneel, offered it in her outstretched palm. The animal snatched it up and swallowed it whole again.

'Good boy . . . Col. Is that your name?'

The wolf gave a small whine as if in reply.

'Col . . . Good. Are you still hungry?' In spite of her own rumbling belly, Vita held out the last piece of bread. The wolf took it from her – more gently this time – then, with a growling yawn, it bent its knees and dropped to the ground.

Whispering a small prayer of thanks, Vita retreated into the corner and sank down into the musty-smelling straw. She'd failed to find out any more about Father's murder, but now people on the outside knew about it, she had to try again with Otho. And this time she'd make him believe her. She gave a shuddering sigh, then rolling over, closed her eyes and did her best to fall asleep.

She was jolted awake by a sudden bang followed by excited yipping and what sounded like a murmured greeting in reply. She drew back against the wall, heart thumping. 'Lupa? Is . . . is that you?'

'Yes. Though that is not my true name.'

There was a rush of air as the wolf-woman strode past, the wolf at her side. Vita wondered if she was angry at her for being sent to the punishment-cell. It was hard to tell. As the pair dropped down in the shadows against the far wall she risked another question.

'So . . . so what is it, then? Your name, I mean?'

The wolf-woman hesitated then puffed out a breath.

'I suppose after what you did earlier you have earned the right.'

Not angry then. Vita heaved a sigh.

'It is Brea.'

'Brey-ah?'

The wolf-woman gave a clipped nod. 'But it is for no one else in this place to know.'

Vita swallowed. 'I understand. I am Vita. I . . . I fed your wolf.' She threw the creature a nervous glance.

The wolf-woman snorted and ruffled the animal's black-tipped ears. 'He will not bite without good reason.'

'I'm not used to wild things.'

'You will be soon enough.'

'What do you mean?'

Brea leant into the shaft of moonlight now shining in through the window above and fixed Vita with a cold-eyed stare. 'Haven't they told you? I am what they like to call a *venator*. A beast-hunter. Little better than the creatures they set us to killing, if you believe in the Roman order of things.' The curl of her lip suggested she didn't. 'The slave that's given to one such as me must feed and water the animals that are trapped and brought here for the show.'

Vita's stomach clenched. 'What sort of animals?'

'Not the ones from distant lands the Emperor orders killed for his pleasure in Rome. Those that roam wild here.'

'You mean bears?'

'It could be, if the beast-trappers catch any. Or else wild boar, or a bull – though I have not been matched with one of those yet.'

A sudden image of the man in the Minotaur's head reared up before Vita. But that – though terrifying at the time – had only been make-believe. In the arena, the beasts' razor-sharp teeth and spike-tipped horns would be for real. She shivered and prayed Fortuna she would have escaped from this place long before the next spectacle.

'How . . . how did you come to be here?'

The wolf-woman clicked her teeth. 'And why do *you* always ask so many questions?'

'That was a question too!'

Brea threw her a sharp look. 'You are quick-tongued. Quick-witted too. I saw that this morning when you used your "weapon" against the giant.'

Vita flushed. 'I'm sorry. I didn't mean to get you into trouble. Especially when you were only trying to protect me.'

The wolf-woman gave a loud sniff. 'There is no honour in an unequal contest. But the Skull-Crusher does not care about such things. He singles out the weak so that all run scared of him.'

'Except you.'

'I am not like the others. The Skull-Crusher knows it. It is why he hates me. And wants to fight me too. But it will never happen in the arena.'

'Why?'

'Because it is forbidden for a man to be paired with a woman. And as I told you, I hunt beasts, not men. Though there *is* a man I would track down and slay if the Horned One would give me sight of his trail.' She shifted on her haunches, her eyes ablaze with a sudden green fire. Beside her, Col sounded a growl.

Vita tensed.

Her cellmate gave a hollow laugh. 'You are like the mouse that lives in fear of the hawk's shadow. If I was going to hurt you, I'd have done it by now.' She gave the wolf's fur another ruffle.

Vita flushed again and drew in a breath. 'Who is he – the one you want to track down?'

At first, Brea didn't answer. When she did, she spoke the words through gritted teeth.

'One of the Eagle-men.'

'The Eagle-men?'

'The red-crests who march in line behind gold birds on poles and take what isn't theirs.'

'You mean soldiers? But they fight to protect us.'

The wolf-woman's lips pressed into a thin, hard line. 'Not where I am from.'

The conversation between the two gladiators flitted back into Vita's head. 'Are . . . are you from north of the wall?'

Brea's eyes narrowed. 'North of the wall? You speak like you are one of them!'

Vita's chest tightened. She wanted to shout back that her father had been a commander in the Imperial Army. That she was proud of him and always would be. But it was clear her companion hated all soldiers, and if Vita confessed the truth, there was no telling what she might do. Besides, she'd been the only one to show her a shred of kindness in this dreadful place . . .

'Sorry. I . . . I didn't mean anything by it.'

The wolf-woman huffed a breath and raked a bunch of dirty-blonde locks back over her shoulder. 'My people are of the Hunter-Folk. We dwell on the far side of the shining sands, where the Black Mount slopes down to the sea.' Her eyes flickered and took on a faraway look, as if she were walking there now. 'We live lightly, take only what we need and in return the earth looks after us. Gives us shelter, food, fire . . . It is a good life . . . *Was* a good life . . .' Her face pulled into a sudden dark frown. She drew Col tight against her and whispered something in his ear.

'So why aren't you there now?'

Brea jerked her head up again, eyes flashing with fresh fire. 'Because those Eagle-men – the ones you say are here to protect us – they took me, bound me with chains and marched me off to their fort. They pitched me against the wild dogs for sport, and when I fought back, they sold me to a man who trained me and set me to fight against bigger beasts. And he sold me to another, and on and on until Nine-Fingers paid a bag of silver and brought me here.'

Vita shivered. Could she really be speaking the truth? Father would never have done such a thing, nor Agrippa, she was sure.

'But how could they?'

The woman shook her head. 'For someone with so many questions inside, you know very little. Where did they steal *you* from?'

Vita's skin prickled. She couldn't risk telling her the truth. She needed another story; one the wolf-woman would believe. A sudden memory of the boy at the Forum sprang up.

She drew back her shoulders and forced herself to meet the wolf-woman's questioning gaze. 'I'm a runaway. I escaped from my master's villa across the river. They found me by the bridge. I . . . I was trying to get to the marshes.'

Brea's face took on a strange, hard-to-read look. 'The marshes? We have friends there. Good friends, don't we, Col?' She patted the wolf's side. He gave a whining yawn and sunk his head between his paws. A small smile played across her lips. 'He is tired out from his day of doing nothing.' Her eyes narrowed. 'What is that?' She jabbed a finger at Vita's throat.

Vita curled her fingers protectively round the owl-key.

'It is something my father gave me.'

'A night-hunter. You call them owls, I think?'

'Owls, yes.' As Vita spoke the word, the familiar sound of Father's pet name echoed into her ears. She bit her lip. He'd called her that because she loved books and learning. But what use had they been to her in saving him? And what use were they now in a place like this? Her eyes welled with tears. She blinked, doing her best to hold them back.

'Your father. Where is he now?'

Vita drew in a breath. 'He . . . he was killed.'

Brea frowned. 'I am sorry. In battle?'

'No.' She hesitated. She had to spin more of this new slave story and quickly. 'It . . . it was in our master's home. Some thieves came while he was away on business . . .' She dropped her head so the wolf-woman stood less chance of seeing through the lie. 'They killed my father and the other male slaves. Maybe my mother and brother too. Or else they took them with them. I'm not sure . . .'

'But you got away?'

She wiped her eyes on her sleeve and nodded.

Brea's jaw tightened. 'That is hard. Our stories. They are not so different.'

'What do you mean?' Vita looked up, frowning.

She sighed and stared off into the distance again. 'One day the Eagle-men came to our village on the hunt for men they could turn into Eagle-men too. My father was the protector of our place. He told the Eagle-man leader he would not allow it. The leader cut him down and watched while his men did the same to the other elders. Then they forced all the young men to go with them. My brother, Fyn, too. He was fifteen frost-seasons old.' She balled her fingers into fists and turned her head away.

Vita's chest gripped. She knew from Father the army did this. Took men from the lands they conquered and turned them into soldiers. It was their way, he said, of increasing their numbers and keeping the local population under control. But she'd never thought what it might be like for the ones it was done to. The ones left behind too . . .

'Did you see it happen?'

Brea heaved another sigh then turned back to face her, eyes dark with pain. 'I was hunting up on the mountain when I saw the smoke. It came from where our village was. But it was thick and black, not grey like the smoke from our own hearth-fires. I ran there as fast as I could. Father lay where the Eagle-man leader had left him. But it was too late. His life-spirit had already gone from him.' She shook her head and stared down at the ground.

'What did you do?'

'I made one of the women tell me what had happened. Then I followed the Eagle-men down to the shore and begged their leader to set my brother free; take me instead. He laughed in my face and said he would take me anyway.

Then he ordered his men to march me to the fort and he climbed up on to his boat and sailed away.'

Vita shivered. This must be him – the soldier the wolf-woman had talked about earlier. The one she wanted to hunt down and kill.

'Did you see him again? Fyn, I mean?'

'No. But I will. I have sworn it on this.' She pulled a small object from the sleeve of her tunic and pressed it to her lips.

'Can I see?' Vita knelt forward.

The wolf-woman hesitated, then held out her hand to reveal a small, rough-edged stone, about twice the size of her thumbnail. As the moonlight caught its surface, the stone glowed with a deep red fire.

Vita drew in a breath. 'It's beautiful!'

Brea nodded. 'I call it my firestone. Fyn gave it to me on our fifteenth birthday, three frost-seasons ago. He told me he found it on the shore. That it would protect me if ever we were parted, until we could be together again.'

'So you are twins?'

She shrugged. 'I do not know that word. But if you mean, did our mother bring us into the world on the same day, then yes.' She sank her fingers into Col's thick, silver-grey fur. He lifted his head and gave a small whine, then dropped down again and closed his eyes.

'You didn't say what happened to her. Did the soldiers –

I mean the Eagle-men – take her too?'

Brea gave another sigh. 'No. She died long before, when we were still young. Though if not for our father's kindness, we might all have gone to the spirit world the day she birthed us.'

Vita frowned. Kindness was an odd way to describe their father's love. But perhaps that's what they called it where she came from.

The wolf-woman's fingers curled over the firestone again and gripped it tight. 'My father should have joined her when he died. But it was denied him.'

'I don't understand?'

'To take a life-spirit without permission means the person cannot enter the spirit world. Not unless the wrong is righted. That is why, when I find the one who stole my father's life-spirit, I will cut the life from him in turn.' She sounded the final words as though each one was the stab of a knife.

Vita shuddered. But what Brea said about her father's spirit filled her with an even greater sense of dread. Because her own father's spirit wasn't at peace yet either; couldn't be until he'd had the proper funeral rites. And maybe not, as she knew some among her own people believed, until the guilty had been punished and proper justice served.

She swallowed hard and did her best to push the thought away. 'But how will you ever do that while you're shut up in this place?'

'I will be free soon. Free to find Fyn, and free to find the Eagle-man leader too.'

'Free? But how?'

A sudden closed look came across the wolf-woman's face. 'It does not matter.' Sliding the stone back inside her tunic, she lay down in the straw and shut her eyes. Moments later the slowness of her breathing told Vita that, like her wolf, Brea too had fallen fast asleep.

She puzzled over what she'd just heard. She knew a gladiator could win their freedom if they fought well in the arena. But even if the wolf-woman was freed, what chance would she stand of ever finding the man who'd done those awful things to her and her family? Especially when she didn't even know his name.

As she glanced at Brea's face, pale and still in the moonlight, Vita's heart gave another quick squeeze. She had trusted Vita enough to share her story. Was there a chance, in spite of their differences, they might become friends? A bubble of hope rose up inside her only to shiver and fizzle out. Because to be friends you had to be honest with each other. And how was that possible when the wolf-woman despised everything Vita and her world stood for?

IX

The next morning, on the bad-tempered cook's orders, Vita found herself in the kitchen cleaning the breakfast things. As she set about scouring one of the dirty porridge pots, she thought again of what the wolf-woman had told her last night about her family and their village. What must it really be like to live in the wildlands north of the wall? Most people, like those two gladiators yesterday, thought the northern tribes were troublemakers; little better than wild beasts. But from what Brea said, her people weren't like that . . .

She frowned. Father might have been wounded by a Blue-face spear. But he would never have approved of what the commander of those soldiers had done to them, she was sure.

The familiar ache seized her heart, twisting it so it felt as if it might tear in two. She let the pot slip back into the greasy, grey water and heaved a juddering sigh. She missed him so much. Mother and Lucius too.

A hand clipped the back of her head. She spun round with an indignant cry.

'You might've been used to daydreaming when you were a fine lady's maid, but there's no time for that here!' The cook glared at her, lips pressed in a pinched white line. 'And if you think that pot's clean, then you'd better give your eyes a good scrubbing too. Get on and do it properly, and quick about it! There's a crate-load of fish still to be gutted and a sack of onions to be chopped. And that's before we can even get started on the cooking.'

Vita clenched her teeth and fished the pot back out of the water. She was halfway through chopping the onions – doing her best to ignore the eye-watering smell – when a loud knock sounded on the door.

The cook slapped down the fish she was gutting with an angry-sounding tut. 'The delivery boy. Late as usual!'

Vita's heart gave a quick somersault. If it was the same one the men had spoken about yesterday, perhaps he'd have more news.

'Well?' The cook's shrill tones jolted her out of her thoughts. 'Are you going to let him in or what?'

Wiping her hands down the front of her tunic, Vita

hurried to the back door. There was no sign of the boy, but someone had dumped a full sack of flour on the floor outside it. She peered along the dim passageway beyond. The door at the other end had been shut earlier, but now it stood open. And through it she could see people – ordinary people – walking past in the sunshine-filled street.

A chance to escape – thank Minerva! But she had to act now. She threw a quick glance over her shoulder. The cook had her back to her and was busy lopping the heads off another pile of slimy brown fish. Vita sucked in a breath and launched herself at the open door.

She was almost there when a thick-set figure stepped into the gap.

'Where d'you think you're going, girly?'

Argus. She gave a silent groan.

'Well?'

She tucked a damp curl behind her ear. 'I-I was just coming to help the boy bring in the provisions. That woman . . . Cook . . . she sent me.' She jerked a thumb back towards the kitchen door.

Argus probed the gap in his front teeth with his tongue then nodded. 'All right. But you can wait for him to bring the stuff in. If you fancied your chances at a spot of freedom, it'd be me old Otho took it out on.' He winked at her then turned and bellowed over his shoulder. 'Hurry up, boy, unless you want me to set that old crosspatch of a cook on you!'

Vita peered longingly past him into the busy street beyond. She'd been so close . . .

'Give him a hand then!'

She started at the sight of a slender, dark-haired boy dragging a sack of flour through the doorway. As she stepped from the shadows, he twisted round to look at her.

Her breath caught in her throat. 'You!'

The boy frowned, before a sudden flicker in his eyes told her he'd recognized her now too. He pressed a slim brown finger to his lips and glanced back at Argus. But the slave was too busy hurling a greeting to someone he knew across the street.

Gesturing for her to pick up the other end of the sack, he led the way, shuffling backwards towards the kitchen door.

As they reached it, the cook appeared, hands jutted on her plump hips. 'There you are, Leander! I've got four baskets of loaves to make for that bunch of hungry great knuckleheads, and thanks to you, next to no time to do it in. Now drop it in the storeroom and fetch the others, quick about it!'

She jerked her head in the direction of a door to their left and bustled off back to her fish-gutting.

As they manoeuvred their load inside, past crates of

turnips and sacks of dried beans, the boy grinned at Vita. 'So the Minotaur trapped you after all, Ariadne?'

A hot rush of blood flooded Vita's cheeks. 'I am *not* Ariadne and this *isn't* a labyrinth, in case you hadn't noticed!'

He made a clicking sound with his tongue. 'You should have come with me when I asked you to. You would be safe now and among friends.'

Vita rolled her eyes. Not that again! 'You're a delivery boy. Which means what you said about not having a master was a lie.'

Leander took the sack from her and thumped it down on the dusty floor. 'Perhaps. Perhaps not.' He shot her a mysterious-looking smile.

'You talk in riddles.'

A loud rapping sounded on the door. 'What are you up to in there? This is no time for canoodling.'

Vita flushed again.

Leander gave a throaty chuckle. 'Come on, before she chops us up and throws us into one of her stews. But after we have finished, I have a message for you to pass on.'

Vita widened her eyes. 'A message? For who?'

Instead of replying, the boy threw her a mischievous wink and slid back out through the door.

As they puffed and panted the rest of the flour sacks into the storeroom, Vita did her best to find out what he knew about her father's death, without giving away who she really was. He'd helped her once, but still, that didn't mean she could trust him. She barely knew him. Besides, he clearly had his own share of secrets too.

But disappointingly, the boy seemed to know little except that a senior magistrate called Marcus Tullius Verus had been found stabbed to death in his grand townhouse at dawn yesterday. The words came easily to him, but for Vita each one felt like a hammer-blow. She took a deep breath to steady herself then asked him if there'd been any other victims. He shrugged and shook his head as if he didn't know. In desperation, she tried another tack.

'Is anyone investigating it?'

He heaved the last of the sacks into place with a groan, then turned back to face her. 'A lesser magistrate called Cassius Agrippa, I think.'

Vita's heart leapt as he spoke the name. 'Agrippa?'

Leander shot her a surprised look. 'You know him?'

'Yes. Er . . . Well, not exactly. He . . . he used to dine at my master's house.'

His eyes sparked with sudden anger. 'I've heard tell he is a cruel man.'

She frowned. Agrippa, cruel? What was he talking about? 'Why do you say that?'

His jaw tensed. 'It is what some people I know say.'

Vita pursed her lips. Who were these people and how

dare they spread such wicked lies? If anyone could catch Father's killers, it was Cassius Agrippa. And if by some miracle either Mother or Lucius were still alive, he'd make sure to rescue them too. Meanwhile, time was running out. Any moment now the cook would be barging in here demanding she get on with her duties.

But as she turned to go, the boy held her back.

'Wait. The message! Do you know Lupa?'

'I share a cell with her. Why?'

'Good. Then give her these.' He snatched up her hand and reaching into a small leather pouch at his waist, pressed a bunch of smooth, round objects into it. 'And tell her... tell her the thunder is coming soon.' His eyes flashed with a look of fresh fire.

'Thunder? What are you talking about?'

He opened his mouth then shut it again. 'I am sorry. I cannot say more.'

The door banged open and the cook stomped in, face darker than a cloud of angry hornets. 'It's the same every time with you. Always flirting with the girls. I've a good mind to complain to your master!' She grabbed him by the ear and yanked him towards her.

'Sorry, lady! Sorry!' Leander held up his hands. But as she dragged him back outside, he turned and threw Vita another quick wink. 'Take good care, Ariadne.'

In spite of herself, Vita let out a giggle.

As soon as the cook had seen him off, she whirled about to face her. 'Wipe that smirk off your face and get back to those onions.' She frogmarched Vita over to the work-bench then let out a horrified cry. 'You're supposed to peel them first, stupid girl!' She jabbed a finger at the mess of shredded skins and onion flesh, then gave her another sharp cuff on the ear. 'And if I catch you and that boy making eyes at each other again, I'll give you a lot worse!'

Vita mumbled a quick apology and picked up the knife. But the moment the woman had turned her back, she uncurled her other hand. Six tiny grey pebbles sat in her outstretched palm. She stared down at them, frowning. What did they signify? And how did the boy – Leander – and the wolf-woman know each other?

She needed to seek Brea out and ask her. But it would have to wait until later. In the meantime she had a mountain of foul-smelling onions to chop.

X

Vita planned to speak with Brea at the midday meal. But when the men filed into the dining hall, she wasn't with them.

It was when the cook sent her to draw a fresh supply of water from the well that she understood why. The wolf-woman was still out in the yard training. In place of the woollen tunic and breeches she'd been wearing earlier, she was dressed in a shorter, sleeveless tunic of lighter fabric, cinched at the waist with a thick leather belt. Her long, well-muscled arms and legs were bare. Her feet too.

She hadn't seen Vita yet. She was too busy twisting a thin wooden pole between her fingers then throwing it into the air and catching it again. Each time she tossed it, she sank to the ground on one knee before rising up to snatch it with ease as it fell.

Col was with her too, ears pricked, fierce yellow eyes following her every move. As Vita set down the bucket to watch, Brea swung the pole back over her shoulder and, with a strange, warlike cry, launched it into the air with all her might. Hurtling across the courtyard, it struck an apple balanced on top of a post and knocked it to the sand-covered ground. With a woofing bark, Col bounded forward, snatched up the apple in his jaws and racing back to his mistress, dropped it at her feet. The wolf-woman knelt and took it from him, then ruffled his fur and murmured something Vita couldn't catch.

Filling the bucket, Vita picked up a beaker from the well-top and, glancing hurriedly about her, set off towards them across the warm sand. At Col's yipped warning Brea stiffened and twisted round, then turned back and gave the wolf a reassuring pat.

'It is all right, friend. She means us no harm.' She jumped to her feet and cocked a pale eyebrow at Vita as if daring her to do otherwise. 'Why are you here?'

Vita swallowed and forced her mouth into a nervous smile.

'To bring you water.' She set the bucket at her feet. 'And these.' Darting another look over her shoulder, she slid a small twist of fabric from her tunic sleeve.

Brea's eyebrows arced in surprise. 'What is that?'

'It's from a friend of yours. Leander.'

'Leander?' She gave a puzzled-looking frown. 'I do not know that name.'

'He knows you.' Vita pushed the bundle at her.

The wolf-woman's eyes widened as she tipped the pebbles into her hand. 'Did this . . . this Leander say anything else?'

'Yes, he said to tell you the thunder is coming soon.'

The muscles in Brea's right cheek twitched.

'Does it mean something to you?'

She touched each of the pebbles in turn then fixed Vita with a penetrating stare. 'Can I trust you?'

Vita's stomach fluttered. She took a quick breath in and nodded.

'How can I be sure?'

'I give you my word.'

'Words are easy to speak. You must offer the gods something if you break it.'

'I swear it then. On . . . on my mother and brother's lives.'

Brea's eyes narrowed. 'And if they are dead already?'

A prickle of cold fear stole across Vita's skin, though in truth she knew she was probably right. 'On my own life then.'

Brea nodded. 'That is better.' She flicked a glance over

at the courtyard door, then drew in a breath. 'You remember the friends I told you of? The ones who live in the marshes?'

Vita started. The marshes. Of course! That was where the boy had claimed he lived too. And he'd said Leander was his slave name. Perhaps the wolf-woman knew him only by his real one. She nodded, keen for her to go on.

'Well, they are coming here.'

'What? But why?'

'To take weapons.'

Vita's throat tightened. 'Weapons? What for?'

'To make everyone free.'

'I . . . I don't understand. Who do you mean?'

'All the ones the Eagle-men and their kind have captured and forced to do their bidding. Like my friends and me. You too.'

'You mean slaves?'

The wolf-woman clenched her jaw. 'That is the Eagle-men's name for them, but yes.'

'But that's impossible. The Governor's soldiers will stop you!'

'Do not be so sure. There was a so-called slave once – a man who led an army of warriors against the Emperor and his Eagle-men in their own land. I have heard it spoken of. And this place – Londinium – has also been laid to waste before.'

'You mean by Boudicca? But she was beaten in the end. The Roman army is ten times the match of a bunch of barbarians – or slaves too.'

Brea's eyes flashed with green fire. 'Again, you speak like one of them! The Eagle-men are your enemies. You, a slave, should know that.'

Vita recoiled. 'What? No . . . Sorry, I don't mean to. It's just that . . . Well, I know what they are like.' She dipped her head to avoid the wolf-woman's gaze.

Brea balled up the stones in her fist. 'And you think I do not? When they have taken my family and my home from me. Bound and sold me like a beast. Made me fight for their pleasure so they can get rich on the blood I and the others like me are forced to spill.'

A sharp-edged voice rang out across the courtyard. 'What are you doing out here, girl?'

Janus. Vita's heart sank. What did he want?

Brea snatched up the bucket. 'She brought me and my wolf water.' She dunked the beaker and took a long hard drink, then scooped up a second cupful for Col. As he lapped at it with his long pink tongue, she looked up and fixed Vita with a hard-eyed stare. 'Go! But remember what you swore. If your words are not true, I will take your life-spirit from you myself.'

Vita gulped in a breath and nodded.

'Vita! Come here this instant!'

Heaving a sigh, she turned and trudged back to where Otho's assistant stood waiting for her in the shadows, fingers tugging at the copper necklet round his scrawny throat.

He glared at her as she approached. 'Hurry, girl! Master Otho has an important visitor. You are to serve refreshments in his rooms.' Seizing her by the arm, he twisted her round and force-marched her back inside.

Vita stumbled along beside him, head spinning at what she'd just heard. This plan of Brea's rebel friends to steal weapons and set all the slaves of Londinium free . . . it was madness. Innocent people were going to get killed. She should warn someone before it was too late. But who would listen to her in this place? And if the wolf-woman found out she'd betrayed her, one thing was sure – her revenge would be swift as a spear-throw and just as deadly.

Janus led her back out into the passage, past the small shrine to Fortuna where one of the other girls said the gladiators made offerings for good luck in the ring. Then, up a flight of wooden stairs and on to a small, dark landing where a jug of wine and a plate of honey-cakes stood ready on a side table next to a large, metal-studded door. As Vita picked up the tray, the gladiator-master's gruff tones echoed out from behind it.

'Of course, Your Honour. A week's time is tight, but I am sure we can arrange things to your satisfaction. And with the generous purse you are offering, we'll make sure it's a spectacle fit for the Emperor Hadrian himself.'

Another, more cultured voice spoke in reply. A voice Vita knew well . . .

'I'm sure I don't need to tell you what a great man he was. But he was my dearest friend too, and while the Governor is away in the north inspecting construction on the Emperor's wall, it is my solemn duty to ensure we honour his memory. With the funeral first of course. And then these games – which if done right will be a fitting tribute to an honourable comrade and citizen who was both brave and just.' The man's voice broke with emotion as he spoke the last words.

Agrippa! Vita stumbled sideways in shock, sending the tray and its contents crashing to the floor. For a heart-stopping moment there was silence. Then a scrape of wood on stone, the sound of brisk footsteps and the rattle and bang of the door.

'What in the name of Mars?' The gladiator-master glared down at her, black eyes flashing.

She steeled herself and took a step forward. She had to let Agrippa know she was here, but as she made to call out a hand clamped her mouth and jerked her backwards.

'I'm sorry, master. She dropped the tray – stupid girl. I will have her bring more wine and clean up this mess.' Keeping a firm hold on her, Janus tipped his head at the mound of broken pottery and bits of wine-soaked honey-cake at their feet.

'She embarrasses me before our guest. Someone else can clean up. Get her out of my sight, now!' Otho shot Vita another furious look, then turned on his heel and strode back inside, slamming the door behind him.

Muttering a low curse, the slave pulled Vita tight against him and bundled her back down the stairs. When they reached the bottom he turned on her and poked an accusing finger in her ribs.

'You made me look a fool back there.'

'I didn't mean to, but—'

'Silence! You're lucky Master Otho didn't give you a beating on the spot. There'll be one coming though, you can be sure of that. In the meantime' – he dragged her over to a door opposite – 'you can sweep up the mess the mice have made in this storeroom. There's a broom inside.'

As the key rattled in the lock, Vita blinked and peered about her. How could the rotten toad expect her to find the broom let alone use it, when she couldn't even see her own hands?

Heaving a sigh, she slumped down on the ground and pulled her knees up to her chin. She'd failed to get free for a second time. And when Janus finally came to let her out, Agrippa – her best, her only chance of help – would be sure to have gone. And then what?

Doing her best to hold down a fresh wave of fear, she went back over what she'd heard Agrippa say. Her heart cramped at the thought of not having a chance to honour Father at his funeral or say a last goodbye. And a grand games staged in his memory in a week's time. She frowned. She wasn't sure what to think about that. It seemed so soon after what had happened – and Father's dislike for the spectacles was well known. And what about Mother and Lucius? There'd been no mention of them ...

The ache in her chest grew stronger still. In a desperate bid to hold back her tears, she reached for the owl-key at her neck and pressed its warm metal to her lips. She *had* to find a way of getting out of here. But how?

A spark of hope flickered up inside her. Maybe if Agrippa came back to see Otho again before the games? Unless the wolf-woman's rebel friends struck first. That would be another way ... She shuddered. Surely it wouldn't come to that? Leaning her head against the wall, she closed her eyes and did her utmost to force the thought back down.

XI

When at last Janus came for Vita, he took great delight in telling her it was 'time for that beating!', then hauled her shivering back to Otho's rooms.

As they waited outside the gladiator-master's door, she prayed for the gods to take pity on her and dull the pain.

When Otho finally opened it, he batted Janus away with an impatient wave of his hand and gestured for Vita to step inside. Resisting the urge to turn tail and run, she drew in a breath and slid past him. The room was lit by a long, oblong window set into the back wall and partly covered by a rust-coloured blind. She glanced around fearfully, only half taking in the scene – the ochre-coloured walls daubed with a badly done mural of a gladiator pair in combat, a heavy wooden desk and a large iron door, slightly ajar, set into the wall behind. Her gaze snagged on the terracotta statue standing on a shelf beside it. Pushing past her, Otho snatched it up and turned back to face her, eyes alight with sudden pride.

'Impressive, isn't he?' It was the statue of a bare-chested warrior. His right hand gripped a curved dagger, his left a small rectangular shield, while on his head he wore a helmet mounted with the crest of a strange, horned creature, half-bird, half-beast.

'The Thracian! That's what I fought as before I won my freedom and was awarded my honorary *rudis* by the Emperor. A proud moment.' Setting the statue down on the desk, he snatched up a wooden sword from a bronze stand and pressed it to his chest.

'We gladiators are the lowest of the low outside the arena. But inside it, the crowd loves us. At least those of us who uphold the gladiator's oath – to fight bravely and, if the Fates decree it, to meet death with courage and fortitude.' He lifted the sword high in the air as if to make a strike, then lowered it again and ran a finger along the wooden blade. 'Back in my fighting days I was top of the tree. The only thing I ever lost was this.' He waggled the stump of his missing finger at her and grimaced.

Vita's stomach clenched. Why make her suffer his stupid stories? Better if he just got on with the beating. At least then it would all be over . . .

But still he droned on, his gaze fixed above her head now, as if reliving past victories. 'I was fearless. Everyone said so. People came from miles around to watch me best my opponents in the ring. And now . . .' His eyes snapped back on her. 'Now they pay *me* to come and watch the ones I train.'

Placing the sword carefully back on its stand, he stepped round behind the desk-top and rattled open a drawer beneath. Vita froze. This was it; any moment now he'd pull out his whip and deal her the first blow. She closed her eyes and muttered another quick prayer.

'What's wrong with you, girl?'

She flicked her eyes open again. Instead of brandishing a whip, Otho sat frowning back at her across the desk, a wooden toothpick clamped between his teeth.

'Nothing, but . . . I thought . . . I mean, Janus said you were going to give me a beating.'

Otho slid the toothpick free and gave a scoffing snort. 'I've got more important things to do with my time! No, I summoned you here to tell you about the new duties I'm assigning you.'

Vita heaved a sigh and offered up a silent thank you to the gods.

'Pay attention, girl!' She jumped as the gladiator-master's hand slammed the desk. 'In a week's time His

Honour, Gaius Cassius Agrippa – the visitor you did your best to embarrass me in front of earlier – has commissioned a grand games. It is to be held in honour of his dear, departed comrade, the great councillor and magistrate, Marcus Tullius Verus, brutally slain in his own home just two nights ago.'

Vita's chest cramped again as he spoke her father's name. But this was her chance! She'd tell him who she really was. Make him believe it whether he wanted to or not! But as she made to speak, he went on.

'Shocking business! The sooner they can track down the no-good slaves that did it, the better.'

Vita stiffened. 'But how do you know it was slaves?'

'You will address me as *master*, unless you want that beating after all?' He jabbed the toothpick at her, black eyes flashing.

'Yes, master.' She spoke the words through gritted teeth.

Otho pulled a strand of stringy meat from his mouth, examined it then wiped it on his tunic sleeve. 'It's what the Honourable Agrippa thinks. By the time the alarm was raised, the kitchen slaves had been murdered. But there was no sign of the house steward. The nursemaid either . . .'

Vita's mouth dried. What was he saying? That Festa and Felix had somehow played a part in her father's death? But that was impossible! Festa had looked after her and Lucius since they were tiny babies. And she'd saved Vita's life too.

As for Felix, he might be a former runaway, but since Father had rescued him off the streets a few months ago, he'd served him loyally. He'd never do such a thing, she was sure of it.

But Otho hadn't finished yet.

'The Honourable Agrippa has offered a reward for their recapture. A very generous one.' The gladiator-master's eyes lit up again as he spoke the words. 'Whoever did it, my guess is they were put up to it by that bunch of runaways they say are hiding out in the marshes.'

Vita drew in a sharp breath. The wolf-woman's rebel slave friends! If Otho was right, perhaps the man who'd brought her here was one of them, and had pretended to be a slave-trader to make a few *denarii* for himself on the side? But then that would mean Father – dear, beloved Father – had been their first innocent victim!

Otho jerked backwards in his chair. 'Of course! You're a runaway too, aren't you?' Tossing the toothpick to the floor, he jumped to his feet and grabbed her by the sleeve. 'If you know something, you'd better tell me now.'

'I'm not, I'm . . .' She bit down on her lip. Rather than waste time trying to persuade him she was Father's daughter, why not tell him about the rebellion instead? With all this talk of runaway slaves being behind Father's murder, he'd be bound to believe her. Then he'd have to call Agrippa back in and she'd be saved. It would mean breaking her oath to the wolf-woman, but if her friends were involved, then they deserved everything they got.

'Well?' The gladiator-master pressed his whiskery face close to hers, enveloping her in a cloud of sour-wine breath.

She was about to answer when she was overcome by a sudden pang of doubt. Father always said you needed proof of someone's guilt before you could accuse them . . . She wavered for a moment, then shook her head. 'I don't know anything, master, I swear it.'

'All right. But if I find out you've been lying . . .' He tightened his grip for a moment, then released her and sat down heavily in his chair. 'Now, back to the reason I sent for you. Agrippa is paying for our premium show – the full range of fighters – *secutor*, *retiarius*, *murmillo*. The Thracian too, of course.' He gave a smug smile and patted the terracotta warrior's helmeted head. 'And from unblooded ones to the star acts, the Skull-Crusher, and your friend Lupa included.'

Vita's stomach tightened.

'Which means . . . Are you listening, girl?'

She swallowed and gave a quick nod.

'Which means we'll be getting a fresh supply of beasts delivered before the week is out. Beasts that will need feeding. And that' – he jabbed a hairy finger at her – 'is where you come in.'

A shiver of ice rippled down Vita's spine. Brea had told

her as much last night – but that was before Agrippa's plans for a new games had been announced.

Otho bent over and picked up the toothpick. 'No need to look like a startled deer. You're small and light-footed. And I'm sure the She-Wolf can teach you a few tricks to keep the brutes at bay.' He gave a mocking laugh then jumped to his feet and jerked his head at the door. 'Now, be off with you.'

As Vita backed through it, a shaft of sunlight caught on something propped inside the half-open iron door behind the gladiator-master's desk. She blinked and raised a hand against the metallic gleam. Otho cast a frowning glance over his shoulder, then, snatching a large, bronze-coloured, 'L'-shaped key from a ring on his belt, slammed the door shut and locked it.

Vita turned and hurried out into the passage. Her head was spinning so much she didn't trust herself with the stairs yet. Instead, pressing her back against the wall, she took a long, deep breath and let everything Otho had told her sink in.

The thought of having to feed the beasts filled her with dread, but the idea that Brea's slave friends might be responsible for Father's murder – perhaps the deaths of Mother and Lucius too – was even worse. She had to know for certain though. And the only way of doing that was to confront the wolf-woman and see what she said. But what

Otho had claimed about Festa and Felix being a part of it. That couldn't be true.

At the thought of the house steward, a sudden memory slid into her head. Something Festa had said after they'd fled the house. That Felix had gone on an errand for Father that afternoon.

. . . but had not yet returned.

So why had Vita found his leather bracelet lying covered in blood outside the dining-room door? A knot formed in the pit of her stomach. Festa told her there'd been two men involved in the attack. The man who'd sold Vita to Otho was one. But could Felix be the other? What if he *had* come back later with his fellow assassin, and the bracelet had come off in a struggle with one of his victims? Rosia? Cottia?

Father?

She shuddered. Could the accusations about Felix be true after all? There was only one way to find out. Ask Brea if he was one of the rebels. And if he was, then Vita would have all the proof she needed and the promise she'd made the wolf-woman would mean nothing. Nothing at all.

XII

Vita carried out the rest of the day's tasks while rehearsing what she would say to the wolf-woman. She had to be careful not to make her suspicious – or worse still, angry. She could do it though, she was sure.

But as Argus led her back to the sleeping-cell, her courage shrivelled until, by the time they had reached the door, it felt no bigger than the size of one of Leander's pebbles.

A loud yip sounded as she stepped back into the gloom, followed moments later by the nudge of a cold wet nose against the back of her legs.

Col stood looking up at her, tongue lolling, eyes gleaming a fiery gold. Beyond him sat Brea, cross-legged in the shadows against the far wall. Her eyes were shut, but they slid open as Vita approached.

'He likes you.'

Vita glanced down at the wolf padding along at her side. 'I like him too.' She brushed her fingertips across the collar of thick fur at his neck, doing her best to hide her fear about the question she needed to ask. 'How—' She gave a small cough and started again. 'How did you come by him?'

Brea sighed and extended a hand to the animal. He bounded over and sank down beside her. She fondled his ears then looked up at Vita again. 'The beast-trappers brought him in when he was still a cub, by accident. The Eagle-men don't approve of us *venatores* hunting wolves in the arena. They say they are – what is your word for it? Sacred to them. I asked if I could keep him. Nine-Fingers thought it could make him more money if I had a wolf at my side, so he agreed.'

Vita swallowed nervously. She couldn't avoid the subject for ever. Best get it over and done with. At least then she'd have an answer. 'Do you know a runaway called Felix?'

The wolf-woman's forehead pulled into a frown. 'No. Should I?'

Vita faltered, unsure of what to say next. Her reaction seemed genuine. But then what if it was the same as with Leander – that she knew Felix by another name?

'Why do you ask me this?' Brea fixed her with a searching stare.

'Because . . .' She swallowed again.

Think, Vita! Think!

'Because the man who is hunting the ones who broke into my master's house came here today to see Otho about a new games he wants him to stage. I heard them talking when I brought them wine. They think this Felix and some other runaways are behind it.'

Brea jumped to her feet. Col did the same, hackles rising. 'Did they say anything else?'

'Not about what you told me, no.' Vita licked her lips. This wasn't going how she'd planned. But if she could get the wolf-woman to say more about the revolt, there was still a chance she'd let slip something that might incriminate the rebels in Father's murder after all. She braced herself and went on. 'When are your friends going to steal the weapons and get the rest of the slaves to rise up against their Eagle-men masters?'

Brea's eyes flashed with sudden fire. 'I said only that they were going to make them free again. It has not begun yet. We must wait for six more nights. It was in the message the boy brought.'

Vita shot her a puzzled frown.

'The stones. There are six. Remember?' The wolf-woman fished inside her tunic and held out her palm.

So that was it! A pebble for each day.

'What if the attack on my fa— I mean, my master's

house was a practice for what is to come?'

Brea shook her head. 'Taran would not be so foolish.'

Vita's ears pricked. 'Taran. Is that your leader?'

The wolf-woman's face took on a guarded look. 'My friends did not act against your master.' She spoke the words slowly through clenched teeth.

'But how can you know that when you've been shut away in here?'

She gripped Vita's arm. 'I told you. We want to free slaves, not kill them. Besides, a hunter does not break cover when surprise is on their side. It is their best and strongest weapon, at least before the chase begins.'

Vita frowned again. What she said did make some kind of sense. But if the men who killed Father weren't the marsh runaways, then who were they?

Brea released her grip. 'This man who came here today, the one who has asked for the new contests, who is he?'

'A junior magistrate called Cassius Agrippa.' Vita's cheeks flushed as she spoke the name.

The wolf-woman narrowed her eyes. 'There is something you are keeping hidden.'

Vita's face grew hotter still. She had to put her off the scent. 'It . . . it is nothing. Just that he is betrothed to my master's daughter.' She spoke the word 'betrothed' in Latin, not knowing what it was in the native British tongue.

Brea looked at her blankly.

'It means I . . .' Vita checked herself. 'I mean, she is to become his wife.' She threw the wolf-woman a quick glance, but she didn't appear to have noticed the slip.

'You mean she is to be his woman?'

Vita flushed again. 'Yes.'

'Did he see you?'

'No. I spilt the wine outside the room and Otho sent me away.'

The wolf-woman gave a sharp, barking laugh. 'That will not have pleased Nine-Fingers.'

Vita pulled a face at the memory. 'It didn't.'

'So is this magistrate good at what he does?'

'I . . . I think so, yes.'

'Well, then you must let him do his work. At least until my friends come for us.'

Vita's stomach knotted. 'And after?'

Curling her fingers round the pebbles, she pressed them against her chest and fixed Vita with a penetrating gaze. 'After, things will change and there will be a different sort of law-making. One that is better for people like you and me. And if this Agrippa has not found the ones who took your father's life-spirit and stole your family by then, I swear I and my friends will do what we can to help you instead. But only if—' Her look grew more piercing.

Vita's heart bumped against her chest. 'If what?'

'If you keep the words of the swearing you have already made.'

'And if I don't?'

'I said I would kill you if you broke them. It would be easy to.' She looked Vita up and down, then let out a sigh. 'But for the sake of your dead father, and mine too, I will not.'

Vita's chest tightened. When she'd come in here to confront the wolf-woman, she'd been convinced Agrippa and Otho must be right about the marsh runaways and their involvement in Father's death. But now? Now she wasn't so sure . . .

Brea was right about one thing though. Agrippa *was* Vita's best hope. Both of winning justice for Father, Mother and Lucius and of getting out of here too. She would go back to Otho tomorrow, claim she did know something about the murders – something that would persuade him she had to speak to Agrippa directly. Meanwhile, if Leander made another kitchen delivery, she could test the wolf-woman's story by asking him about Felix too.

Brea gripped her by the shoulder. 'Well?'

Vita blinked and gave a hurried nod.

'Good.' She pushed the stones back inside her tunic. 'Now we must rest. You too, Col.' She ruffled the wolf's shaggy head. 'We will need all our strength and wits for what is to come.'

❧ XIII ❧

But the chance to speak to Otho either the next day or in the days that followed never came. The only time Vita caught sight of the gladiator-master was out in the yard when she was on water-fetching duty and he was busy supervising the men's training, yelling at them to 'jump higher', 'run faster', 'fight harder'.

Time passed in a blur of drudgery and exhaustion. All the slaves were worked hard, but it felt like the pinch-mouthed cook and the gladiator-master's wily assistant kept the dirtiest jobs for Vita and found fault with every-thing she did. And with only a bucket of cold well-water in the cell to wash in, her hair and skin got grimier and grimier as the days went on.

There was no hint of a return visit by Agrippa to discuss arrangements for the games, and no sign of Leander either. Cook must have done what she'd threatened and complained to whoever his master was, because now the food deliveries were made by other boys. As for the beasts, there was no further talk of when they might arrive, though Janus taunted her about her new duties whenever he got the chance. Vita refused him the satisfaction of showing her fear. But it was a different story at night when her dreams were plagued by visions of skin-piercing teeth and flesh-ripping claws.

She was terrified of what the planned revolt by Taran and his band of runaway slaves would mean for families like hers if it went ahead too. Though a part of her – what Father would call the less honourable part – hoped if they did launch their weapons raid, it would come before the beasts turned up.

When they were locked back in the cell for the night, she and the wolf-woman spoke little. In part because they were both so worn out; in part because Vita was fearful of any more clumsy slips of the tongue that might give away her true identity.

Meanwhile, the games were all the men could talk about. That and the feast the night before, when everyone taking part would get the chance to gorge themselves on the finest food and wine at Cassius Agrippa's expense. The question on everyone's lips when they met for meals in the dining hall was who would be paired to fight who. They were even placing bets on it, and who might live or die – though according to Cook such a thing was strictly forbidden.

Vita was on floor-sweeping duties by the main entrance, thinking for the hundredth time how barbaric it all was, when a loud rap on the door made her start. Agrippa? Murmuring a quick prayer to Fortuna, she pulled back into the shadows and waited. A few moments later, the door to the accounting room swung open and Janus hurried out. Glancing along the passage, he muttered something under his breath, then smoothed a hand over his tunic and darted up to the door.

He pulled the hatch back and peered out, then, producing a key from his waist-pouch, he unlocked the door and rattled it open. A hooded figure slipped inside. Relocking the door, the slave gestured for the visitor to follow and scuttled back into the accounting room.

Vita heaved a disappointed sigh. It wasn't Agrippa. If it were, Janus would have made much more of a fuss and escorted him straight to Otho's rooms upstairs. A trades-man then, calling in about the supply of goods for the upcoming games. She picked up the broom again. As she drew closer to the door, Janus's voice sounded from behind it, nervy and high-pitched.

'When exactly are we to expect the beasts?'

Vita's stomach lurched. This was it – the moment she'd been dreading. She crept forward and pressed her ear to the crack. There was a creak of wood, like someone shifting in a chair, before the other man replied.

'Tomorrow at dawn. Ten in total.'

She froze. That voice! The way it rasped out the words, like the man's throat was full of stones.

'Very good. And of what sort?'

'Home-grown. Wild hogs and a bear, to be set against each other. And the prize beast for the She-Wolf to be delivered straight to the arena.'

It was him! The man who'd brought her here. The assassin – or one of them anyway. The ground turned to river-mud beneath her. She staggered sideways, clutching at a nearby cupboard for support.

Janus's high, braying laugh sounded in reply. 'A rare treat for the crowd!'

The other man gave a loud snort. 'Cassius Agrippa is not one to pass up the chance of a crowd-pleaser to win himself a few extra votes.'

'Yes, Master Otho said he was hoping to fill the vacancy left by the Honourable Verus of exalted memory. Such a tragedy for a man to be cut down in his prime like that. The Honourable Agrippa must miss his friend sorely. But I'm sure he will prove a popular choice with the citizens.'

Vita frowned. So Agrippa was going to put himself forward for Father's position as senior magistrate.

A bitter-sounding laugh jolted her out of her thoughts. 'No doubt – my master always gets his way.'

Master? Her breath caught in her throat. Had she heard right? Was this . . . Agrippa's man?

She flinched at the sudden scrape of wood on stone.

'Now, I must go. The trappers expect payment before they will deliver the beasts.'

'Of course. Let me show you out.' The door swung open.

Vita shrank back into the shadows and watched, heart in mouth, as Janus led the man to the entrance and let him out.

If he was part of Agrippa's household, then she'd been wrong about him being one of the runaways. Perhaps what the wolf-woman had told her was true and her rebel comrades really did have nothing to do with Father's death. But what possible motive could this man have for murdering his master's oldest friend? She shook her head. It didn't make sense.

She was so lost in the storm of her own thoughts, she didn't hear the footsteps returning until it was too late.

'What are you doing skulking about out here?' Janus glared at her suspiciously. 'The men need feeding. Off to the kitchen with you and look sharp about it!' He gave her a shove in the ribs.

Resisting the powerful urge to shove him back, Vita snatched up the broom and marched off in the direction of the dining hall.

XIV

Cook scowled at Vita as, head still spinning, she trudged in through the kitchen door.

'About time too! Fetch me some water and then you can pluck and joint the fowl.' She jabbed her knife at a crate of limp-headed chickens on the workbench. 'The men are to have meat from now on. Master's orders. To help build them up for what lies ahead.' She picked up the bucket and rammed it against Vita's chest.

As Vita stepped into the open a menacing roar split the air. She glanced across the training yard. Instead of the usual sight of men slashing at targets or punching grain-sacks, the whole lot of them were stood in a semicircle, backs towards her, jeering loudly and shaking their fists.

Otho must have pitched a pair of the gladiators against each other so the rest could watch. But as Vita lugged the bucket to the well, desperately trying to make sense of what she'd just learnt, another cry went up. Higher-pitched this time and joined by a volley of frantic barks too. The wolf-woman? Tossing the bucket aside, Vita sprinted over to where the men stood and wormed her way through the mass of sweaty bodies to the front.

Her heart jolted as she came out into the open. Two figures stood facing each other, legs braced, hands gripped on their weapons, as if squaring up for a fight. One was the wolf-woman. And the other . . . Vita's scalp prickled. The other was the Skull-Crusher.

But this couldn't be right! Men were forbidden to fight against women. That's what Brea had told her. So why didn't Otho stop them?

Vita scanned about her, but there was no sign of him. The assistant-trainers were there, but they were cheering and yelling insults with the rest.

Another volley of barks ricocheted around the yard. Col! But where? She shaded her eyes. And then she saw him, a silver-grey shape pacing behind the bars of a wooden cage by the wall on the far side.

The wolf-woman was on her own . . .

A torrent of Germanic curse-words ripped through the air behind her. Vita turned to see the Skull-Crusher lumber towards Brea, his wooden training sword pointed straight at her. She stood her ground, but as the Skull-Crusher took another step forward, she twisted her pole slantwise across her body, readying herself to ward off the approaching blow.

Vita shuddered. She still wasn't sure whether to believe her or not. But she couldn't stand here and watch her face this brute alone. She had to act, and quickly!

A sudden, ear-shattering howl drowned out the men's cries and all at once Vita knew what to do. Gathering her tunic, she gulped in a breath and dashed towards the cage. As she drew close, the wolf froze mid-howl, then dropped his head and gave a low, menacing growl.

'It's all right, Col. It's me.' Heart racing, she shoved the tips of her fingers through the bars. The animal sniffed them and gave a small whine.

'Good boy. Now, quickly! Your friend needs us.'

No sooner had the words left her lips than a thundering bellow sounded behind them, followed by cries of 'Get her!' and 'Show her who's boss!'

Vita's chest gripped. Time was running out. She snatched hold of the door-latch and yanked it open. 'Go save her, Col!'

But the wolf didn't need an invitation. He shot past her, a blur of grey fur, making straight for where the giant stood, sword poised and ready to strike. With a howl of fury, he leapt at the Skull-Crusher, barging into him and jolting his weapon from his hand. Cronos gave a roar of surprise and staggered backwards. For a heart-stopping instant it looked as if he would fall. But at the last moment, he righted himself and spun round, arms spread, legs splayed.

Throwing back her head, the wolf-woman uttered a warlike scream and charged. But she was no match for him and, thrusting out a muscled arm, the brute knocked her to the ground face down. Sounding another gut-wrenching howl, the wolf sprang again. But the Skull-Crusher jerked up his knee and caught him square on the flank, sending him crashing into the sand. Raising his foot high above the animal's head, he turned to his comrades and bared his teeth in a grinning leer. They yelled back at him, baying like a pack of blood-hungry hounds.

Vita darted a look at the wolf-woman, but she hadn't moved.

She couldn't let him do this.

Begging Minerva for her protection, she snatched up Brea's pole and ran at the giant with a shrieking cry. He swung round frowning, then snarled at her and made a swiping lunge. She jumped sideways but lost her footing and fell sprawling to the ground. As roars of laughter echoed about her, a giant shadow loomed over her, blotting out the light. Muttering a quick prayer, she shrank up into a ball and waited for the blow.

'What, Cronos? So you fight girls and dogs now?'

Vita snapped her eyes open and pushed up in time to see a stocky figure barging his way to the front of the crowd.

Otho! A wave of relief surged through her.

The Skull-Crusher wavered, then, kicking a shower of sand over her, he stepped back and let his arms fall to his sides.

The gladiator-master drew alongside him. He threw Vita a furious glance then turned back to face the giant. 'You will get your chance in the sun in two days' time, Skull-Crusher. Gaius Cassius Agrippa is paying good money to see both you and the She-Wolf perform. So I won't have the goods damaged before the show. Do you understand me?'

Cronos growled and spat into the sand – but it was clear the fight was over.

After the doctor had examined Brea and Col and declared no serious damage had been done, Otho ordered them confined to the cell for the rest of the day and for Vita to take them food once the gladiators had been fed.

When she finally managed to escape Cook's clutches, the shadows outside were already lengthening. As the door to the cell slammed shut behind her, she saw that a wooden truckle-bed had been shoved against the wall. The wolf-woman lay on it motionless, her back towards the door. Col sat on the ground beside her, eyes closed, sides heaving in and out.

A spike of guilt snagged Vita's chest. Poor Col!

As if in answer, a low whine sounded from beside the bed. Biting her lip, she tiptoed over and set the tray of food she was carrying down on the floor. Her cellmate didn't stir, but the wolf blinked and, lifting his shaggy head, sniffed the air. Vita pushed a bowl of raw chicken scraps towards him.

'I'm sorry, Col. I didn't mean for you to get hurt.' She gave a low sigh and combed her fingers gently through his fur.

'It is not your fault.' The wolf-woman jerked upright and swung her bare feet to the ground. 'You used your wits, like a good hunter should. The Skull-Crusher is the one to blame for this.' She ran a hand over the back of her neck and winced.

'So . . . so what happened?'

'What always happens. He waited for Nine-Fingers to be gone then picked a fight with me.' She rotated her right arm and pulled another face then switched her gaze back on Vita. 'It is the second time you have saved me. Though the way you chose the first time was more unusual.' Throwing Vita a wry-looking smile, she helped herself to the bowl of chicken and vegetable stew from the tray and began to shovel it down.

Vita glanced at her as she ate. Should she tell her about Agrippa's man?

As if sensing the thought, Brea lifted her head. 'Something troubles you?'

'A man came to see Janus today, about the beasts. They are bringing wild hogs and a bear tomorrow morning at daybreak. The man said there would be another – a prize beast, he called it – for you to fight.'

Brea dropped her spoon and fixed her with a glittering green stare. 'What is it?'

'He didn't say. It is to be delivered straight to the arena. But . . . well, there is something else too.'

Brea frowned. 'Another beast?'

'No. It is about the man.' She hesitated, then, making up her mind, drew in a breath. 'He is one of the ones who killed my father.'

The wolf-woman's eyes widened. 'You know this?'

'Yes. I recognized his voice. But . . .' Vita chewed on her lip. 'There is more.'

'What?'

'He works in the household of Cassius Agrippa.'

Brea's face pulled into another frown. 'The one who was going to take your master's daughter for a wife?'

Vita gave a quick swallow and nodded.

'So why would his servant do such a thing?'

'I . . . I don't know. Unless . . .' The familiar doubt clawed at her chest. 'Unless . . . do you know anyone who works in Agrippa's household?'

The wolf-woman's eyes flashed with sudden fire. 'You still think my friends had something to do with this? I have told you before, they would not risk all they have planned for by doing such a thing now. You should look for another to blame.' She shoved the bowl back down on the tray and turned her back on Vita, mouth pressed into a thin, hard line.

'But . . . but who?'

The wolf-woman twisted round to face her again. 'I do not know. Maybe this man was only doing what his master commanded?'

Vita's eyes widened. What was she saying? That Agrippa had given the order for Father to be killed? 'No, that's not possible!'

'Isn't it?' Brea cocked a pale eyebrow. 'Your master and this Agrippa, they are friends?'

'Er . . . yes.'

'Friends can turn into enemies. Look at the Eagle-men's tale of the two wolf-brothers. Ree-muss and the other one.'

She meant Romulus and Remus – the twin brothers, raised by wolves, whose story was part of the founding of Rome. Romulus had killed Remus over a dispute about which hill they should build the city on.

Vita's eyes widened. 'What do you mean?'

'Maybe like the wolf-brothers, your master and Agrippa argued over something and Agrippa was angry and wanted revenge?'

Her stomach jolted. It couldn't be . . . could it?

She cast her mind back to the day of the murder. Father seeming troubled when she'd gone to see him in his study. Then, bumping into Agrippa on the way to the play and his mention of the urgent meeting her father had summoned him to. And returning home after to find her parents arguing over whether to tell her something. Something serious, though she'd never got the chance to find out what.

But it wasn't to do with Agrippa catching her sneaking off to see the play, because as she'd discovered when she got back, he hadn't told them. What else? Could the wolf-woman be right? Had he and Father had an argument? Perhaps. But even if they had, Agrippa would never hurt Father. He'd saved his life on the battlefield and been honoured as a hero for it.

'I can see you do not like my story.' The wolf-woman's words jerked her back to the present. 'But still, I think it is worth testing. As you have tested me about my friends. Maybe then you will believe me.' She threw Vita an accusing look.

She flushed. 'What do you mean?'

'You could set a snare for him.'

'How?'

'In two nightfalls' time. There is to be a great feast, remember? This Agrippa is the one who has asked for the games, which means he and his friends have the right to meet with all those who will fight. There will be food and wine. Songs and dancing too. And Nine-Fingers will expect the ones who work for him to attend on the guests, including you.'

'So . . .'

'So you can test him then.'

'How can I do that if I'm meant to be serving?'

Brea tapped a finger to her head. 'You have quick wits. You have shown that more than once. There is still time to think of something. And I will help if I can. But I need you to do something in return.'

'What is it?'

The wolf-woman's eyes narrowed. 'I will tell you tomorrow, after the feeding of the beasts.'

Vita slumped at the reminder of her new task. 'I'm not sure there will be any "after".'

The wolf-woman reached out and squeezed her arm. 'There will. All you need to do is remember these three things. Keep low, move fast, and do not let the beast get between you and your way of escape.' She held Vita's gaze for a moment, then, whistling for Col to jump up beside her, she stretched out on the truckle-bed and closed her eyes. The wolf followed suit, and in a few short moments the pair of them were deep asleep.

XV

While her two cellmates slept soundly, Vita tossed and turned, going over what she and the wolf-woman had talked about.

There was no point trying to work out what favour it was the wolf-woman wanted of her. She'd find that out soon enough, if she survived her encounter with the beasts. But could Brea be right about Agrippa? And if she was, what possible motive could her father's friend have for committing such a terrible crime?

Friends can turn into enemies.

Vita frowned. Could an argument between friends ever be serious enough to make one murder the other?

She shook her head. Whatever the legend said Romulus

did to his brother, she couldn't believe it of Agrippa. But then the same question came circling back again. Why would his servant do such a thing? Unless he *was* one of Taran's men, after all?

Her stomach knotted as a fresh thought occurred. What if both he and her parents' own house steward, Felix, were the rebel leader's spies – planted in the households of two of Londinium's most important men to search for information useful to the rebels' cause? Was that the reason for Father's urgent meeting with Agrippa? Perhaps he'd found out who the pair really were and wanted to warn him but then, somehow, the spies learnt he was on to them and silenced him for good? Except if that was true, then surely they would have tried to kill Agrippa too, or at the least, fled back to their hideout in the marshes?

She heaved a sigh. She didn't know what to think any more. And as the time for the rebellion drew ever closer, she was no nearer to getting justice for Father or to finding out what had happened to poor Mother and Lucius either. Though if the beasts got the better of her in the morning, none of it would matter anyway. A shiver of fear rippled through her. Reaching for the owl-key, she turned to the wall and squeezed her eyes shut to blot out the thought.

Argus came for Vita at dawn.

As she prepared to go with him, Brea gripped her by the

shoulders and fixed her with a steady, green gaze. 'Remember what I told you and all will be well.'

Vita gave a quick nod, then, gulping in a breath, she drew herself up to her full height and marched out through the cell door.

As the slave led her across the courtyard, his hand clamped firmly around her arm, she glanced at the wooden targets and other fighting gear lying like a bunch of toys abandoned in the sand. In two days' time, the men who'd been using them would fight each other with real weapons in the arena – and some would not come back.

Argus ground to a halt in front of a low thatched building, its walls studded with a line of window-holes fitted with thick iron bars. A volley of sharp, grunted squeals echoed from somewhere inside followed by a low, angry-sounding groan. Vita stiffened. The man had said one bear – but how many hogs? Before she could ask, Argus picked up a pair of wooden buckets and thrust one at her.

'Feeding time!'

Her stomach heaved at the contents – a mix of vegetable peelings, chickens' heads and lumps of half-rotten meat.

The slave threw her a gap-toothed grin. 'It's not so bad, girly. Not when you get used to it.' Lifting the bar, he dragged the door open and pushed her inside.

She gagged against the cloud of thick, musky air.

Thrusting her sleeve against her nose, she peered about her. At first it was hard to see anything at all. But as her eyes got used to the light she made out two large pens, each one fronted by a set of heavy iron bars and a large, bolted door. A fresh burst of squeals and snorts sounded from the one to her right.

'Old Growler first.' Argus tossed his head at the left-hand pen. 'Mama Boar and her babies second.'

Vita's stomach turned over. 'You mean there are piglets too?'

Argus poked a grubby finger under his eyepatch and gave it a good scratch. 'Makes for a better show if the bear's pitched against the sow and her brood. Mind you, thanks to the trappers butchering her own young, she's sore enough to make mince-meat of anything.'

Vita's blood curdled. Would the bear make mince-meat of her too?

Argus jabbed his finger at a bulky, oblong shape to the left of the cage door. 'The trough's over there. If you want my advice, get in and out sharpish!' He rattled back the bolt and shoved her forward.

Vita offered up a silent prayer to Fortuna, then, heart pounding, she slid through the gap into the gloom-filled pen beyond.

She scanned about her, but there was no sign of the bear. Keeping her back to the bars, she held her breath and edged sideways towards the trough. She was almost there when a huffing snort sounded from beneath a pile of straw less than two strides to her right. She watched in horror as a pale brown snout poked out and waved from side to side.

Argus shouted a warning.

As if on cue, the beast uttered a low, rumbling growl. Vita turned to flee, but it swung round in front of her, black eyes gleaming and lifting up on its haunches, blocked her path.

A stab of cold panic spiked her chest. She'd done what the wolf-woman had said she must never do. Let it get between her and the way of escape. She froze, her entire body rigid now with fear. But then, as the bear dropped down on all fours, a desperate thought struck her. Raising the bucket high above her head, she flung the contents in the creature's direction, dodged to the side and . . .

RAN!

She was halfway to the door when her right foot skidded on something wet and foul-smelling, sending her crashing to the ground face down. A roaring growl sounded loud in her ears. It hadn't worked. It was still coming for her. She made to push up, but her lungs were empty and her arms and legs refused to move.

Something took hold of her ankles and yanked her backwards, her arms flailing. She tried to scream, but her mouth was stopped with a plug of mud and straw. And now the creature was rolling her over. She could feel its hot breath on her face. Sense its great claw-studded paws preparing to strike. She gave a choked sob and closed her eyes, waiting for the final death-blow.

A rattle of metal sounded and a dark shape reared up in front of her. Spitting the straw free, she cried out and threw up her hands.

A loud belly-laugh split the air. 'Not bad, girly – though I wouldn't bet my *denarii* on you in the arena.' A single glittering eye peered down at her from out of the gloom.

Vita sucked in a great mouthful of air. 'I . . . I thought you were the bear.'

The slave laughed again. 'No.' He turned and looked behind him into the pen. 'She's too busy filling her belly with those tasty morsels you just lobbed at her.'

Shaking, Vita hauled herself up to sit against the wall.

A sharp, oinking grunt sounded from the pen next door.

She tensed. Argus puffed out a breath. 'It's all right. I'll see to the porkers this time.' Snatching up the second bucket, he drew the club from his belt and marched over to the door. As it clanged open, an explosion of frenzied squealing ripped through the air.

A mix of surprise and relief coursed through Vita. She hadn't expected him to come to her aid like that. Fortuna must have heard her prayers after all. But what about next time?

A blood-freezing groan sounded to her left. Scalp prickling, she turned to see a brown snout and twitching black nose poking through the bars of the left-hand pen. The bear stayed there for a moment, its breath coming in heavy, laboured snorts. Then, with another sad-sounding groan, it pulled back into the darkness again.

Vita's chest squeezed. In spite of what had just happened, she couldn't help feeling sorry for the creature. She must be missing her cubs. And as if that wasn't bad enough, in little more than a day's time, she and the boar would face each other in a fight to the death.

As she turned away, a second, even more chilling thought dawned. That unless Taran and his men succeeded in freeing them first, the wolf-woman and Col would be forced to face the same fate too.

XVI

As Vita stepped back inside the cell, Brea shot her a grim-faced smile. 'I see you listened to what I told you.'

'Thank you, yes.' Her cheeks coloured at the lie.

'Good, so now I will explain the thing I need you to do.'

Vita felt a fresh prickle of unease. In the excitement – and sheer terror – of feeding the bear, she'd forgotten all about the promise she'd made the wolf-woman the night before.

As she listened to what Brea wanted, her misgivings grew. But if she was to get the wolf-woman's help to test Agrippa at the banquet later, she knew she had little choice but to go ahead with what she was asking. And it had to be done today – the wolf-woman made that clear. Tomorrow

– the day of the games – would be too late.

Her chance came when Cook sent her with a message to Janus asking to discuss some last-minute arrangements for the banquet.

When Vita knocked on the accounting room door, the slave made a big fuss about having to interrupt his work. But being sure the patron of the games and his friends were fed well was too important a thing to leave to chance. Scooping up a stylus and wax tablet, he closed the door behind him and stalked off muttering in the direction of the kitchen.

As soon as he'd disappeared from view, Vita lifted up the door-latch and darted inside. Her nose pricked at the familiar smell of papyrus and ink and for a brief instant she was back at the table in her bedchamber, her pen racing across the page as she put the finishing touches to her poem.

Her eyes stung with tears as the present came crowding back in. Those days had gone for ever. It was foolish even to think of them. What mattered now was discovering the truth about Father's murder and bringing the ones who'd committed it to justice. And rescuing Mother and Lucius too . . . If, by a miracle of the gods, they were still alive.

She blinked and scanned about her. But aside from an abacus, a rack of wax tablets and a pen and metal ink-pot, there was nothing else on view. She darted round to the other side of the desk and peered beneath it. A drawer! If what she was looking for was anywhere, surely it would be in here. She tugged at the knob, but it stayed stubbornly shut.

Seizing a stylus from the tablet rack, she poked the pointed end in the lock and wiggled it up and down. At first it met no resistance. But then, after more jiggling, it caught on something which felt like the workings of a bolt. She slid it slowly across and this time, when she pulled on the knob, the drawer juddered open. She scanned the contents. A pile of papyrus scrolls, a bag of coins. And something else too. A thin square of dull grey metal, its surface scratched with lines of spidery writing.

Great Apollo I beseech you, strike down the one who dared jeer at me behind my back when I visited your temple yesterday. May he be afflicted by the pox and may he die a beggar, with not a <u>single</u> sestertius to his name.

A curse tablet. She'd seen plenty like it on her trips to the temple with Mother. People rolled them up and threw them into the pool to ask for the gods' help in returning stolen things and punishing the thief, or else teaching an enemy a lesson. She snorted. Just the sort of mean-minded thing that weasel Janus would do!

But as she made to put it down again, a sudden terrible thought struck. What if everything that had happened to her was a punishment from the gods too? For going to the play when she shouldn't have . . . Her jaw tightened. No. It was a man who'd killed Father. For a reason she didn't yet know. But she was going to find out and bring him to justice, whatever it took.

She tossed the tablet aside and carried on rifling through the drawer. She'd almost given up hope when her fingers snagged against another, rougher piece of metal fixed between two nails on the underside of the drawer lid. She slid the thing free and held it up in front of her.

It was what the wolf-woman had sent her here for – the spare key to the weapons store. It had the same curved handle and 'L'-shaped hook on the end as the one she'd seen Otho use to lock the iron door in the wall behind his desk. Now all she had to do was pass it through the main door-hatch to one of Taran's men who'd be keeping watch nearby.

Vita stared down at the key. If she took it, she would be helping to arm the rebels. She shivered. Father would never have approved of such a thing. But Father wasn't here, and if all else failed, this might be her only chance of escape. Heart racing, she slid the key inside her tunic sleeve. But as she pushed the drawer shut, a patter of footsteps sounded along the passageway outside. Her mouth dried. If it was Janus, she was done for. Darting into the corner nearest the door, she pressed herself against the wall and waited. The footsteps ground to a sudden halt. She closed her eyes. This was it. Any moment now, he'd come in and catch her red-handed. But as the latch lifted, a grumbling voice echoed along the passage.

'Janus! I haven't finished with you yet.'

Cook! Vita held her breath.

'Jupiter's beard!' The latch banged down again. 'What does the old crow want now?' There was a loud huffing sound and the footsteps pattered away again.

Vita waited as long as she dared, then, checking the passage was clear, she slipped back outside and into the shadows by the main entrance. She could only hope now that Brea's friend Taran was as good as his word.

Sliding the door-hatch back, she stood on tiptoe and pressed her face to the grille. The sun was fully up and she blinked, blinded for a moment by the glare. Then, shading her eyes, she scanned what little she could see of the street outside – a row of tumbledown houses to the right, a small, overgrown vegetable patch to the left.

But save for a young girl scattering corn at a bunch of dusty-looking chickens and the hunched figure of an old man propped sleeping against the wall of the nearest house, the place was deserted. She frowned. What was she meant to do now?

She was about to turn away, when the man gave a small cough and lifted to his feet. As he emerged from the shadows and walked up to the door, Vita's heart skipped a beat.

'Hello, Ariadne.'

'You again!'

Leander looked pleased with himself. 'You didn't know it was me? Well, that is the art of a good disguise. You can be anyone you want to be, if you study the part well enough. But you will know that already after your star performance on the stage.' He threw her a mischievous grin.

Her stomach tightened. This was her chance to ask him about Felix. Find out once and for all if the wolf-woman had been telling her the truth. She did her best to smile back.

'That is better.' He frowned. 'But I was expecting Lupa. Is she all right?'

'She's training for the games . . . She asked me to steal the thing you came for instead.' Vita pulled the key from her sleeve and held it up to the grille.

Leander sounded a low whistle. 'A girl of many talents. It is good to have you on our side.' He made to take the key, but Vita snatched it out of his reach.

'I have a question for you first.' She glanced back over her shoulder. Still no sign of Janus, thank the gods!

Leander's face pulled into another frown. 'Go on.'

'Is there a slave called Felix living with you and your friends in the marshes? He . . . he has a terrible scar on his right arm.'

The boy's gaze narrowed. 'Why do you want to know?'

She gave a quick swallow. 'He was a slave in the house I used to work in. But he ran away. I . . . I thought he might have gone to join you.'

He hesitated, then dipped his head in a nod. 'Yes, he is one of us.'

A knot of cold fury gripped Vita's throat. So Felix *was* one of the rebels. 'I knew it! He's a murderer. You all are!' The accusation shot from her like a lightning bolt from a thundercloud.

The boy's eyes widened in surprise. 'What in the name of the gods are you talking about?'

'Your leader, Taran, sent Felix to spy on my father. But Father must have found out what he was up to, so he *killed* him.'

'Your *father*?'

'Yes, Marcus Tullius Verus!' She clamped her mouth shut. She hadn't meant to tell him. But it was too late now.

'But . . . but I thought you were a slave?'

She puffed a breath. 'Felix's partner made the same mistake too. But I'm not. It was a disguise so I could go and watch that wretched play.'

'Is this some sort of story you are spinning me, Ariadne?'

She drew back her shoulders and fixed him with a proud stare. 'No. I told you, I am Vita, daughter of Marcus Tullius Verus. The magistrate your comrades cut down in cold blood with his own army sword.'

He frowned. 'You are wrong! It is true Felix was spying for us. But he did not kill your father. He respected him.'

The knot in Vita's throat tightened. 'You're lying!'

Leander held up his hands. 'I am not. Please, hear me out!'

Vita threw another look over her shoulder, but the passage was still empty. She bit down on her anger and nodded for him to go on.

'The one you call Felix was a good friend of Taran's from the times before.'

'What times?'

'It does not matter. But you should know that he asked Taran if he might stay with your father when the rebellion happened, so he could protect him and his family. And Taran agreed.'

She shook her head. 'I don't believe you!'

'But I am speaking the truth, I swear.' The boy put his hand to his chest and met her gaze with his own steady-eyed one.

She frowned. 'But if that's true, why did Felix go missing the afternoon my father was killed? And why did I find the bracelet he wore covered in blood at the scene?'

Leander's eyes clouded. 'I do not know. But we have not seen him since that day either, though he was expected back in camp to make a report.'

Vita gnawed her lip, suddenly less sure of herself. 'All right. But why did your friend Lupa say she didn't know anyone called Felix when I asked her?'

The boy's expression brightened. 'That is easy! We do not use our slave names in the camp, only our real ones. It is one of our rules. But I had to know his in case Taran ever needed me to take him a message.'

She frowned, remembering again how the wolf-woman hadn't recognized Leander's name either.

'Did Taran plant a spy in Cassius Agrippa's house too?'

He shook his head. 'I would have known if he did. Why do you ask?'

'Because one of the murderers – the man who brought me here and sold me to Otho – works for Agrippa.'

Leander's face pulled into a puzzled frown. 'What does that mean?'

Vita lowered her shoulders and let out a sigh. 'I . . . I don't know.'

But she did know, didn't she? Because if what this boy said was true, then it could mean one of only two things. Either Agrippa's man had killed Father for his own reasons. Or else, on his master's orders . . . She clutched her arms about her and let out a groan.

Leander gripped the bars of the grille. 'Do you believe me?'

She dropped on to her heels and closed her eyes, letting

her mind flit through everything he'd said. But in her heart of hearts she knew already that what he'd told her was the truth.

'Vita?'

She blinked, drew in a juddering breath and lifted on to her tiptoes again. 'I . . . I think so, yes.'

'So will you give me the key?'

She turned it over in her hands considering, then looked back up at him again. 'Will people die?'

He frowned. 'We do not want to kill people. Only to free those who do not want to be slaves. But if the soldiers try to stop us . . .'

She nodded. He couldn't give her any guarantees, she knew that. Taking another breath in, she poked the key through the grille.

'Thank you!' He flashed her a smile, then his eyes clouded again. 'I am sorry about your father. I would have liked to have met him.'

She bit her lip and gave a small nod.

'I must go now and deliver this to Taran.' He held up the key before pocketing it in the pouch at his waist. 'And I must tell him what you have told me too. But I will try to help you, I promise. And in the meantime, Lupa will protect you. You can be sure of that.'

He turned to go then spun round to face her again. 'I almost forgot. Tell Lupa our plans have changed. We will use the games as cover and break in while everyone is at the arena.'

Vita frowned. 'But won't the weapons be needed at the games?'

'Some, but there are plenty to spare in the weapons store.'

He raised a hand in quick salute, and before she had a chance to reply, turned and darted back off down the empty street.

As she watched him go, her chest cramped at a sudden thought. She should have asked him about Mother and Lucius when she'd had the chance. He might have known something...

'What are you doing loitering at the front door, girl?'

She started. Janus! Swallowing hard, she forced herself to turn and face him. 'Nothing. I... I felt faint. I had to get some air.' She pointed at the open door-hatch.

The slave's beady black eyes darted to it then back to her. 'A likely story. Now off to the kitchen with you. Cook's flapping about like a chicken in a fox's den with all the work still left to do for the Honourable Agrippa's banquet this evening.'

Gritting her teeth, Vita dipped her head and slid past him without another word.

⚞⚞⚞ ✴ XVII ✴ ⚟⚟⚟

The kitchen was a hive of activity when Vita arrived. The other girls were already hard at work, one plucking pheasants, the other grinding cinnamon with a pestle and mortar. And a scrawny male slave she'd not seen before was busy hacking a pig carcass into steaks with a heavy iron cleaver.

The moment she saw Vita, Cook pounced and marched her over to a barrel of oysters steeping in seawater. Thrusting a small, stiff-toothed brush at her, she ordered her to scrub the shells and arrange them in nests of slippery green seaweed on a pair of large silver platters.

As Vita set about her task she mulled over her conversation with Leander. She was as sure as she could be he'd told her the truth about Felix. But it still didn't explain how the steward's bracelet had come to be lying outside the dining room and covered in blood. Or what had happened to him either. Unless . . . Her chest tightened. What if the bracelet had been planted to make the authorities suspect he was to blame? Her throat clawed at the thought.

And now fresh doubts about Agrippa wormed their way into her mind. She'd always thought of her future husband as fun-loving and a little bit mischievous. But not in a bad way. When Leander had made that comment about his supposed cruelty the other day, she'd been shocked, never believing for a moment it could be true. But what if there was another, darker side to him? A side that would make him capable of murder?

Perhaps the wolf-woman was right. But still, as with her earlier suspicions about the rebels, Vita had to find a way of proving his guilt. And with the banquet and the rebellion fast approaching, she was running out of time . . .

Cook had confirmed Vita and the other girls would be needed to help serve the guests. She'd also said there were to be entertainments – acrobats and dancers; actors too. Vita frowned. What was it Leander had said to her earlier?

You can be anyone you want to be, if you study the part well enough.

He'd accused her of being a story-spinner too. She heaved a sigh. She had been once, though not in the way he meant. But maybe it was time to dust her old tale-telling talents off and put them to good use after all? A thrill of excitement ran through her. It needed more thought, but yes, she could definitely see a way . . .

After all the chores had been completed to Cook's satisfaction, Vita was sent back to the cell with a bag of make-up things and instructions from Janus to 'make Lupa presentable for the feast'. But when she crossed the threshold, she did a double take. For there on the truckle-bed, in place of her wild-looking cellmate sat a strange woman in a long white gown, skin pale as goat's milk, a plait of bright blonde hair hanging down her back.

'Brea? You look . . . beautiful.'

The wolf-woman jerked round to face her and gave a bitter-sounding laugh. 'Why? Because I have cleaned the dirt from my face and hair? Or because I am wearing these fine Roman clothes?' She snatched up a handful of the white cloth and wrinkled her nose in disgust.

Vita flushed. 'No. I mean, I don't know, I—'

But Brea wasn't listening. 'Nine-Fingers wants us to look our best for the ones who are coming to view us later.'

'You make it sound like animals at a market.'

Brea's eyes blazed with sudden anger. 'It is what we are to them. To be prodded and poked before they decide which ones of us will live and which will die.' Her look sharpened. 'What of the key?'

'It was in the desk drawer. I gave it to the boy Taran sent – the one who brought the stones.'

'Good. That was well done.'

Vita felt a small flush of pride at her words.

The wolf-woman uncurled her arms and swung her legs to the ground. 'Did he say when Taran and the others will come for the weapons?'

'Tomorrow, during the games.'

'That is a wise choice. The men not picked to fight will be locked in their cells. And they and any slaves Nine-Fingers leaves behind on guard will have the choice to join us.' She pursed her lips and sounded a sharp whistle. Col scrambled out from beneath the bed and bared his teeth in a yawn.

'Not long to go now, my friend.' Scooping up a leather pouch beside her, Brea fished out a piece of dry-looking bread and held it out to him.

Vita gave a small cough. 'The boy told me Taran and your friends are not to blame for my father's death.'

Brea shot her another sharp look. 'I told you this. It is strange that you should believe him and not me.'

Vita's chest tightened. She had a sudden urge to tell her what she'd told Leander. About who her father really was. But how would the wolf-woman react? No. She couldn't risk it. She bent and ruffled Col's fur instead.

An awkward silence hung between them until finally, the wolf-woman cleared her throat and spoke again. 'You did what I asked of you, so now I will keep my promise in return and help you lay a trap for the one called Agrippa. Have you thought more on what to do?'

'Yes, but I am meant to help you get ready.' Vita held out the bag of make-up things Janus had given her.

Brea snatched it from her with a snort of disapproval. 'I can do that myself.' She emptied the contents on to the bed and raked through them, listening carefully while Vita set out her plan. When she'd finished, the wolf-woman tipped her head to one side as if considering.

'It is not the sort of trap I am used to setting. But if this man has done what you fear, then he is no ordinary prey.' Her face pulled into a pale frown. 'The danger is that he sniffs you out before you have struck your blow. I will do what I can to shield you, but it is a risk.'

Vita's stomach gave a quick flutter. What she said was true, but still, she had to try. 'Thank you.'

'It is not done yet.' Brea glanced up at the window. 'The light is fading. You must ready yourself too.' She jerked her head at a blue gown draped across the foot of the bed.

As Vita bathed her hands and face in the water-bucket and changed into the gown, all the possible ways her plan could go wrong crowded into her head. Though she pushed each away in turn, there were always more jostling to take their place.

When she'd finished, Brea beckoned her over again. As she sat down beside her, the wolf-woman snatched up a bone comb and reached for a strand of Vita's hair. She started and pulled away. Brea clicked her tongue. 'I am not going to harm you. You should know that by now.'

Vita flushed, and with a quick muttered 'sorry', nodded for her to go on.

It was painful at first, but as the tangles gave way and the wolf-woman's strokes grew smoother, Vita closed her eyes and let herself imagine she was back at home with Mother helping get her ready for her birthday feast. Listening to her talk of the special menu she'd prepared, feeling the soothing touch of her fingers and knowing that in spite of her scolding, she still loved her.

She lowered her head and gave a choked sigh.

Brea dropped the comb and drew Vita round to face her. 'What is wrong?'

'Nothing. I was thinking of my mother. That is all.'

Brea nodded. 'Mothers are important. I miss mine too. She dwells in the spirit world now, waiting for my father. But I have this gift from her.' Lifting the hem of her robe, she revealed a small blue-grey shape tattooed on the skin above her left ankle-bone.

Vita bent in close to get a better look. 'What is it?'

'A mountain hare.' The wolf-woman traced its outline

with the tip of her forefinger. 'Here are its ears, and here, its front and back legs, arched and leaping.'

'It is beautiful. How was it done?'

'With the point of a needle and water mixed with the powder from burnt wood. It hurt when it was made, but it will never wash away. Fyn has one too.' Her eyes darkened as she spoke his name. She shook her head, then dropped the hem back down and stared off into the distance. 'My mother had the same mark the night my father found her in the cave.'

Vita's eyes widened. 'A cave? What was she doing there?'

'Getting ready to bring me and my brother into the world. Father had been out hunting and got caught in a rainstorm. If he had not taken shelter there, we might all have died.'

Vita frowned. 'I don't understand.'

'She had run from another place, across the water, on the far side of the hills. A place she no longer felt safe in, thanks to the Eagle-men and their kind.' Brea's jaw clenched.

The knot in Vita's chest tightened again. Her instinct not to reveal the truth about herself to the wolf-woman had been right. Her hatred of the 'Eagle-men' was clearly as passionate as ever.

'So . . . so your father – he is not your blood father?'

– 150 –

'No. But he cared for us like he was. It is why, if I find the Eagle-man who took his spirit, I will take his too.' Brea drew in a breath and turned her head away.

'What does the hare mean?'

At first she didn't answer, but when she turned round to reply, the track of a single tear glistened on her left cheek.

'For us it means the life that never dies – like the moon that fades each morning and is born again each night.'

Vita's heart squeezed at the memory of her father on that final afternoon, his brown eyes full of love and pride as he handed her the writing-box. His last gift. She fumbled for the owl-key at her throat.

They sat in silence in the gathering shadows, each lost in their own thoughts until the thud of heavy footsteps shook them back again.

Brea glanced at the door then back at Vita. 'It is time. Are you ready?'

She gave a quick swallow. 'I . . . I think so.'

'Good. Let us set the trap and see if our prey will take the bait.'

XVIII

Vita and Brea followed Argus along the passageway. As they turned the corner a hubbub of male voices echoed towards them from up ahead. The men who were to fight tomorrow had been released from their cells and were crowding through the door that led into the dining hall. Each was clean-shaven and dressed in a fresh grey tunic, with the exception of Cronos who still wore his fighting gear and carried a great bronze helmet under his right arm.

Vita shivered. He looked more like he was preparing to do battle with Agrippa and his guests than dine with them. She was about to say something to Brea, when Janus elbowed his way towards them.

'Put the She-Wolf in there with the others. And make

sure you keep her out of the Skull-Crusher's way or you'll have the Master to answer to.' He nodded at Argus then gripped Vita's arm. 'Come with me, girl. You're to help set the table before our guests arrive.'

But instead of taking her to the dining hall, the slave pushed her towards the door that led into the courtyard. As she stepped across the threshold, Vita blinked and looked about her in wonder. Dusk had fallen and the sky, a beautiful shade of indigo blue, was dotted with pale stars. Rows of padded couches scattered with brightly coloured cushions had been arranged on the sand to form three sides of a rectangle looking out on to a long wooden table in the centre of the training ground.

Cook, wearing a spotless white tabard over her brown tunic, was bustling about placing terracotta finger bowls and piles of fine linen handcloths on the smaller tables in front of each couch. The two other kitchen girls, dressed in the same pale blue gowns as Vita, were busy lighting wicks in the great dishes of oil mounted on iron stands at intervals around the dining area.

Vita jumped at a sudden sharp jab in the ribs. 'Stop standing there gaping and fetch water for the finger bowls.' Janus jerked his head in the direction of the well.

Squashing the temptation to jab him back, she picked up an empty bucket and did as he said. As she hauled it over to the nearest table, she glanced about nervously.

No sign of the actors yet. They had to be here or her plan would be doomed . . .

She was about to offer up a quick prayer to Minerva when a commotion sounded behind her. She turned to see Janus marching back into the courtyard followed by a gaggle of figures dressed in patched cloaks and hoods. Two of the taller ones, clearly men, lugged a wooden chest between them. The rest carried musical instruments or baskets full of wooden hoops and balls.

The slave jolted to a sudden stop and turned round to face them, his lips pinched in tight annoyance. 'You can change over there.' He pointed to where a wooden screen stood blocking the far corner of the courtyard from view. 'The dancers and acrobats are to come on first. The actors will perform after the gladiators have been brought in and the guests have finished their main course. Master Otho will give you the signal.'

One of the men carrying the chest set his end down, gave a quick bow and spoke up in strong, bold tones. 'Thank you, sir. Would you be so good as to ask your girl there to bring us something to drink? We've had a long, dusty journey and our throats are in need of a bit of oiling before we perform, aren't they, friends?'

There was muffled laughter and cries of 'Yes!' and 'Bring wine!'

Janus puffed out a breath. 'Very well! Vita, go and fetch

two jugs of wine from the stores.' Vita's heart gave a quick somersault. This was her chance! As she turned to go, Janus grabbed her wrist and hissed low in her ear, 'Be sure to make it more than half water. We don't want to waste any more of the Master's fine wine on those vagabonds than we have to.'

She nodded and hurried away. But when she reached the storeroom, she filled both jugs full to the brim with undiluted wine – she needed the actors on her side. By the time she brought the tray over to where they were camped, they were already busy helping themselves to a bunch of costumes and masks from the open chest. The time had come. She only hoped she could persuade them to help her . . .

But as she set down the tray, one of the actors – who like the others, wore his hood low over his face – spun round and made straight for her. Before she could stop him, he'd grabbed hold of her arm and was yanking her off into the shadows.

'Get off me!' She made to twist free.

He pulled her closer and tugged back his hood. 'No need to struggle, Ariadne. I am your friend, remember?'

Her eyes widened. 'Leander?'

'At your service!' He put a hand to his chest and gave a small bow. 'Though, as I have told you before, that is not my real name.'

'But I don't understand. What are you doing here?'

He flashed her a smile. 'I have come to rescue you.'

'Rescue me? How?'

'It is all arranged.' He jerked a thumb at the costume-chest. 'All you have to do is find a moment to slip away and hide inside it, and we will smuggle you out with us when we leave.'

She glanced at the actors, disappearing now behind the screen to change. 'So they are on your side?'

'Yes, like many others. So what do you say? Will you come with us?'

Vita threw another look at the chest, then over to the main building. 'What about Brea – I mean Lupa – and Col?'

'They need to stay. If they disappeared the whole place would go into lockdown and we would have no chance of taking the weapons tomorrow.'

She frowned. It didn't feel right to leave them behind. But what the boy said was true. Besides, what use would she be to them after tonight anyway? And if, for some reason, things didn't go as Taran and his friends planned tomorrow, she might never get free. Which made it even more vital to test Agrippa tonight while she still had the chance . . .

She drew in a breath. 'All right, but I need your help with something first.'

Leander listened carefully as she told him her plan, then blew out an admiring breath. 'Clever as well as brave. Wait here.' He touched her arm then darted over to the screen and slid behind it. He returned a short while later, eyes sparking with excitement.

'It is agreed. But you must be ready to leave the moment we are done. If this man is guilty, we cannot be sure what he might do next.'

Vita licked her lips. He was right. If Agrippa was guilty, what she was about to do – what *they* were about to do – would be like poking a dangerous beast with a stick. And she didn't want to be around when he struck back . . .

Leander nodded over at the dining area. 'You had better go. The boss-man looks like he is about to make an announcement.'

As if on cue, Otho's voice boomed out across the courtyard. 'To your stations!'

'Good luck!' He gave her hand a quick squeeze, then picked up the tray and hurried back to join his comrades.

Vita felt a sudden twist of guilt. She'd been so ready to blame the rebels for Father's murder, and here they were putting their own lives at risk to help her. What if she'd been wrong about them and it had been Agrippa all along? Well, if her plan worked, she would find out soon enough . . .

She sucked in a breath then turned and hurried back

towards the dining area, slipping quickly into line beside the other girls.

A hush fell around the courtyard. Everyone turned their heads to where the gladiator-master, now clean-shaven and dressed in a smart woollen tunic and matching breeches, was standing to attention, chin back, chest puffed out like a cockerel.

'Your Honour, distinguished guests.' He gestured to a group of well-dressed men and women who had appeared in the doorway behind him, and dropped into a low bow.

Vita's throat tightened. This was it – the moment she'd been waiting for. Dreading too.

And now here he came: Gaius Cassius Agrippa – her father's best friend. Or, if the wolf-woman was right, his murderer . . .

XIX

Vita watched, heart pounding, as Agrippa stepped out into the cool evening air. He was dressed in his magistrate's toga – fine bleached wool, edged in purple – and a pair of expensive-looking, gold-tooled leather sandals, his fair hair clipped close to his head in the latest fashion. But it was the gleaming gold torc round his neck awarded for valour on the battlefield which most caught her eye.

As the rest of the guests followed in his wake, she kept a lookout for any sign his servant might be here too, though it would be impossible to identify him from sight alone.

Otho bowed low again, gesturing for Agrippa to take his place in the dining area. But to Vita's horror, instead of going the most direct way, he turned and strode along the line of slaves straight towards where she and the other girls were standing. A familiar waft of frankincense made her stomach churn. She hunched her shoulders and pressed her chin tight to her chest, willing him not to recognize her.

'My slaves are here to do your bidding, Your Honour.' That was Otho, hurrying along at his side. As their footsteps approached, he barked an order. 'Fetch wine for our guests, girl!'

Vita froze. Did he mean her? She daren't look up, not when Agrippa was so close. Gritting her teeth, she kept her head bowed and stood her ground.

'Must I tell you twice?' There was a sudden rush of air as the girl beside Vita jolted into life and hurried off to carry out the gladiator-master's orders.

As the two men walked past her, Vita heaved a sigh. The rest of the guests came after, the men talking loudly among themselves about the day's business, the women complaining to each other about the price of linen, ill-mannered tradesmen and the laziness of their house-slaves. She recognized the voices of two of her father's fellow magistrates among them and it took all her resolve not to leap out as they passed and beg for their help. But it was too risky. Besides, she had to be certain she was right about Agrippa first.

While he and his guests took their places, Janus

instructed the girls to serve the first course. Vita made sure to keep her distance, attending to a group of guests furthest from the grand couches where Agrippa and the two other magistrates reclined.

As she spooned dressed oysters and portions of fried eggs mixed with nutmeg and honey on to their plates, snatches of the conversation from Agrippa's table wound their way towards her.

One of the other men spoke first. 'Dreadful business! An affront to Emperor Hadrian himself. And such a tragic loss.'

'You speak right, friend. As I said in my speech at his funeral earlier, he was like a brother to me. I miss him more than words can say.' Agrippa gave a choked cough and fell silent.

Vita's heart clenched. So the funeral had happened. But before she could think any more about it, the other man went on.

'You have my heartfelt sympathies, man. But how is the investigation going? And what of the Honourable Verus's family? Have you been able to make any progress in finding out what has happened to them?'

'Sad to report we suspect his own house-slaves are responsible. But I'm afraid I cannot say more at this stage. As for my beloved Vita and her dear mother and brother, there is no trace yet. But when we catch the culprits, you can be sure they will suffer the full force of the Emperor's justice.'

Vita caught her breath. So there was still a chance Mother and Lucius were alive! But surely that was all the more reason to wait before staging the games? She dared herself a quick glance over at Agrippa. He was dabbing at the corner of his eyes with his linen handcloth. She felt a flicker of sympathy. He seemed genuinely upset . . .

The second magistrate addressed him now. 'I hear we are in for a great spectacle tomorrow?'

Agrippa dipped his head. 'It is the least I can do to honour a lifelong friend and brave comrade-at-arms.'

The other man cleared his throat. 'I suspect your generosity will be richly rewarded. You can count on my vote for senior magistrate for sure.' He reached out and patted Agrippa on the shoulder.

'Mine too and a good few others of our brethren, I shouldn't doubt,' the first magistrate chimed in. 'With Cronos and Lupa heading the bill, how could we, or any other citizen who receives your hospitality in the arena, resist?' He gave a knowing laugh and the other man joined in.

Agrippa coughed and dabbed at his eyes again. 'That is kind of you, brothers. And if I am given the honour of being elected, I shall be sure to look after your interests as best I can.'

'We would expect nothing less,' the second magistrate replied.

So it was true. Agrippa *was* standing for Father's position as senior magistrate. Vita was desperate to hear more, but as she made to draw closer, Otho waved at her and the other girls to stop serving and announced to the diners that the acrobats and dancers were about to perform. A man carrying a large wooden drum took up position in the space in front of the couches and set up a steady beat. A few moments later, two young women in floating white gowns slid into view and began to twirl in time to the rhythm. Some of the guests stopped to watch, but most, including Agrippa, carried on talking and eating. The dancers were joined shortly after by two bare-chested men dressed in loincloths who began to juggle handfuls of wooden hoops and balls high above their heads.

As Vita helped the others clear the empty dishes, a bell sounded from somewhere inside. Otho hurried into the middle of the dining area. He chased the dancers and acrobats away, but signalled for the drummer to remain.

'Your Honour.' He gave a low sweeping bow before Agrippa's table. 'The moment has come for you to meet tomorrow's warriors. May I present our fighting pairs.' He signalled again to the drummer and threw a quick nod at the door.

As the beat struck up again, the first pair of gladiators

marched out side by side. Vita drew in a breath. It was the two men who'd helped tend the young volunteer Cronos had attacked in the training yard. They'd been friends then. Now, pitched against each other in the arena, they'd be deadly enemies.

She stole another look at Agrippa. He was sitting up straight now, his attention fixed on the pair as they approached his table then bent their heads in unison and dropped down on one knee. They stayed in the pose until Otho clapped his hands. Then, jumping to their feet, they bowed again and strode away to take their places at the long dining table in the middle of the training ground. Another gladiator pair followed and then another, until Vita had counted at least twenty pairs in total. But neither Cronos nor Brea were among them.

Otho raised his hand and the drummer fell silent.

'And now, Your Honour and distinguished guests, the moment you have been waiting for. The chance to meet the stars of our show.' He nodded to the drummer again who set up a new and faster beat.

All heads turned back to the door. For a moment the space remained empty, then a tall figure in a long white gown stepped into it. Vita's heart quickened.

Otho clicked his fingers for the wolf-woman to advance. She paused, then, slowly, shoulders back, head held high, made her way along the row of couches. But as she swung through the gap to face Agrippa and his magistrate friends, something in her attitude changed. A jerk of the head, a sudden tensing of the limbs. Vita swallowed. Something was wrong. Keeping to the shadows, she slid behind the line of diners, creeping as close to the back of Agrippa's couch as she dared.

Otho thrust his arms wide as if making an extravagant gift of Brea to the magistrate. 'Introducing Lupa, the great She-Wolf. Queen of the beast-hunts this side of the Emperor's great wall and the other.'

There were cries of shock and disgust from the women and grunts of approval from the men. All the while the wolf-woman stood motionless before Agrippa's table, her face white as marble, her eyes burning with a strange green fire.

Agrippa cast his cool grey gaze over her, then gave a clipped nod. 'Very good. Well, let us see how you fare against the challenge I have set for you tomorrow.' He flicked a quick sideways look at Otho. 'I trust she and her wolf are in the peak of condition? It would be a shame if this contest were to prove her last.'

Brea's gaze didn't flinch, but her hands curled into two tight white balls.

'Of course, Your Honour.' Otho inclined his head. 'She has received only the best food and care. Like the men.'

As Agrippa looked her over one last time, Vita was

reminded of the wolf-woman's words – how she and the others were treated as no better than beasts.

'Very well. You may go and join the rest.' He waved her away with a flutter of his handcloth and pressed it to his lips.

But Brea stayed where she was. Vita's stomach knotted. What was wrong with her? Hadn't she heard him?

Agrippa stiffened and fixed her with narrowing eyes. 'I said, you may go.'

The wolf-woman's fists balled even tighter. She stood there a moment longer, then turned and swept from his presence without giving the customary bow.

There were more shocked cries and one of the magistrates called 'Dirty Blue-face' at her retreating back. She jolted to a stop. For an awful moment Vita feared she might turn and run at him, but instead, pulling herself to her full height, she strode off to take her place at the gladiators' table without a backward glance.

Otho muttered something under his breath, then turned to face Agrippa again. 'Apologies, Your Honour. She's got the blood of the beasts running through her veins.'

Agrippa gave a curt nod. 'Like all those other barbarians who refuse to be tamed. She and her opponent will be well matched tomorrow then.' Murmurs of agreement and peals of approving laughter echoed around him. Dipping his head again in acknowledgement, he turned back to Otho and clapped his hands. 'Bring on the main attraction.'

'At once, Your Honour!' Otho clicked his fingers again. As the drummer picked up the beat, a second figure filled the doorframe, a great bronze helmet in one hand, a wooden training sword in the other.

The knot in Vita's stomach grew tighter still. Cronos! He must be loving this attention. Everyone was transfixed by the sight of the Skull-Crusher, head newly shaved and gleaming with a fresh polishing of oil, the craggy face beneath pulled into a menacing frown.

As the gladiator drew to a halt in front of Agrippa's couch, the drummer lowered his sticks and the courtyard fell silent. Cronos straddled his legs, then thumped his sword against his chest and bared his teeth. Agrippa's face paled and for a moment his eyes came the closest Vita had seen to filling with fear. But then suddenly, his expression changed. Springing to his feet, he spread his arms and turned a smiling face to his guests.

'A worthy champion. He is all I hoped he'd be and more. We shall look forward to watching him live up to his name tomorrow when he faces the winners from the earlier bouts.'

Otho gave another low bow. 'Indeed, Your Honour.' He waved the Skull-Crusher away. The giant gave a loud snort, then turned and marched off to where the other gladiators sat. As he passed behind Brea, he lurched to a stop and, lifting his hands, cracked first one set of knuckles against her ear then the other. But to Vita's relief, the wolf-woman refused to react, leaving him no choice but to lumber off and take up a seat at the opposite end of the table.

A sharp double-clap sounded – the signal for the main course to be served. Vita's heart gave a jolt. Not long now before she would have to slip off and join the actors. Her mouth watered as she passed round the platters of succulent-looking roast pigeon breasts, herb-baked river-fish and plump, milk-fattened snails. But it was quickly replaced by a flush of bitterness at the sight of Agrippa, bull-ring glinting on his little finger as he excavated the bones of a stuffed dormouse from between his teeth. How could she even think of food right now? And guilty or not, how could he either?

She glanced over at the gladiators. They were busy guzzling from beakers – or in some cases whole jugs – of wine and helping themselves to carcasses of roast chicken from the wooden platters in front of them. All except Brea, who instead of joining in with the feasting, sat bolt upright, her gaze fixed on Agrippa and his magistrate friends.

Vita frowned. The moment she'd set eyes on him, the wolf-woman had begun behaving strangely. Was she trying to unsettle him in readiness for what Vita had planned? Or was it something more? A twist of fresh guilt spiralled up inside her. If she made her escape with the actors, she might never get the chance to find out.

She peered across to the far corner of the courtyard. They had changed into their costumes now – flowing robes of red and black, and painted masks which hid their faces. She shivered. It was almost time . . .

Heart pounding, she piled a set of empty terracotta bowls on to her tray and marched away as if heading for the kitchen. But when she reached the entrance porch, she set the tray down behind a low stone wall, and using the shadow of the buildings as cover, slid round to where the actors were gathered.

As she approached, Leander stepped out to meet her, costume in hand. 'Here. Put this on.' He thrust a black cloak at her. 'And this too. I thought it would serve well for the story.' His eyes sparked with mischief as he handed her the mask.

Her breath froze in her throat at the sight – a Roman centurion's face, fashioned from panels of beaten tin with a red-crested helmet and cheek-guards edged in brass. And the eyes – black and sightless. Like Father's the last time she'd seen him . . . would ever see him again . . .

She pushed it back at him with a shudder. 'No, you wear it. Find me another.'

'All right.' He shrugged and rummaged in the chest again.

This time when he handed her the choice, her heart gave a quick squeeze. It was an owl – its face covered in real brown and white feathers, its beak fashioned from a polished hazelnut shell. But most striking of all were its wide-staring eyes, picked out by the artist in circles of red and black dots.

'Will it do?'

She stroked a finger over the feathers and nodded. It would do. It would do very well.

Leander helped her into the cloak, then fastened the mask's leather ties around the back of her head. As he slid the centurion mask over his own face, Otho's voice rang out across the courtyard again.

'Your Honour, it is time now for the final part of this evening's entertainment. A play from our company of actors.'

Leander gripped Vita's hands in his and fixed her with a steady brown gaze. 'Ready?'

'Yes.' She made a small adjustment to the mask and took a deep breath. The time had come to discover the truth. If the goddess Minerva would only grant her the wit and the words . . .

XX

The drum started up and the actors set off, marching in time towards Agrippa and his guests. As they approached the gladiators' table, Brea twisted round, a puzzled look on her face. Vita frowned. She must be searching for her. Would she realize it was her beneath the mask? Even if she did, there was no way of telling her that the plan had changed: that Vita would escape with the actors as soon as the performance was done.

When they reached the dining couches, Otho signalled for the drumming to stop. An actor wearing a blood-red robe and the mask of a solemn-faced man stepped forward and gave a low bow.

'Your Honour and most noble guests . . .'

It was the lead actor, the one who had called for wine earlier.

'This evening, we are honoured to present a great tragedy. A tale of mistaken trust and wicked deceit. But wait! Our narrator – the gifted writer from whose head this story of treachery and murder has sprung – will do a much better job of telling it than I.' He turned and extended a hand to Vita.

This was it. Time to set the trap. Swallowing hard against the rising tide of fear, she stepped out to face the audience. But as she drew in a breath to speak her first lines, her throat gripped, forcing the words back down. Trembling, she took a step backwards. She couldn't do this. She wasn't brave enough.

As if in answer, a voice whispered low in her ear. 'Spin your story, Ariadne. For your family's sake.'

Her heart cramped. Leander was right. Father deserved justice. And while there was still a chance Mother and Lucius were alive, she must do everything in her power to save them. Curling her fingers into fists, she drew back her shoulders and took another breath.

And this time both the air and the words flowed freely.

Pitching her voice low to avoid being recognized, she set the scene for her story, while the actors stepped in around her, taking on the parts of the characters she intro-duced. Going over things earlier, she'd decided to alter certain details to avoid arousing Agrippa's suspicion before the play had the chance to run its course. So Festa, Rosia and Cottia became three male house-slaves – which better suited her cover story with Brea too – while Father, played by the lead actor, was transformed into a rich merchant with a wife, and twin daughters.

At first she was petrified she would become tongue-tied again or else forget what to say. But the more she went on, the stronger her voice grew. And all the while, in spite of the constant churn of fear in her stomach, she forced herself to watch Agrippa for any telltale sign of guilt.

In the beginning he scarcely looked up, preferring instead to continue feasting on the platter of devilled larks' tongues one of the kitchen girls had brought him. But then, as Vita introduced the merchant's loyal soldier friend, and Leander – wearing the centurion's mask – took centre stage with a flamboyant bow, he jerked up his head and fixed him with a sharp stare. Vita glanced at Leander. His small nod told her he'd seen it too. She gulped in a breath and carried on.

As she told the story of the two men, how they'd grown up together like brothers, then joined the army, fought side by side and sworn they would gladly die for each other, Leander and the lead actor breathed life into her words with exaggerated gestures: extravagant embraces to show friendship, arms punching the air to celebrate victory, or hands pressed flat to the chest when solemn vows of brotherhood were exchanged.

The whole audience was watching the play intently now, Agrippa included. Buoyed up by their attention, the words spilt effortlessly from Vita's lips as she led them deeper into her story. Now she told of how the first man left the army, became a successful wine merchant and married a beautiful woman from across the sea. How he grew rich, but was also respected by one and all for his nobility and kindness. How he helped to set his soldier friend up in trade in the same town. But then alas, the two men had fallen out, and after a bitter argument, the friend had hatched a plot to have the merchant killed.

As she revealed the friend's treachery, one of the girls approached Agrippa's couch to serve more wine. He waved her away impatiently and turned back to the play, his forehead pulled into a brooding frown. Vita's heart skipped a beat. The performance had definitely unsettled him. But she had to be sure. Time to strike the final blow . . .

'So one dark night, the friend sent two of his followers to the merchant's house armed with newly sharpened knives.'

There were gasps of horror as two actors wearing the masks of demons edged towards the merchant and his family, their hands shaped into daggers and raised high above their heads.

'And the men . . .' Vita took another breath in and spoke more forcefully so that all would hear. 'The men drew their deadly blades and slew the house-slaves and all the merchant's family.'

At Vita's words, the actors playing the killers' victims pressed their hands together to beg for mercy. But the devil-masked pair grabbed them and thrust their fists against their chests as if striking them through the heart. First the three slaves, then the merchant's wife and children crumpled to the ground. Now only the actor playing the merchant was left standing.

More horrified gasps sounded all around. Even the gladiators, who'd been busy carrying on with their feasting, fell silent. As for Agrippa, he sat ramrod-straight, eyes darting first left then right, a sheen of sweat coating his pale forehead.

Vita shot another look at Leander. He nodded again and stepped swiftly up to the merchant. He mimed the drawing of a sword from beneath his cloak, then paused and waited for her to speak the final words. Her stomach gave a quick somersault. She had to hold her nerve. Everything depended on it. She closed her eyes and reached for the owl-key beneath her cloak.

Please, Minerva, grant me the courage and the words . . .

She blinked and forced herself to meet Agrippa's now iron-hard gaze. She was safe behind the owl-mask – so why did it feel as if he could see straight through it?

Clenching her jaw, she did her best to shake off the feeling and carried on.

'And last to die was the merchant. Most foully cut down with his own *gladius* by the friend he loved – in cold and jealous blood.'

As the words left her mouth, Leander thrust the make-believe sword into the back of the merchant. The actor clutched his hands behind him as though trying to pull the weapon free, then sank to the ground and lay still.

For a moment there was total silence as if all watching – Vita, Leander and the actors, Agrippa, his guests, even Otho and the gladiators – had been turned to stone. Then, slowly, uncertainly, one by one the audience began to clap. As the applause built around them, the actors stepped forward, linking hands to take their bows.

The only one who didn't join in was Agrippa. Instead, he sat there unmoving, his face ashen-pale, the fringe of his hair damp with sweat.

And that was the moment when Vita knew for certain. That Gaius Cassius Agrippa, her father's best and oldest friend, was the man who had ordered his death.

A tide of boiling fury surged up inside her. She would accuse him now. Why not? The others here who knew her father would surely come to her aid. Heart pounding, she took a step forward. But as she went to tear the mask from her face, a hand gripped her arm.

'Come with us. Now!'

Leander tried to drag her away, but she dug in her heels, refusing to move. 'It's him! I have to say something before—'

'Hey!' A voice boomed out behind them.

Vita's heart sank. Otho. Leander was right. There was no time. But as the pair turned to run, she was yanked backwards, the mask ripped from her head.

'You!' The gladiator-master loomed over her, face as black as a thundercloud.

'Leave her alone!' Leander raised his fists, but before he got the chance to strike a blow, a hefty-looking gladiator grabbed him from behind and locked a muscled arm around his neck.

'Please. He didn't mean anything by it.' Vita shot the boy a warning look. Frowning, Leander lowered his hands. Otho hesitated, then growled for the gladiator to release him.

As Leander stumbled free, Vita urged him with her eyes to go while he still could. He wavered, then with one last anguish-filled glance, he turned and hurried off to join the actors, already busy packing up their things.

She was about to heave a sigh when footsteps sounded behind her and a familiar cloying scent of pine-sap mixed with lemons pricked at her nose. She thrust her head down as Agrippa swung round to face them.

'What is the meaning of this?'

'My humble apologies for the trouble, Your Honour.' Otho's voice sounded suddenly nervy. 'This slave-girl of mine' – he shook Vita by the arm – 'has ideas above her station.'

'A slave, eh? Well she knows how to tell a good story, that is for sure.' A hand cupped Vita's chin and before she could stop him, he'd forced her head back up. As his eyes met hers, they flickered for an instant before drawing into an unreadable stare. He switched his gaze back to the gladiator-master.

'Give me a moment alone with her.'

'But of course, Your Honour.' Doing his best not to show his astonishment, Otho gestured for the magistrate to step inside. As he made to accompany them, Agrippa rounded on him sharply.

'I said, *alone*!'

The gladiator-master gave a low bow and stepped back frowning into the courtyard.

Agrippa waited until he was out of sight then spun round to face Vita, his grey eyes filled now with concern.

'It is so good to see you, dearest Vita. Thank the gods you are safe! But how in Jupiter's name did you come to be in this place?' He reached out to take her hand, his gold ring glinting in the light. She shivered and took a step backwards, arms clutched tightly against her chest.

Agrippa gave a small cough and withdrew his hand. 'Of course. How insensitive of me! I have not offered you my condolences yet. I still cannot quite believe my dear friend is gone.' Shaking his head sorrowfully, he angled his right palm across his chest and gave a solemn bow. But when he lifted up again, his face wore a new, fiercer look. 'Rest assured we will catch that renegade house steward and his runaway friends. Though I confess I never did understand why your father gave that street-dog a second chance. And to see how he has rewarded him for his kindness.' He shuddered and turned away, a knuckled hand pressed to his mouth.

'But . . . but it wasn't Felix. It was your own man!'

Agrippa twisted back to face her again, eyes wide with shock. 'What are you saying?'

'I saw him after I went back to the house.' Stifling a sob, Vita forced herself to go on. 'Or rather, I heard him. He knocked me out, then brought me here and sold me to that . . . that man out there.' She jerked her head in the direction of the courtyard. 'And then he came back about the beasts and I recognized his voice.'

Agrippa's eyes narrowed. 'The beasts, you say?' He dropped his gaze, then looked up again and gripped her arm. 'Of course! I understand now. You thought because he was my man, that I was somehow responsible for your father's murder. But Vita, he and I were lifelong friends. Set to be family soon too.' He paused and flicked her a sidelong glance, then went on. 'Why would I ever do such a terrible thing?' As he spoke, he twisted the ring on his finger so that the red stone set into it shone like a single glittering drop of blood.

Vita's chest tightened. It was true she had struggled to find a motive . . . But then the magistrates' words from earlier wound back into her head.

'Because . . . because you want to take his place as senior magistrate.'

Agrippa pulled back, eyebrows arcing in bewildered surprise. 'Is that what he told you?'

'No, but—'

He puffed out a breath. 'I didn't think so. Your father was my biggest supporter! Surely you must know that he intended to nominate me at the next elections? Besides, even the most ruthless of politicians would never risk committing such a cruel and heartless act for the sake of waiting a few more months.' He shook his head and gave a long, drawn-out sigh. 'I am disappointed in you, Little Owl.'

Vita stiffened. That was Father's special name for her. His and his alone.

Agrippa glanced at her again and forced a tired-looking smile. 'You are scared and still grieving his loss. And of course you will be worried for your mother and little Lucius too. But please, you must know that I am doing all I can to find them and to hunt down the ones responsible.' He raised a hand and tucked a stray curl behind her ear.

She gave another quick shiver. 'But your servant—'

He held up a hand. 'I will question him. And if he is guilty then he will suffer the ultimate punishment. In the meantime . . .' He heaved another sigh. 'I think it best for your own safety that you stay here tonight. I will escort you to my villa in the country after the games tomorrow. In the meantime, I will speak to the gladiator-master. Make sure you are well treated.'

He made to stroke her cheek, then appearing to think twice, dropped his hand down to his side. 'Take good care and I will come for you again tomorrow, I promise.' Adjusting his toga he threw her a final sorrow-filled look, then turned and stepped back out into the courtyard.

Vita let out a breath and slumped against the wall, head spinning. Could he be speaking the truth? It was possible . . . Maybe the man who worked for him had been part of a break-in that went wrong. And he was right: Father *had* said he'd support him in his candidacy for senior magistrate. But then why had Agrippa looked so upset during the play? She hadn't imagined it. Leander had seen it too.

Her stomach twisted. Leander! She darted to the door and peered outside. Agrippa was deep in conversation with

Otho, while the guests were busy sampling the desserts or else making merry with more wine. But there was no sign of the boy, or the actors either. If only she'd gone with him when he asked her to!

She needed to speak with Brea. Tell her what Agrippa had said, see what she thought. She glanced across to the gladiators' table. The wolf-woman was still there, pinned between two men who were clearly the worse for drink.

Vita pulled her cloak tight about her. But as she darted forward, a bony hand grabbed her arm and spun her around.

'No you don't!' A pair of weaselly black eyes glinted at her from the shadows. 'I'm taking you back to the cell before you can play any more disgraceful tricks. The Master will decide your punishment once he's finished with our guests.'

XXI

Back in the sleeping-cell, and with only Col for comfort, Vita closed her eyes and fell into a fitful sleep. She was startled awake by a rattle and clang of metal. For a moment she thought it might be Otho come to apologize and show her better quarters. But then a loud woof sounded in her ear and a set of paws pattered past her towards the door.

'Hello, my friend. I have missed you too.'

Brea bent and ruffled Col's head, then loped over and squatted in front of Vita, eyes glinting silver in the moonlight. 'What happened to you?'

Vita jerked upright. 'I'm sorry. Leander came with the actors so the plan changed. He . . . he was going to rescue me.'

'I see he did not succeed.'

Vita flushed. 'No.'

'Did the trap work?'

She licked her lips. 'I . . . I don't know.'

The wolf-woman tensed. 'What do you mean?'

Vita hurriedly collected her thoughts and, making sure not to say anything that would give away her true identity, told her a version of what had passed between her and Agrippa after the play. When she confessed her doubts about his guilt, Brea gripped her by the shoulders and fixed her with a bright, burning stare.

'Let me tell you something more about this Agrippa. Something I learnt myself tonight.'

'What?'

'You and I, we hunt the same prey.'

Vita shook her head. 'I don't understand.'

The wolf-woman heaved a sigh. 'It is not the first time we have met, that snake and I. But he was an Eagle-man then, in the lands beyond the wall their Emperor now builds.'

Vita's eyes widened. 'Agrippa was there when they raided your village?'

'He was not just there. He ordered it done. The stealing of the people's spirits. The burning of our homes. The taking of my brother too.' Brea pulled herself to her feet and turned her face to the window.

'You mean he was the commander?'

She gave another sigh and turned back again to Vita. 'Yes, if that is what you call it.' She walked over to the truckle-bed. As she dropped down on it, Col leapt up to join her.

'Are you sure it was him?'

'I would know that spirit-stealer anywhere!'

Vita's stomach gripped. If Agrippa was capable of killing Brea's father and slaughtering all those villagers in cold blood, then he was more than capable of ordering Father's murder too, whatever the motive. She lifted up and slid over to where Brea was sitting.

'Did he recognize you too?'

Brea shook her head. 'No. I was a girl then. Besides, men like him see me and my people as beetles to be crushed into the mud and forgotten. Though as the Horned One teaches, it is often the smallest creature that has the sharpest sting.' As she spoke the last words she flexed the knuckles of her right hand.

'What do you mean?'

The wolf-woman's eyes narrowed. 'This. That now my path has crossed with his, I will hunt him down and take his lifeblood from him as surely as he took it from our father.'

Vita shivered and turned her head away.

'What is wrong? You must want the same for your

father. Your mother and brother too?'

'Yes, but . . . but not like that.'

'How then?'

'By arresting Agrippa, bringing him to trial and proving him guilty in a court of law. Then, after that is done, he will be sentenced to death and executed.'

The wolf-woman gave a loud snort. 'The Roman way! You should leave that to the one who called himself your master. You know the snake's guilt. We both do. Better to strike quickly and have done with it.'

'But that wouldn't be just. Or fair either.'

'Was it just or fair when he ordered my father's throat cut and yours butchered?'

Vita's heart spiked with fresh pain. Brea was right to want vengeance. She wanted it too. And with Agrippa almost certain to be elected to her father's position, perhaps the wolf-woman's method was the only way to get it. Though she would need to overcome the beasts in the arena first.

A prickle of fear slid across her skin. 'Are you frightened? About tomorrow, I mean?'

Brea frowned. 'Of course. A hunter lives in fear, always. It is what helps keep her alive.'

'But what if—' Vita bit down on her lip, afraid to speak the words.

'What if I die?'

'Yes?'

Brea shrugged. 'Then it will be my time to cross over into the Horned One's realm. And if I have deserved it, the ones left behind will sing songs of me.' She gave a wry smile.

'Like Boudicca?'

The wolf-woman's eyes narrowed again. 'Yes, but not the way the Eagle-men and their kind sing of her.'

'What do you mean?'

'Boudicca is their name for her, but it was not her true name, the one her people knew her by. And the Eagle-men make her sound wild and fierce for their own ends. To show how brave they were in fighting her. Why they lost battles against her too. She *was* fierce, but for her people's sake, and for what the Romans call *justice*' – she spoke the word in Latin – 'though the Emperor and his Eagle-men showed none to her and her tribe.' She shook her head. 'You did not know her.'

Vita puffed out an angry breath. 'Well, you didn't either!'

'No, but the one who first spoke these words did.' Rising to her feet, the wolf-woman stepped out into a shaft of moonlight and lifting her face to it, began to tell a story.

But it was a song really. And beautiful; more beautiful, though it pained Vita to admit it, than anything she had ever written herself. Because it had passion and fire. And because it felt true.

'Flame-haired, dauntless queen of her people,
dwellers of eel and marsh flatlands.
Gentle mother of two fair daughters,
loyal wife to a noble king.
Fairer than swan.
Swifter than eagle.
Stronger than bear.
Braver than wolf.
Friend of the downtrodden,
defender of right.
When the enemy came,
she was ready.
Ready to meet them with chariots and spears.
The Horned One spoke and she let the hare guide her.
Let the hare guide her and show her the way . . .'

Brea went on, telling of how when the great queen's husband, the ruler of the Iceni tribe had died, she had been betrayed by the Roman Emperor, Nero, and tricked out of her right to rule. How, after the men of his army had dishonoured her and her two young daughters, she had sought her revenge by raising an army against them. She fought bravely, defeating them first in one battle and then the next, until at last she and her warriors had ridden on Londinium and burnt it to the ground. And then how she had pressed on to the town of Verulamium and won there too until the Roman army caught up with her and managed to defeat her in one last desperate attack.

But though her words sang with a magic that made Vita's spine tingle and put her own ones to shame, their stories ended in the same way.

'Do you know what happened to the queen's body after?'

Brea raised her shoulders in another shrug. 'It was never found.'

'And what about her daughters? People say they died too.'

The wolf-woman's forehead pulled into a frown. She opened her mouth as if to speak, then closed it again and, tilting her head back, gazed silently up at the moon.

XXII

Vita was woken at dawn by the sound of the door rattling open.

'Come with me, girl!' Janus scowled back at her, arms folded, fingertips drumming against them.

She frowned. Why was he still ordering her around? Surely Otho would have told him who she really was by now?

She threw a quick look at the wolf-woman and Col. The wolf was awake, eyes fixed on the door, but Brea was still sleeping. Vita made to wake her, then thought better of it. She would need every bit of rest she could get for their time in the arena later. Taking a deep breath in, she slipped over to the door and out into the passageway beyond.

'Where are you taking me?'

Instead of answering, the slave seized her by the elbow and, banging the door shut, marched her away. Her stomach clenched. Maybe Agrippa had changed his mind. Decided to come for her before the games.

But rather than taking her to the main entrance, Janus bundled her up the stairs and along the passage that led to Otho's rooms. When they reached the door, he raised his fist and gave a sharp *rat-a-tat-tat*.

Otho's voice boomed back from the other side. 'Enter!'

What if Agrippa was with him? Vita steeled herself. But when the door swung open, there was no sign of the magistrate, and the gladiator-master himself was all beaming smiles.

'Come in, girl.' He dropped the chicken leg he'd been eating and beckoned her forward. But when Janus made to follow, he batted him back. 'You, stand outside!' Shooting Vita a sneering look, the slave turned and scuttled away.

Vita stood blinking in a shaft of early morning sunlight, waiting for the apology that would surely come.

But it didn't. Instead, Otho lifted up from his chair and strode round to stand in front of her. 'To be honest, I'm surprised he picked you after that business yesterday. But with a bit of work perhaps . . .' He tipped his head on one side and looked her up and down.

Her heart sank. In spite of Agrippa's promise last night,

it was clear he hadn't told the gladiator-master who she really was.

'Stop scowling like that, girl. It doesn't become you.' He reached out and pinched her right cheek between a greasy thumb and forefinger. 'You must be all sweetness and smiles for the role you will play today.'

Vita's breath froze in her throat. What 'role' had he 'picked' her for? She shook her head. Whatever it was, she didn't want to wait to find out.

She clutched at Otho's tunic. 'You have to let me go! Please!'

The gladiator-master yanked a whip from his belt. 'Slaves should be seen, not heard!' He rammed the leather handle against her lips, then lowered it again and snatched up a sack from the desk behind. 'Now take this and change into it.'

'What is it?'

'Your costume. The Honourable Agrippa had it delivered first thing.' He fished a length of pale yellow fabric from the sack and held it up in front of her. It was a gown, made of the finest linen, its hem and neckline embroidered with a line of delicately stitched white stars. Stars sewn by Vita's own fingers. She clamped a hand to her mouth and gave a small cry.

Otho's expression darkened again. 'Jupiter's beard! What's wrong with you? Most slave-girls would sell their own mothers for such a thing.'

The knot of fear in Vita's stomach tightened. The gown was the one she'd worn for her betrothal feast. What did it mean? Was Agrippa planning to marry her after all? But in that case why humiliate her by having Otho continue to treat her like a slave?

The gladiator-master pushed past her and flung open the door. 'Janus! Take her to the dining hall for breakfast duty. Then back to the cell with her to put this on.' He shoved the dress at Janus. 'And while she's about it, she can help ready the She-Wolf too.'

The slave twitched a hand to the copper necklet at his throat. 'Very good, master. But won't the beasts need feeding and watering as well?'

Otho frowned then shook his head. 'The risk is too great. If she were to be damaged in any way . . . No, that numbskull Argus can do it instead.'

'As you wish, master.' Janus slid Vita a sour-faced look, then dipped into a bow.

Her stomach squeezed with a mix of pity and relief. Pity that the poor creatures would soon be forced to fight each other in the ring. Relief that she'd not have to face them again. Though if her fears were right, what lay ahead of her now would likely be a whole lot worse . . .

The gladiator-master gave a loud grunt and stomped back round to his chair. 'And remember—' He snatched up the half-eaten chicken leg and jabbed it at his assistant. 'The new arrangements are to be kept secret, or you'll have not only me but the Honourable Cassius Agrippa to answer to.'

'Of course, master.' Bowing again, Janus grabbed Vita by the arm and dragged her from the room.

As he marched her off into the gloom, she racked her brains as to what the 'new arrangements' Otho had spoken of could possibly be. She threw a sideways glance at the slave's pinched face. There was no point asking him. He'd never dare disobey his master. But something told her she wasn't going to like them. Not one little bit.

After breakfast, Argus was waiting for her at the door to the sleeping-cell. 'I wouldn't go in there if I were you. Old Boodicki has got herself all done up in her war-gear. A proper fright she looks too.' He grimaced, then his face changed and a look of sudden sadness came over it.

'You know, you put me in mind of my own girl, Anna. Thirteen she was when my old master sold her to a trader from across the sea. I tried to stop him and was sent here with this and a new name in punishment.' He jabbed a thumb at his eyepatch. 'She was a beauty like you. But I'll not see her again. Not in this life anyway.' He shook his head and blowing out a breath, handed Vita a yellow bundle of cloth. 'Here! The Master's pet spider told me to give you this. I don't know what they've got planned today, but whatever it is, I hope Fortuna favours you.' Throwing her an awkward smile, he swung the door open and stepped aside.

Battling a fresh sense of dread, Vita gulped in a breath and giving him a quick nod, slipped into the cell beyond. As she crossed the threshold she gave a small cry of surprise. The wolf-woman had changed again. The long white gown was gone, replaced by a sleeveless woollen tunic of dark green, a heavy leather breast-shield buckled over it, and a matching pair of breeches cropped and laced tight at the knees. These were the clothes of a hunter; but a hunter like no other. For instead of its usual pale colour, Brea's skin was a dazzling swirl of bright blue patterns. Circles and spirals coiled around the lower part of her legs, while others curled along her arms, over her shoulders and up the side of her neck. Most fearsome of all was her face. One half was shaded blue, the other left ghostly white, and framed by a mass of snaking blonde plaits tipped with small silver beads which glittered and chinked at every turn of her head.

Vita clutched the gown tight to her chest and took a step back.

The wolf-woman clicked her tongue. 'You have no need to fear me. We are on the same side, aren't we, my friend?' She reached down and pulled Col to her, stroking the length of his silver-grey flank.

Vita blinked. 'Yes. Sorry, it's just that—'

'You had not bargained with meeting a Blue-face?' Brea shot her a mocking smile.

She flushed and gave a small nod.

'Well, I will tell you something. Until the Eagle-men took me for their slave, the only marks on my skin were this' – Brea pointed to the hare on her ankle – 'and the cuts and scratches the land gave me when I was out hunting.'

She switched her gaze to where a wooden bowl half-filled with a dark, shining liquid sat perched on the end of the truckle-bed. 'But this paint gives the ones paying what they want – the wild Blue-face woman and her wolf. And who am I to deny them?' She gave a scornful-sounding laugh. 'Here. Finish things!' She snatched up a brush from beside the bowl and thrust it at Vita.

'How?'

'I am Lupa, the She-Wolf, so make a wolf's head, here.' She jabbed a finger at the unpainted side of her face and sat down on the edge of the bed.

Dropping the gown, Vita took up the brush and with trembling fingers, dipped it into the liquid. Then, sliding a quick sidelong glance at Col, she took a deep breath and traced two ears and a pointed snout on to the pale skin of Brea's cheek.

When she'd finished, the wolf-woman picked up a small

round mirror made of what looked like polished tin. She peered at Vita's handiwork then gave a nod.

'Not as skilled as the hare, but it will be enough for those savages watching us, together with this.' Reaching for a bundle behind her, she unfurled it to reveal a light woollen cloak hung with fragments of assorted animal pelts. She stared at it for a moment, then heaving a sigh, pulled it over her shoulders and dropped down on one knee.

'Now I must ask the Horned One's blessing.' Bending her head, she closed her eyes and muttered a string of strange-sounding words Vita didn't understand.

Vita gathered up the gown and drew back into the shadows to change. As she slipped it over her head, her heart clutched at the familiar smell of the lavender-water Festa sprinkled over their clothes before packing them away. Everything about her old life had gone and nothing could ever bring it back. The only comfort was knowing that Father and Mother couldn't see her now. She stifled a sob.

'Why do you cry? Is it your father?' Brea came and stood by her side.

Vita wiped at her eyes and nodded.

The wolf-woman's jaw clenched. 'I know that feeling.' She reached out and squeezed Vita by the shoulder. 'So, why did Nine-Fingers send for you?'

'He gave me this.' Vita held out the skirts of the gown.

'Agrippa wants me to wear it.'

Brea arched her eyebrows. 'Why?'

She hugged her arms about her. 'I . . . I don't know.'

The wolf-woman's eyes blazed with a sudden fire. 'Do not fear him. It makes his power over you greater. I will avenge them, your family and mine. Of that you can be sure.' She curled her right hand into a fist and struck it against her heart.

A prickle of guilt rippled up the back of Vita's throat. If the wolf-woman knew who Father really was, avenging his death would be the last thing on her mind. Doing her best to push the thought back down, she forced herself to hold Brea's gaze. 'How?'

'The Horned One will show me the way.' As Brea spoke the words, she drew herself to her full height and stared over Vita's head into the darkness beyond.

Vita wanted desperately to believe her. But Agrippa was a powerful man, and there'd be an army of soldiers at the games ready to act at the slightest sign of trouble. Besides, it was the wolf-woman, not him, who would be facing death in the ring.

The thud of heavy footsteps jolted her from her thoughts. A bristle-covered face appeared at the hatch. 'It's time, Boodicki.'

As the door swung open, Brea turned and gripped Vita by both shoulders. 'Ready, friend?'

Vita sucked in a breath and nodded. But it was a lie. Because how could she possibly feel ready with not the slightest clue of what the enemy had planned?

❧❧❧ XXIII ❧❧❧

As the three of them stood waiting in the passageway, Vita stared wide-eyed at the line of gladiators ahead, each now dressed in the specialist gear which marked them out as a particular type of fighter. She knew the names of some – the *retiarius* with his net and trident; the *murmillo* with a helmet topped with a fish-fin crest. But of others she was less sure. None were armed. She guessed Otho would only issue their weapons to them once the men were safely under lock and key inside the arena.

Each man knew that his life would be forfeit if he fought badly and disappointed the crowd. She understood all too clearly now why Father disliked the games. There was no justice in it, despite what others might claim. The weak were the ones to suffer, while brutes like the Skull-Crusher would always come out on top.

As the queue began to shuffle forwards, a man's voice echoed out from behind one of the locked cell doors. It was quickly joined by others and matched with the steady *thump-thump-thump* of fists on wood.

'Victory! Victory! Victory!'

A fresh shiver ran through her. Their friends might be willing them all to succeed, but that was impossible. There would be winners – she glanced at the towering figure of Cronos up ahead. But there would be many losers too. And for some it would mean certain death, unless the goddess Fortuna favoured them.

But what of Brea and Col? She threw a look at the wolf-woman. She and Vita were from different worlds, with a whole lot more than an Emperor's stone-and-earth wall to divide them. But Brea had been good to her. Kind even, in her own wildlands' way. She owed her the truth about who she really was, before it was too late . . .

She was about to draw close and confide all when a familiar, weasely voice sounded in her ear. 'Come with me.'

As Vita made to twist free of Janus's bony grip, Brea sprang towards them, fists raised, a snarling Col at her side.

Quick as lightning, the slave whipped a thick-bladed knife from his belt. 'Keep back, Lupa, or you'll have the Master to answer to.'

Vita flashed Brea a warning look and shook her head. The wolf-woman hesitated, then lowered her hands and, frowning, took her place in the queue again.

Jamming the knife in its sheath, Janus marched Vita past the line of waiting gladiators and up to the door of the accounting room. He gave a quick knock, then pulled it open and shoved her inside.

As the door banged shut, the stocky figure of the gladiator-master stepped from the shadows and came to stand in front of her. He looked her up and down and stroked his chin approvingly. 'Yes, I can see now. The Honourable Cassius Agrippa does indeed have very good taste. But he has requested one small finishing touch.' He jerked his head at Janus. 'Bind her!'

Before Vita had a chance to react, the slave plucked a coil of rope from the desk and bound her wrists together. As she made to protest, Otho snatched something down from the shelf behind and held it up in front of her.

Vita's heart jolted. It was the owl-mask. The one she'd worn last night. If she'd had the tiniest remaining doubt about Agrippa's guilt, it was replaced now with a terrible, sickening certainty. He'd lied about everything. And now, unless she could convince Otho, she would pay the ultimate price.

'Listen to me – please! Agrippa . . . He's a murderer. He killed my father. He—'

'How dare you speak ill of our patron? Time to silence that lying tongue of yours!' Forcing her head down, Otho shoved the mask over her face and fastened it tightly in place with the ties.

She went to cry out, but someone had fixed a thick woollen pad across the mouth, making it impossible to speak. Snatching in a breath through the hole in the mask's beak, she shook her head from side to side. But there was no shifting it. Heart pounding, she peered helplessly out through the eyeholes.

The gladiator-master stood there, hands on hips, admiring his handiwork. 'Fit for a hero's rescue.' He gave a satisfied-sounding grunt.

Vita's stomach gripped again. Hero's rescue? What in Minerva's name did he mean? She tried again to speak, but the wool stuck to her lips and made her choke.

'I'd keep quiet if I were you. It's what a good heroine does best after all.' Otho gave a growling laugh, then waved a hand at Janus. 'Take her outside to join the others. She and Lupa can walk either side of the beasts in the parade. But keep her on that lead.' He jabbed a thumb at the length of rope dangling from her wrists. 'Once a runaway, always a runaway.'

She frowned. A parade? But of course – she remembered now. When a show happened at the arena, the performers were expected to process along the streets for the benefit of the crowds. A cold chill ran down her spine. Whatever Agrippa had planned, there was no chance of rescue by the rebels when they came for the weapons now.

As the slave thrust her out into the morning sunshine, she blinked and peered about her. The gladiators stood two abreast in a line in the street up ahead, each man paired with his fighting partner. All except Cronos the Skull-Crusher, who swaggered in proud isolation at their head. As she was dragged past the line of men, the air filled with whistles and mocking laughter, but Vita held her head high and walked on.

Halfway along, two carts broke the line, each pulled by a pair of white oxen, their harnesses decorated with vines, and each bearing a great wooden cage. Her spirits lifted for a moment as she saw Brea standing to one side of the rear cart, Col pacing up and down alongside. But there was no way of attracting the wolf-woman's attention and she kept her eyes fixed straight ahead.

Then, as they drew closer, an agonized-sounding groan exploded from the cage above. Vita stiffened and looked up. A large brown shape sat humped behind the bars, its snout muzzled with a loop of thick rope, its back legs fixed to the floor by two heavy-looking chains. The female bear, and judging from the shrieks and squeals now echoing from the first cart, the other cage must hold the sow and her young.

In spite of her fear, Vita's heart cramped. These animals would be made to fight each other to the death. But whichever of them won, it would surely die too – the crowd would demand it. And what of Brea? What beast would Agrippa make her face?

A distant drumbeat started up. Finally, the carts' wheels ground into action and their part of the procession got underway. As the carts rattled round the corner into the main street, the first spectators came into view. They were guarded at intervals by sharp-eyed soldiers on the lookout for troublemakers.

The crowds grew thicker and louder as they neared the Forum. Doing her best to ignore them, Vita gritted her teeth and focused on the road ahead.

As they pulled on to the street that led to the arena, she became aware of a slim, dark-haired figure in a patched tunic shadowing her along the edge of the crowd. Her heart gave a quick bump. Leander? She couldn't be certain. But if it was, maybe some of his rebel friends were with him too? Vita still wasn't sure what she felt about the revolt, but it was a comfort to think she and Brea weren't completely alone.

And now, here was the arena rising up in front of them, its great timber walls easily the height of ten men. She'd seen it only once before, on a trip a few years ago to visit one of Father's friends in his grand villa north of the town boundary. It had been rebuilt since then. Part of the Emperor's building schemes taking place all across the Empire – a symbol of his power and strength, like the wall being put up in the northlands. She shivered at the sight of the huge entrance arch, its gates thrown wide to receive them, a row of soldiers standing to attention on either side.

On their approach, a bunch of soldiers stepped out to push back the crowds milling around the souvenir and food stalls set up next to the arena walls. They were almost level with the gates now, close enough for her to read the entrance posters announcing the programme for the day. Her eyes skimmed down over promises of dancers, executions, the beast fight and gladiatorial rounds to the description of the main attraction: *The Grand Finale*.

Lupa – Queen of the Blue-faces and her man-killing wolf to hunt a prize beast of the host's choice.

Then *Cronos the Skull-Crusher* to fight the winner of the earlier heats.

So Brea and Col had star billing alongside the dreaded Skull-Crusher. But what was the 'prize beast'? And where did she – Vita – fit into it all? A tide of fresh panic rose up inside her. But what was this at the bottom?

These games are brought to you by your generous host, the most Honourable Gaius Cassius Agrippa, War Hero and Magistrate, in memory of his esteemed and much missed friend and comrade-in-arms, Marcus Tullius Verus, Councillor and

Senior Magistrate. May the gods watch over his spirit for all eternity.

A surge of hot fury swept the panic aside. How dare he! If she could, she would scrawl 'Murderer' across the poster in giant blood-red letters. And it would be Cassius Agrippa and not Brea fighting the 'prize beast' to the death. But then, as angry tears pricked, a familiar voice sounded low in her ear.

That would not be justice, Little Owl.

Father? She spun round, looking wildly about her.

Janus turned and reined her in. 'Stop your fussing, or I'll feed you to our flea-bitten friend there.' He jabbed his head at the bear then yanked Vita forwards again.

As they passed under the archway, she balled her fingers into two tight fists. Father had believed in justice Roman-style, but look what had happened to him. Like Brea had said, to be avenged against Agrippa – that's what mattered now. In any way she could, and whatever the cost.

XXIV

As the gates slammed shut behind them, Vita jerked to a stop behind the cart and peered about her. They were standing in a semicircular courtyard of dirty yellow sand, its roof open to the sky. A high, straight wall stood in front of them, broken by a passageway in the centre leading up to what looked like a second set of wooden gates further on. A mix of drumbeats and the buzz of excited voices echoed along it, coming from what she guessed must be the main arena beyond.

A sudden loud bang made her jump. She pivoted round to see a soldier step smartly away from the entrance gates now securely barred behind them. He joined his comrade, and they marched the line of gladiators forwards into the passage and through a door on the right, halfway along. There was a distant chink of keys and the rattle-clang of metal. A few moments later, the soldiers re-emerged.

Janus gave them a clipped nod. 'Put the She-Wolf and her beast in the cell opposite the Skull-Crusher.' He swung back to face Vita. 'And you can join them. It would be a pity to part such good friends. Besides' – he gave a spiteful-sounding laugh – 'it will give you the chance to discuss battle tactics together.'

Vita's heart lurched. Battle tactics? What did he mean by that?

There was a loud scuffling sound from the other side of the cart followed by a sharp growl, then bitter cursing. Moments later the soldiers reappeared, one shoving Brea forwards at sword-point, the other nursing a bloodied hand while doing his best to herd a snapping, snarling Col.

The wolf-woman started at the sight of Vita in her mask. But before she could say anything, the soldiers drove her and Col the same way they'd taken the gladiators. Tightening his grip on the rope, Janus dragged Vita after them.

Stepping through the door, Vita squinted through the mask's eyeholes, doing her best to make sense of the gloom. They were in a low-ceilinged room, its walls lined on either side with a pair of iron-barred cells, each lit by the flickering flame from a single oil lamp. The gladiators had been split into two groups and thrown into the cells on either side of the door. The soldiers marched them past these and up to a smaller cell on the left-hand side.

As they rattled open the door, a rumbling growl sounded from the darkness behind them. Vita spun round to see the Skull-Crusher's snarling face pressed hard against the bars of the opposite cell. She shuddered and turned quickly away, struggling against her bonds to reach for the owl-key at her throat.

But Janus was there before her. 'What's this?' He snatched up the key and held it to the light. 'A pretty thing, to be sure. It would be a shame if it got lost. I'll keep it safe for when – I mean, *if* – you return.' He snapped the cord from around her neck and looped it through the belt at his waist.

Vita gave a muffled cry and made to snatch it back, but with her hands so tightly bound it was hopeless. And then she was being jostled into the cell after Brea and Col, and it was too late.

As the men's footsteps dwindled away, she sank to the floor with a groan. Brea dropped down beside her, eyes full of concern.

'Did Nine-Fingers put the night-hunter's face on you?' She jabbed a finger at the mask.

Vita tried to answer, but the only sound that came out was a small, ragged sob.

'Wait.' Gently the wolf-woman tilted Vita's head and undid the ties. As she pulled the mask clear, Vita gasped a dry-mouthed thanks.

'Here.' Dragging a wooden bucket from the corner, Brea pressed a ladleful of cold, peaty-tasting water to Vita's lips. 'Better?'

Vita gulped down a second mouthful and gave a grateful nod.

Letting Col drink from her hands, Brea took a long draught from the ladle herself, then picked up the mask and ripped the woollen pad free.

'Why did they put you in it?' She balled the pad up and tossed it into the far corner of the cell.

Vita coughed and drew in another breath. 'So that I wouldn't be recognized, I think.'

Brea shot her a sharp-eyed look. 'What do you mean, *recognized*?'

'Er, nothing . . .' She gave another quick cough. 'What's going to happen to us?'

Before the wolf-woman could answer, a voice thundered out of the gloom opposite. 'You are going to die.'

It was followed by an explosion of rough laughter from the men in the neighbouring cell. 'That's it, Cronos. Tell old Lupa and her pretty little kitchen maid friend how it is!'

Vita scrambled back from the door, heart pounding.

'Do not listen.' Brea pulled round, squatting to block her view. 'He seeks to find a weak spot to make us doubt ourselves and fail.' She took Vita's face between her hands and fixed her with a fierce green stare. 'But we are smarter than that. Smarter than him too.' She threw a tight-lipped glance over her shoulder then turned back to face her. 'Come, I will undo your bonds.'

As Brea loosened the rope, the words of the Skull-Crusher rang again in Vita's ears. If what he and Janus said was right, then it meant only one thing. That she was destined to appear in the arena too. A jet of hot panic surged through her. She shook her head and gave a choked moan. She couldn't fight. She didn't know how . . .

Brea tossed away the rope and gripped her by the shoulders. 'Are you sick?'

She shook her head and bit back against the tears. Brea was right. Whatever Agrippa had planned, she mustn't let herself think about failing. What she needed now was a story. One to give her the strength for whatever lay ahead; to show what might be possible if the gods were on their side.

She swallowed again and drew in a breath. 'I'm all right. Will you tell me again about Boudicca. I mean, your hare-queen?'

Brea gave her a searching look then nodded. 'Here, friend.' She patted the straw beside her. Col let out a yip, then circled round and settled down in the gap between them, head resting on his paws. 'Ready?'

Vita nodded. Leaning into the wolf's warm body, she closed her eyes and let the words weave their magic, banishing her fears, for the moment at least, and filling her head with a dream of victory.

As Brea spoke the final lines of the song, Vita sat back against the wall with a sigh.

'That was beautiful, thank you. But . . . but what happens now?'

The wolf-woman grimaced. 'We rest and wait.'

Vita's stomach clenched again. She had to stay calm. Do what she could to conserve her strength. She reached for the owl-key again, then remembered and stifled a cry.

Brea shot her a frowning look. 'We will get it back from that thief, you will see. Now, do as I say and take your rest while you can.'

Vita was jolted from a sleep full of leaping hares, thundering hooves and smoking ruins by the grip of a warm hand on her shoulder. She blinked and sat up. Brea knelt before her, the patterns on her skin darting and twisting like living snakes in the light from the now sputtering oil lamp.

'How long have I been asleep?'

'Long enough. It is nearly time.'

'How do you know?'

'The others have been taken off to fight. All except that one.' As she jerked her head towards Cronos's cell, a flurry of loud snores rumbled out through the bars.

'But what about the beasts? The bear and the boar?'

'They will be gone now.'

'You mean . . . dead?'

Brea frowned but gave no reply.

Vita gritted her teeth, trying not to show her fear. 'What should I do? When they come for us, I mean.'

'We must stand strong together, like the flame-haired queen and her people did. Use our wits – our eyes, our ears. Our hearts too. And if the Horned One wills it, we will succeed.' She heaved a sigh, then, standing, stepped up to the bars and peered towards the door.

A distant roar sounded above the noise of the Skull-Crusher's snores. Trembling, Vita slid to her feet and joined her.

'Here.' Brea reached inside her leather breastplate and pressed something cool and rough-edged into her hand. 'Take this.'

Vita uncurled her fingers and sucked in a breath. It was the wolf-woman's precious firestone. She looked up at her, frowning. 'But . . . but won't you need it?'

Brea clasped a hand to her breast. 'I hold its light here, always.' Her eyes clouded, then cleared again. She flashed her a quick smile.

Vita felt a sudden surge of warmth followed by a sharp stab of guilt. Brea had trusted her with her brother's gift. She had to confess the truth to her while she still had the chance. Tucking the firestone into a gap in the hem of her gown, she rehearsed her opening words then straightened again and took in a breath.

'I . . . I need to tell you something.'

The wolf-woman cocked a blue-stained eyebrow. 'What is it?'

'The truth.'

'The truth of what?'

'Of who I am.'

Brea frowned. 'What do you mean?'

Vita stalled for a moment. Then, pulling back her shoulders, she forced herself to meet her gaze and told her everything. About Father once being an 'Eagle-man' commander and how he'd taken Agrippa under his wing. How Agrippa had saved him on the battlefield and of the friendship between them. Then – tears spilling now from her eyes – about the day Father was killed. The break-in, her flight from the house with Festa, then her return to make the terrible discovery of Father's lifeless body, Mother and Lucius gone. And after, how she'd been mistaken for a slave by Agrippa's man because of her disguise. Finally, in faltering sentences, she mustered the courage to tell the wolf-woman that it was she who was betrothed to Agrippa, not her fictitious master's daughter.

As the wolf-woman listened, her lips pressed tight and her eyes hardened to two glittering chips of green ice. When Vita had finished, she stared past her into the darkness without uttering a single word.

After what felt like an age, Vita dared herself to speak again. 'Aren't you ... aren't you going to say something?'

The wolf-woman stiffened and blinked, then swung round to face her, the beads in her hair rattling like a storm of hailstones. 'You choose to tell me this now? That I am to fight alongside an Eagle-man's daughter? And not only that, but the friend of the one who cut my father's life-spirit from him!'

Vita's stomach clawed. 'He killed my father too! Father ... he was a good man. Kind and just and honourable. A man who treated his slaves well and wanted ordinary people to have better lives. The opposite of Agrippa. I swear it on my life!'

'Perhaps. But it doesn't change that you lied to me. How can there be trust between us now?'

'I'm sorry. I was afraid to tell you before.'

'You should be more afraid now.'

A shiver ran along Vita's spine. She'd ruined everything. The wolf-woman hated her. Just as she'd known she would. And now, as they were thrust into the arena together, whose side would she be on?

The sound of approaching footsteps broke through her thoughts. The wolf-woman threw her a sharp-eyed look, then reached down and ruffled Col's ears. 'May the Horned One be with you, my friend.'

Vita's heart cramped. Brea would never call her 'friend' now. Her desperate need to tell the truth had made certain of that. And now . . . now she would have to face whatever was to come alone.

She blinked and looked up. Three shadowy figures had appeared at the cell door. Janus and the two soldiers. It was time.

The slave clicked his tongue at the sight of Vita, unmasked and free of her bonds. 'Bind the girl's wrists and put her back in the mask. And muzzle that beast too!' He jabbed a finger at Col.

Vita bucked against the soldier's grip, but it was useless to resist.

As they were marched out through the door, a pair of giant hands gripped the bars of the cell opposite. 'Make your peace with your god, She-Wolf. And pray your death is a quick one.' A glistening ball of spit arced through the air and landed on the wolf-woman's painted arm. She jerked to a stop, then, head held high, marched on in silence.

When they reached the passage, Vita shot a look back into the courtyard. The carts and oxen had been taken away, leaving only the cages. One of them was empty, a wooden ramp leading from the open door down to the sand. But the door to the other was shut, the bear still slumped inside. She frowned. Hadn't she been meant to fight the boar?

Janus slid her a sly look. 'We're keeping her back. In case there's any clearing up to do.'

Vita's throat dried. She could only guess what he meant by that. But the sow and her young would be dead now for sure. As she turned her face away, the sounds of the arena rushed in again. Laboured grunts and gut-wrenching cries, the clash and scrape of metal, the swooping 'Oohs' and 'Ahhs' of the crowd.

'One pair to go, She-Wolf. And then you will have your chance to shine.' Janus threw the wolf-woman a sneering smile. 'Can you guess which beast His Honour Cassius Agrippa has chosen for you?'

But the wolf-woman ignored him and kept her eyes focused on the gates ahead.

He curled his lips. 'It matters not. You'll find out soon enough. As for you—' He gave Vita a quick poke in the ribs. 'I hope you've practised your screaming. The crowd will expect it.'

A fresh wave of panic surged up inside her. She forced it back down and looked straight past him, following the wolf-woman's lead. At the same moment, an agonized yell split the air, followed by a deafening roar and the loud, rhythmic chant of *Kill! Kill! Kill!* Vita shuddered. She might not have witnessed a real fight before, but she could guess what had happened. A man had fought and lost and now Cassius Agrippa was asking the crowd to help decide his fate. Who was it out there? The man with the mangled ear and his friend? Or another pair? It didn't matter. Soon, one of them would be dead, cut down by the other – unless the patron of the games showed him mercy. But as bitter experience had so recently taught, Agrippa was not a merciful man . . .

The crowd fell quiet and now the only sound in Vita's ears was the *thump-thump-thump* of her own heart. She shivered. This was it – the moment when he would decide. She flicked a quick glance at the wolf-woman. She stood statue-still, her tightly-clenched knuckles the only clue as to what her true feelings might be. Beside her, Col sniffed the air and gave a low whine.

And then, with a strangled cry, the silence was broken. The crowd erupted into a thunderous bout of cheers and applause punctuated by cries of 'Agrippa! Agrippa! Agrippa!' Cries which confirmed that the Honourable Agrippa had indeed not been merciful.

Vita closed her eyes and whispered a prayer for the dead man's soul. But the shrill blast of a trumpet caused her to snap them back open. Another blast, and the gates before them swung slowly apart.

As the soldiers jostled them forwards, the wolf-woman turned and fixed Vita with a grim-eyed stare. 'Remember: eyes, ears, hearts.'

She swallowed and gave a quick nod back. Had Brea forgiven her? She was about to find out.

XXV

The soldiers marched them through the gates, hands gripped on the pommels of their swords. As they stepped out on to the sand, the air about them exploded in a frenzy of cheers and wild yelling, accompanied by the thunder of trumpets and the steady beat of the drums.

Vita peered through the eyeholes of the mask, pulse pounding. The arena was vast, much bigger than she'd imagined. Tiers of spectators clad in a mosaic of different colours rose up around them, arms waving about their heads like frantic insects, faces a blur. She'd never seen so many people crammed into one place – most of them men, though a bunch of well-dressed women sat tucked away in the topmost tier of seats under a bright yellow awning.

Friends of her parents would be here. Not that they'd recognize her beneath the mask. And Agrippa too of course. She shuddered at the thought.

A trio of attendants in grey tunics were busy raking a set of bright crimson patches in the sand, then scattering a fresh layer from a bucket to cover them – the last traces of the ones who had lost their fight and been put to the sword. Vita bit her lip and turned away.

The soldier beside her nudged her and tipped his head at a statue standing in an alcove set in the arena wall – a woman bearing a horn full of brightly coloured fruit. 'What fate does Fortuna have in store for the pair of you, eh?'

Vita's skin prickled. She had prayed to Fortuna often. But she knew as well as anyone the goddess could be the bringer of bad luck as well as good.

The soldier gave his companion a knowing wink. Then the pair swung them round and marched them towards a set of wooden steps leading to a grand tented platform set in the first tier of benches above.

As they drew closer, her heart beat even faster. For there, beneath the red canvas awning, its supports decorated with swags of white linen tied with twists of ivy, sat a row of richly dressed people: the men in dark woollen togas of the kind people wore at funerals, the women wearing fine-woven gowns of the same colour, their white painted faces topped by hair curled and primped in the latest styles. And at the centre, on his own high-backed chair, the blond upright figure of Gaius Cassius Agrippa – her one-time husband-to-be, and now her deadliest enemy.

Vita's stomach gripped. She still didn't understand. What could possibly have made him want to murder his best and oldest friend? A man he now claimed to honour with these games . . .

As he gazed about him, hand raised, pale-skinned face shining with a look of self-satisfied pride, a burst of fresh rage coursed through her. She had liked him once. But oh, how she hated him now! She glanced at the wolf-woman, but she appeared unruffled, her expression still giving nothing away.

The soldiers drew to a stop in front of the steps and, thrusting their arms across their breastplates, gave a clipped bow. The familiar figure of Otho, now dressed in a smart cream tunic and light-brown cloak, stepped out from behind Agrippa's chair. He signalled for the wolf-woman to drop to her knees. Ignoring him, she bent and freed Col's snout from the muzzle instead.

Agrippa's face pulled into a tight frown. Dismissing Otho with an impatient wave, he rose to his feet and held up his right hand for silence. A sudden hush fell over the crowd. He nodded and cleared his throat.

'Honourable magistrates, councillors, friends and

citizens! As you know, tradition dictates that the beast-hunt should take place in the morning, before the combat of the gladiators. But to honour our dear departed friend and comrade, Marcus Tullius Verus . . .' He paused as a groan of anger mixed with sympathy rippled through the crowd. 'I know, citizens, I know. Rest assured we will hunt down whoever is responsible and deal them the justice they deserve.' He waited a moment for the crowd to settle before continuing.

'In the great Verus's honour I have arranged for something a little different. A spectacle featuring one of the Londinium arena's greatest stars – one worthy to grace our grand finale!'

The crowd burst into another round of cheers and applause. Agrippa looked about him smiling and raised his hand again. 'We have before us the fearsome hunter, Lupa, and the savage creature from which she takes her name.' The crowd gave another loud whoop as he gestured to the wolf-woman and Col. 'But as your host I have decided we should mix the wildness of the lands beyond the wall with a little Roman civilization. So, please join me in welcoming a special surprise guest at today's games – the fair Princess Ariadne!' He flung out his arm towards Vita, then eyes narrowing, began a slow handclap which was quickly imitated by the crowd.

An icy shiver rippled across the back of Vita's neck.

Had he found out somehow about her appearance on the stage, or was the choice of name just a coincidence? And what did he have planned? Whatever it was, it was bound to be his own version of events, just like the lies he'd been spreading about Father's murder.

But Agrippa was speaking again. 'Those who know their history will remember the story of the beautiful young Princess Ariadne, kept prisoner by the fearsome Minotaur in a great labyrinth deep beneath her father's royal palace.' There were loud gasps and cries from the spectators, many of whom clearly didn't realize he was twisting the story, making it suit his own ends.

At a sudden signal from Agrippa, the soldier guarding Vita spun her round and marched her over to a wooden post which had been hastily erected in the centre of the arena as the magistrate spoke.

Agrippa's taunting tones rang out again behind her. 'But fear not, my friends. A hero stands waiting in the wings. Not the great Prince Theseus from the story of old, but our very own blue-faced warrior queen!'

The air exploded with more thunderous roars. Vita turned in time to see the wolf-woman's guard force her arm into a hero's salute.

Keeping a firm grip on her, his companion untied Vita's wrists and looping the rope round her middle, used it to bind her to the post instead. The more she struggled, the tighter the soldier pulled and the louder the crowd cheered.

Agrippa's voice echoed out across the sand. 'So, we have our princess – a reluctant one, I'll grant you – and our brave hero and her sharp-fanged companion. But we are missing something, surely?' He cupped a hand to his ear, clearly revelling in his role as scene-setter-in-chief.

The voices of the spectators swelled into a single, repeated chant.

Beast! Beast! Beast!

Vita froze. In the shock of the moment, she'd forgotten about the prize beast.

'Are you ready?'

YES!

'Are you sure?'

Around the arena, men jumped from their seats and punched their fists high in the air.

YES!!!

Agrippa nodded to Otho. The gladiator-master plucked a pair of iron-tipped spears from a stand behind him, then thudded down the steps and out on to the sunlit sand. As he strode towards the wolf-woman, the two soldiers withdrew to the platform and took up their positions on either side of Agrippa's chair. Muttering something in the wolf-woman's ear, Otho thrust the spears at her and retreated up the steps.

Agrippa turned from one side to the other, courting the applause of the crowd. 'Let the spectacle begin!' He jerked up both arms, held them there for an instant, then plunged them down to his sides.

Fresh cheers erupted all about them, but the wolf-woman stayed stock-still, a spear gripped tight in each hand, head tilted back in cold defiance. Agrippa glared down at her, his forehead pressed into an icy frown. Behind him, Otho flapped his hands in a frantic attempt to get her to obey. But still she refused to move.

The mood of the crowd began to cool and there were angry cries of 'Get on with it,' and 'I want my money back.'

Losing patience, Agrippa spun round and signalled to the soldiers. But as they started forward, the wolf-woman leapt into action. Clashing the spear-poles together, she thrust them high in the air. Then, pulling her cloak about her, she turned and set off at a slow-paced stride towards the post where Vita was tied, Col padding along at her side.

Vita watched, heart in her mouth, trying to guess what her next move would be.

The wolf-woman continued to advance, looking neither left nor right. Then, at less than an arm's reach from the post, she dug both spears in the sand, dropped to one knee and gave a low bow as if paying Vita some kind of mock tribute. The crowd roared its approval. At the same moment, the wolf-woman twitched the edge of her cloak aside to reveal a flash of silver at her waist.

Vita's stomach clenched. It was a knife. She had a knife! As the wolf-woman slid her hand to the blade, the memory of her last words before they left the cell whirled back into Vita's head.

You should be more afraid now.

'Please, no!' She twisted against the post, but the rope held firm.

The wolf-woman's face pulled into a puzzled frown. Then, eyes widening, she gave a sharp shake of her head. Using the cloak as cover, she drew the knife, and flipping it handle outwards, thrust it at Vita with a conspiratorial look.

Her stomach gave a quick somersault. It was the same bone-handled blade Janus had pulled on her at the gladiator school. But how? The hint of a smile danced over Brea's pink and blue lips. Miming for Vita to conceal it in the folds of her gown, she shot her a final look of defiance. Then, springing back to her feet, she ripped open the ties of her cloak and flung it to the ground.

The audience burst into raucous cries of *Lupa! Lupa! Lupa!*

As the noise built to an ear-piercing howl it was joined by the single blast of a trumpet. A gate in the wall to their right swung slowly open. Drawing back her shoulders, Brea turned to face it, a spear in each hand, Col poised and ready at her side.

To the sound of a loud drumbeat, two burly men dressed in leather tunics stepped into the space beneath the gateway arch, each one holding the looped end of a rope. Directing a low bow at Agrippa and his guests, the men hooked their right shoulders through the loops and began to pull. Then, as the lengths of rope tightened, a new sound cut through the noise of the crowd: a furious bellowing which filled Vita's heart with a sickening dread.

She glanced desperately back at Brea and Col. The fur on the wolf's back had risen into a long silver-grey ridge. Beside him, the wolf-woman tossed back her plaits and shifted from one bare foot to another, muscles tautening beneath her blue-patterned skin.

As the men strained ever harder on the ropes, the crowd began to yell and stomp their feet in time to the drums.

Pull! Pull! Pull!

Suddenly the ropes fell slack. One of the men yelled a warning and the pair flung themselves towards a set of steps in the wall as a dark, boiling cloud of dust rolled through the arch. As it cleared, the biggest, blackest bull Vita had ever seen galloped out on to the sand.

The crowd went wild, roaring its approval, but the wolf-woman and Col stood their ground. Vita made to cry out, but her tongue stuck to her teeth.

The bull thundered to a stop and looked about, then tossed its pointed white horns and snorted a breath. It hadn't spotted them yet, but it was only a matter of time. As she threw another panicked glance at Brea, an unwelcome memory flashed into Vita's head. The wolf-woman had said she'd never had to face a bull before. She and her wolf were brave and swift on their feet, but against such a powerful adversary, would that be enough?

Her heart gave a sudden jolt. What was she thinking? Three against one had to be better than two. She scanned around her. All eyes were fixed on Brea and the bull. Sliding the knife up, she turned the sharp edge against the rope and began to saw.

The bull gave another toss of its head and set off zigzagging across the sand, the ends of the rope tied round its middle flailing about like a pair of whipping black snakes. But then, reaching the halfway point between the gate and the post, it pulled up again, swung its head round and stared straight at them.

And now the crowd switched from roaring to jeering, egging the beast on to do its worst. Vita's stomach clenched. In a moment or two it would be certain to charge. As though reading her thoughts, the creature dipped its head and pawed at the ground with a shining black hoof. She threw another desperate look at Brea.

The wolf-woman had angled the spear in her left hand

so the tip was pointed straight at the bull's chest. Slowly, surely, she raised the other one to shoulder height. Then, sliding it into a throwing position, she growled a terse command to Col. The wolf pulled back, readying himself to spring.

Vita blinked against the sting of the sweat now trickling into her eyes. She was almost halfway through the rope, but she needed more time. Time Brea couldn't hope to give her.

As she bent her head to the task again, a piercing whistle sounded in front. She jerked up to see Col shoot forward, head down, teeth bared. She froze, convinced the bull would gore him. But at the last moment, the wolf pulled up short, and keeping just out of reach, danced in front of it, leaping from side to side on nimble grey paws. The bull gave another furious-sounding bellow and made to charge, but Col kept sidestepping it, forcing it to change tack.

Gritting her teeth, Vita sawed again at the rope. Just a few . . . more . . . strokes . . .

Now the spectators were up on their feet, screaming at Brea to use her weapons. But instead she stood there motionless, eyes fixed on a spot in the distance as though in some kind of trance.

Then it happened. As Col danced back across the bull's path, it swerved and caught him unawares, landing a sharp kick against his flank. With a piercing yelp, he tumbled across the sand and lay still. And now the bull was bearing down on Brea instead, black eyes rolling, strings of white foam dripping from its nose and mouth. Frantically Vita redoubled her efforts with the knife. She had to get free. She had to—

The bull had lowered its head. It was going to charge!

Suddenly the wolf-woman rocked back on her left heel. Then, raising her right foot off the ground, she drew back the spear in her right hand and loosed it at her opponent with a savage cry. It sped through the air, iron tip flashing in the sunlight. As it neared the target, it hung for a heart-beat, as if stopped in time, then shot forwards, piercing deep into the bull's right shoulder. The creature gave an ear-splitting bellow and rocked to one side. For a moment it seemed about to fall. Then, to Vita's horror, it righted itself, lowered its head again and charged.

As Vita hacked through the final strands of rope, Brea rocked back a second time and launched her remaining spear. But instead of finding its mark it flew wide, clipping the bull on its horns, and rebounded sideways to fall uselessly in the sand. The crowd gave a collective groan.

Vita watched in dismay as the bull careered about in confusion, only to spin round and fix its eyes back on Brea – now weaponless and standing directly in its path. She had to do something. But what? She glanced down at the knife. It was all they had. But would it be enough? A sudden picture of the net-fighters at their training sprang up before her.

Tossing the rope to the ground, she whipped up Brea's discarded cloak and, with the crowd's frantic cheers ringing in her ears, dashed to the wolf-woman's side. Brea's eyes widened, then narrowed again as Vita thrust both cloak and blade at her. With a quick nod, she snatched them up and turned back to face her opponent.

The bull stood its ground, halfway between them and the gate, the blood from the spear-wound coursing down the front of its heaving black chest and splashing in crimson drops on to the yellow sand below. Though still standing, it was clearly weakened. Sensing it too, the crowd set up a slow handclap. But the beast wasn't finished yet. With a roll of its eyes, and another thunderous bellow, it dipped its horns and readied itself for yet another charge.

Brea squared up to it, cloak gripped in one hand, knife in the other. Vita's chest clutched. They had to distract it somehow. She glanced at Col, but he was still out cold – or worse. It was down to her then.

Gulping in a breath, she hoisted her skirts and yelling Brea's war-cry at the top of her voice, whirled out across the sand. The bull snorted and tossed its head, unsure of who to lunge at first. There were jeering hoots and cries of 'Run away, Princess!', but Vita didn't care. All that mattered now was saving her friend.

The beast made its decision and turned to face Brea again. In desperation, Vita circled round behind it and let out another battle-cry. It wavered for a moment, then swung about to face her. But as it drew back on its hooves, a blue-painted figure with wild snake-tail hair leapt out and flung a billowing black shape over its horns. The bull tossed and bucked, but the more it struggled, the more tangled up in the cloak it became, until finally, with a loud groan it toppled forwards and thudded to the ground.

As the crowd roared its delight, the wolf-woman darted forward. Crouching before the fallen creature, she laid a painted hand on its side and mouthed words impossible for anyone but her and the bull to hear. Then, redoubling her grip on the knife, she raised the blade high above her head and plunged it through the cloth, deep into the animal's flesh. The bull gave another snorting groan, then with a final great shiver, it fell still.

A wave of relief flooded through Vita, only to dry up again at fresh sight of Col. She dashed towards him, the cheers of the crowd echoing dimly in her ears. But Brea was there ahead of her, kneeling panting at his side.

'Is he . . . ?'

'Dead? No. But winded. Bruised too.' Brea sucked in another breath, then stroked the wolf's head gently and whispered words to him in the language only they shared. He lifted his head and blinked at her, then slumped back into unconsciousness.

'Poor Col. What shall we—'

Brea seized her by the wrist and threw her a warning look. Vita stiffened. What was wrong? She glanced about her. Moments ago the crowd had been cheering their beloved Lupa's name. But now there was deathly quiet, all eyes fixed on the platform above.

A single slow handclap echoed around them as Agrippa stepped down from his chair and out into the light. 'Bravo, Lupa. Your skill and courage is second to none – for a Blue-face.' His mouth pinched in disgust as he spoke the insult. 'Is that not true, good people of Londinium?'

Jolted from their silence, the crowd broke into a round of deafening applause. He let it go on for a moment, then held up a hand. 'To celebrate your bravery, I have another test for you and the lovely Princess Ariadne. A spectacle never before seen, either here or in the Emperor's great arena in Rome. Are you ready, citizens?'

Resounding cries of 'Yes!' and 'Bring it on!' echoed about them.

Vita's stomach shrank up inside her. She shot a questioning look at Brea. The wolf-woman returned it with a puzzled shrug. But they didn't have long to wait for an answer.

A creak of wood sounded behind them. As they turned, the gates they'd come through earlier juddered slowly open again. For a moment the space between them stayed empty. Then a giant helmeted figure lurched into it. And now the crowd set up another chant.

One that sent a shiver of ice up and down Vita's spine.

CRONOS!
CRONOS!
CRONOS!

XXVI

A prickle of cold sweat formed on Vita's forehead. Beast-hunters were never pitted against gladiators in the arena. Or women against men. That's what Brea had said. But it was clear Agrippa didn't care about playing by the rules. She had to try and stop things. Reveal who she really was.

Heart pounding, she snatched at the ties binding the mask. But it was no use – they were knotted fast. And now the Skull-Crusher was on the move, lumbering towards them, an oblong shield bearing the image of a black gaping skull in his left hand, the blade of his sword – a real one this time – flashing this way and that in his right.

She twisted round to seek Brea's help, but the wolf-woman had gone to retrieve the second spear. Cronos was still coming, now slamming the flat of the blade across his shield in time to the crowd's gleeful chants. Vita's instincts were telling her to flee, but she forced herself to stand her ground instead. He might be stronger than the three of them put together, but they weren't beaten – not yet!

The giant thudded ever closer, urged on by the crowd. In his full fighting gear, he looked even more fearsome than usual. Naked except for a black-skirted loincloth belted round his middle and a breastplate and arm-guard for protection. His muscles rippled beneath a layer of glistening body oil, making the scars on his torso dance like a nest of twisting vipers.

But it was his helmet which filled Vita with the most dread. It was fashioned from heavy bronze panels which encased his entire head. Even his eyes were hidden from view behind eyeholes criss-crossed with silver-coloured grilles, though she could sense his gaze behind them, sizing her up; deciding where to make the first strike. She shivered and drew her arms about her, then checked herself and dropped them back down to her sides. Brea was right. If she showed the giant she feared him, all would be lost.

As if in reply to her thoughts, a snake-haired shadow fell across the sand. The wolf-woman came to stand alongside her, spear in one hand, Janus's knife in the other.

'Are you ready?'

Vita fisted her fingers and nodded.

'Good.' The wolf-woman dug her spear-pole into the sand. 'And remember, together we are swifter than eagle, stronger than bear, braver than wolf.'

Vita's heart lifted at the words of the hare-queen's song. If the Horned One and Fortuna were both on their side, perhaps they might stand a chance after all. With a hurried glance at the goddess's painted eyes, she gripped Brea's wrist and chanted the words back at her, loud and defiant above the mounting cries of the crowd. The wolf-woman flashed her a grim smile, then switching her gaze to the Skull-Crusher, spoke through gritted teeth.

'Wait for my signal.'

'But what shall I do?'

'You will know when the time comes.' She pressed the knife into Vita's hand.

Vita glanced back at their opponent. He was only a few strides away now, shield raised, sword at the ready. But before he could land the first blow, Brea leapt forward, jabbing at him with her spear. He juddered to a stop and, hunkering down behind his shield, rocked from one foot to the other.

Brea did the same. Slowly, the pair began to circle each other, striking out with their weapons when the other drew too close. All the while the crowd screamed and shouted the name of their chosen hero as if their own lives depended on it.

Time and again the Skull-Crusher forced Brea back, barging with his shield and slashing at her with his sword. But each time, she proved the more agile of the two, darting aside, or parrying him with quick jabs and thrusts of her spear. What she lacked in muscle and weight, she made up for in fleetness of foot, worrying at him the way she'd once told Vita a wolf might harry and wear down its prey.

And sure enough – though it seemed like a miracle – Cronos started to show signs of tiring, grunting with each shield charge and snorting out great breaths with every stab. The crowd had noticed too. The calls for Lupa drowned out those for the Skull-Crusher now. Vita flicked her gaze back to Brea. She was still moving well. Was it possible the gods would let her win? She threw the statue of Fortuna another glance and offered up a hurried prayer.

But the goddess couldn't have heard, because no sooner had Vita spoken than a stone shot through the air, clipping the wolf-woman on the side of her face. As she cried out and raised up a hand, Cronos took his chance and lunged, thrusting at her with his sword then slamming the edge of his shield down on her bare toes.

She gave another cry and stumbled backwards, toppling to the ground with a groan. The crowd went wild, leaping from their seats and yelling for Cronos to launch another attack. Vita's throat gripped. If she didn't act now, it would all be over. Tightening her hold on the knife, she dashed in between them, slashing the blade from side to side in a frantic bid to halt the giant's advance.

Cronos lurched to a stop. He was so close now she could smell his sweat. She snatched a look back at Brea, but she was still on the ground, hand clutching her right foot, face twisted in pain. She had to win her time to recover. She sucked in a breath and spun round to face the Skull-Crusher again.

'Leave her alone, or ... or—'

The giant gave a menacing growl and took another step forward. But instead of striking Vita down, he cast his shield aside, then, to gasps of shock and surprise, tore at the buckles fastening his helmet and dragged it clear of his head.

'Or what?' He tossed the helmet down between them and drew his lips into a sharp-toothed leer.

Vita's chest spiked with fresh fear. She opened her mouth, but no answer came. Because how could she ever hope to stop a monster like Cronos?

'Time ... to ... DIE!' The giant snatched up Vita's arm and, ripping the knife from her trembling hand, rammed it into his belt. She struggled against him, but his grip only tightened. He pulled her against him and raised his sword. Then, eyes shrinking to two granite chips, he peered at the platform above them.

Heart racing, Vita followed his gaze to where Agrippa

sat, his face lit with a look of cold cunning, a finger stroking the gold torc at his throat. As the chants of *Cronos!* began to build again, the magistrate rose slowly to his feet. Balling his right hand into a fist, he thrust it in front of him, slid his thumb out to the side and looked about him.

And now a new and blood-chillingly familiar chant filled the air.

Kill! Kill! Kill!

Vita's heart shrank up in terror. She twisted around, desperate for Brea to come to her aid. But though the wolf-woman was on her knees now, she was clearly still in great pain. And there was no sign of life from Col either. The Skull-Crusher forced Vita back round to face the platform. As her eyes locked with Agrippa's, his lips curled into a knowing smile. He lifted his gaze to the crowd, waited a moment longer, then tipped his thumb and sliced it up and down like a knife stabbing the air.

The spectators erupted in a bloodthirsty roar. Head spinning, Vita made a last-ditch bid to get free, but Cronos yanked her back by the hair and forced her down on her knees. As his giant shadow loomed over her, a hard, barking laugh sounded from the platform above. Vita's chest cramped, but with anger this time, not fear. Agrippa had got the better of them. If Mother and Lucius were still alive, she would never find them now. And she would never get justice for Father either.

As the cold blade of the Skull-Crusher's sword pressed against her throat, Vita closed her eyes and murmured a final prayer to the gods. But before the giant could administer the death-blow, an ear-piercing war-cry ripped through the air. She snapped her eyes open in time to see Brea step back and send her spear hurtling at the gladiator. Tossing Vita to the ground, he swung to avoid it. But he wasn't quick enough and the spear struck him hard in the left shoulder. He staggered sideways with an agonized bellow, then righting himself, grabbed at the spear and tried to drag it free. But it was no use – it was in too deep. Roaring with anger, he pounded towards Brea, sword up and ready to strike.

Vita's throat knotted. She had to help her. But without a weapon she was powerless. She cast about looking for something – anything she could use. A gleaming shape in the sand snagged her eye. The giant's helmet! A sudden memory sprang up of the great Prince Perseus battling the fearsome gorgon, Medusa. Of how he'd tilted his shield like a mirror on her hissing snake-haired head and, making her magic work against her, turned her to stone.

Stories could be weapons too . . .

She heaved the helmet up, and as the Skull-Crusher swung back his sword to strike, angled the great curved crest so it caught the sun's rays and beamed them back into the gladiator's eyes. Cronos cried out and stumbled backwards, hand raised against the glare. At the same moment, Brea swiped up his discarded shield and, turning it on its side, rammed it into the giant's thick neck. He twisted round with a groan, arms flailing, and toppled to the ground face down.

Cries of shock echoed around the walls. Then a fresh chant of 'Lupa!' started up and soon the whole arena was yelling the wolf-woman's name.

But Brea hadn't finished yet. Striding over to where the injured gladiator lay, she yanked the spear from his bloodstained shoulder, and turning on her heel, sprinted to the foot of the platform steps. Agrippa hesitated, then stepped forward, his lips drawn into a tight smile. He'd be forced to declare her the victor. The crowd would expect it and he couldn't dare risk going against them. But as he went to give the signal, instead of bowing her acceptance, the wolf-woman jerked back her spear and with another ear-splitting shriek, hurled it straight at him.

As the spear shot through the air, Agrippa stood there, eyes wide, mouth gaping, as if struck by Medusa's magic himself. The wolf-woman's weapon would have found its mark too, but for the quick thinking of one of the soldiers who leapt out and smashed it away with his sword.

A spine-freezing silence fell over the entire arena, and now all Vita could hear was the frantic drumming of her own heart. She watched in horror as the soldier recovered the spear and offered it to Agrippa with a hurried salute. The magistrate stood there for a moment, white-faced and speechless, but as the crowd began to shout his name, the colour returned to his cheeks and his eyes sparked back into life. He snatched up the spear with a grim-faced nod and brandished it above his head.

'Who strikes at me, strikes at Rome!' He glared down at Brea as cries of angry agreement echoed back from the crowd.

The wolf-woman stood her ground, fists clenched, eyes burning back at him with a defiant green fire. But Agrippa pretended not to notice. He scanned about him, a look of triumph on his face.

'And what, good people, is the punishment for such a crime?'

Death! the cry went up.

Death! Death! Death!

XXVII

Vita balled her fingers into fists. Her friend wasn't going to die. Not if she could help it. She darted to the wolf-woman's side. Then, as the cries of the crowd faded, she took a lungful of dusty air and yelled up at Agrippa with all the power she could muster. '*You* are the one who deserves death! You killed my father. Brea's too . . .'

A flush of pink bloomed on Agrippa's cheeks. He opened his mouth, then shut it again. Around him his fellow magistrates and other guests exchanged puzzled looks and exclamations of surprise. Vita's heart gave a quick jolt. She'd got him! Now all she had to do was to drive home the blade. But as she steeled herself to strike the killer blow, Agrippa's eyes sharpened to two iron-grey points.

'This slave-girl is a runaway, my friends.' He turned to face his guests, arms outstretched. 'And as we know, a runaway can never be trusted. They'd rather murder us in our own homes, like her brutish friends did to our poor dear colleague, Marcus Verus, than submit to the rule of Roman law.'

Heads nodded and there were murmurs of agreement.

'No, he's lying. I'm Verus's daughter. I can prove it – look!' In desperation Vita grabbed the rim of the mask and tried to prise it off. But it stayed stubbornly in place.

With a pitying look, which he made sure his guests saw too, Agrippa raised his arms to the crowd as if seeking their opinion on what to do next.

'Get them off!' came a voice. More joined in until the whole arena thundered with a single cry.

'*Off! Off! Off!*'

Agrippa gave a small bow, then signalled to the soldiers. Jumping to attention, they leapt down the steps and advanced towards Vita and Brea, swords raised. Vita spun about looking for an escape, but more soldiers were closing in around them now. Heart pounding, she turned back to Brea. But the wolf-woman stood there unmoving, her gaze fixed on Agrippa, as if her look alone would somehow be enough to strike him down.

Agrippa stared back at her, his eyes glittering with cold fury. 'The crowd has decided. Take the She-Wolf and her dog – if it still lives – to the cells. We will execute them here tomorrow with the rest of the common criminals we didn't get through today.'

Vita stumbled forward, hands clasped to her chest. 'No, please!'

But Agrippa was in no mood to listen. 'And as for this one . . .' He jabbed the bloody spear-tip at her. 'Deliver her to my house. I'll punish her myself. That is if you do not object, Gladiator-master?' He turned back to Otho, who had little choice but to bow his stony-faced agreement.

What came after happened in a sickening blur. The troop of soldiers force-marched Vita and Brea away across the sand, one falling back to muzzle the still-groggy Col with a rope and drag him whimpering along behind. All the while, Vita kept her head down, doing her best to ignore the shouts and insults of the crowd. But try as she might, she couldn't block out the heart-rending thought which repeated like a drumbeat in her head. That she'd failed Father. Mother and Lucius too. Agrippa had escaped justice – both her kind and Brea's – and now, no one would ever know the real truth.

As the gates creaked shut behind them and they stepped into the passage, the noise of the crowd faded and Vita's ears filled instead with a barrage of angry-sounding groans. It was coming from the courtyard up ahead. The two men who'd led the bull into the arena were standing in front of the bear's cage, jabbing her in the flanks with a pair of sharp sticks.

Her heart, still pounding frantically, gave an extra, sickening squeeze. Why couldn't they just leave her alone?

'You can stand that fleabag down,' the lead soldier yelled at them. 'And don't bother feeding her either. She'll have plenty of fresh Blue-face meat to chew on in the arena tomorrow, eh, Lupa?' He shoved Brea in the back with the end of his sword to gales of his comrades' coarse laughter.

The two men in the courtyard gave each other a quick shrug and tossed their sticks to the ground. But as they turned to go, the bear lifted up on her haunches and with a growling roar flung herself at the cage. There was a loud splintering sound and then, as she charged again, a resounding crack of wood. Before either of her tormentors had a chance to react, she tore free of her shackles and barrelled through the gaping hole in the bars, knocking them both to the ground.

The soldiers drew into a panicked huddle and fell back inside the passage, swords drawn. Seizing the moment, Brea snatched Vita by the hand and, shrilling a whistle at Col, sped them out into the courtyard. They were almost at the gate when Vita tripped and fell. As she scrambled to her feet, the bear lumbered round, blocking her path. She fixed Vita with her glittering black eyes and for a heart-stopping moment she was sure the creature would charge.

But instead, after sniffing the air between them, she gave a loud snort and turned her attention back to the two attendants cowering now behind what remained of the cage.

'Come!' Brea grabbed her arm and yanked her over to where Col stood waiting at the gate. A few moments later they were outside and sheltering breathlessly behind a pile of canvas stacked up against the arena wall.

Brea slid the muzzle from Col's snout and shot Vita an approving nod. 'You did well, Verus's daughter.'

She flushed. 'Thank you. I'm sorry about not speaking the truth to you, it was—'

The wolf-woman held up her hand. 'This is not the time for words of regret. We must go. I to join Taran, you to the marshes. Speak my name there and our people will take you in.'

'But will I see you? After, I mean.'

'If the Horned One wills it. But first I must find the spirit-stealer again and claim what is mine.' She made a swift, slicing motion with the edge of her hand.

Vita shivered. Much as she hated Agrippa she was glad she wouldn't have to witness such an end. 'May your gods watch over you.'

'And yours, you.' Brea clasped her by the hand. Then, throwing a quick glance over the top of the canvas, she slipped out on to the street and with Col hard on her heels, set off down a nearby alleyway and away out of sight.

It was only then that Vita realized she was still wearing the mask. She had to find a way of getting it off before the streets grew busy with the spectators returning home. Keeping to the shadows, she made her way along the arena walls. Most of the stalls had packed up now, but there were still one or two displaying their wares, including one selling souvenir weapons. The stallholder was busy dealing with a customer. Holding her breath, she slunk in close and snatched up the nearest blade, its handle fashioned in the shape of a gladiator. The stallholder, alerted by the customer, spun round.

'Hey, thief!' As he leapt towards her, Vita tossed down the knife and made a dash for the open street and . . .

. . . straight into the arms of a soldier.

'Not so fast, owl-girl!'

Her heart sank. It was one of the arena guards. She struggled against him, but his grip was too strong.

'Your runaway days are over.'

'But I'm not a slave. Please, you've got to listen to me!'

'Enough of your lies!' In one swift move, the soldier whipped out his sword and jabbed it against her chest. 'My orders are to take you to the Honourable Agrippa's house and that's exactly what I'm going to do.'

The shadows were lengthening when they reached the street where Agrippa's townhouse lay. As the soldier marched her to a stop in front of the grey walls, Vita gave a quick shiver. A week ago she'd been preparing to come and live here as Agrippa's wife. But she was his prisoner now, and once she stepped through the door, she feared she would never see the daylight again.

The soldier's knock was answered a few moments later by a burly man dressed in the patched tunic of a house-slave. As he caught sight of Vita's masked face his eyebrows forked in bewildered surprise. But when the soldier explained, he led them off along a gloomy hall, through a deserted kitchen and out into a shadow-filled courtyard beyond.

He drew to a stop in front of a low wooden building. Producing a key from the leather belt at his waist, he unlocked the door and stood to one side.

As the soldier bundled Vita through it, she spun round in a last frantic attempt to save herself. 'Please. Don't do this, I beg you. I—'

The door banged shut in her face and a key grated in the lock. She hammered against the wood. But it was no use. As the men's heavy footsteps echoed out of earshot, she heaved a sigh and turned back into the room.

There were no windows, but the smell of dried herbs and a whiff of ripe cheese told her it was Agrippa's food-store. As her eyes grew used to the darkness, her suspicions were confirmed by the sight of shelves stacked with pots and jars, and a row of twin-handled oil amphorae propped on the floor beneath.

A sudden rustling sound made her start. She froze. It was coming from a long basket pushed up against the wall. Mice? It must be. A week ago she'd have screamed out loud and demanded that one of the slaves deal with them. But she'd faced a lot worse since then. And right now she had more important things to worry about – like how to get out of here before Agrippa turned up.

The rustling sounded again. And now there was a low moaning noise too. Heart racing, she snatched up one of the jars and crept towards the basket. But as she slid up the wooden pin holding the lid in place, it began to lurch from side to side. Jar at the ready, she flipped back the lid with her toe and peered inside.

A pair of round eyes blinked back at her. 'Mmmm! Mmmm! Mmmm!'

Lucius. He was alive! With a choked cry, Vita threw the jar to the ground. But as she reached in to pull him free, he shrank back from her, eyes wide with terror.

'What?' And then she realized. 'It's all right, brother, it's me, Vita. This is just a stupid mask. See?' She tapped the beak with her fingers.

He wavered, then gave a small nod.

'Come on, let's get you out of here.' Lifting him clear of the basket, Vita set him down on the ground and undid the gag tied across his mouth. He gasped in a parched-sounding breath and collapsed against her, his body convulsing with great shuddering sobs. She cradled him in her arms, rocking him gently from side to side.

'You're safe, little brother. I'm with you now.'

As his sobbing lessened, she drew him to his feet and, gripping his shoulders, looked him in the eyes. 'Where's Mother?'

He shook his head and began to cry again.

Doing her best not to think of what that might mean, Vita dabbed at his cheeks with the edge of her gown. 'Hush, now. Let's untie your hands, then you can help me with this thing' – she tugged at the mask – 'and we can tell each other what we know.'

A short while later they sat side by side on top of the basket. Vita, now free of the mask, stroked her brother's curls and did her best to hold back tears of her own while she listened to his story. How he'd been helping Mother get things ready for Vita's feast when they'd heard Rosia cry for help. How Father had appeared in the dining room, but before he'd had the chance to investigate, a hooded man had burst in on them. How he'd threatened them with a knife, and when Father tried to defend them, the man had knocked him to the ground. But then a second man had arrived and struck Lucius over the head and that was the last he remembered until he'd woken up here in this storeroom.

He looked up at her when he'd finished and gulped back another sob. 'Father's dead, isn't he?'

And now in spite of herself, the tears came. Vita let them fall for a few moments, then took a deep breath and met his anguished gaze. 'Yes, he is. But his spirit has gone to the Underworld now. And we will see him again when it's time, I promise you.' She felt a stab of guilt as she spoke the words, remembering again the claim that the spirits of those wronged in life could never find rest until justice had been done. And how that seemed further away than ever now. She shivered and made to draw Lucius close again, but he pulled away.

'Why did those men want to kill him? And ... and what have they done with Mother?'

She shook her head. 'I don't know about Mother. We must pray to the gods she is still alive and being kept prisoner somewhere, like you. But the men weren't acting alone.'

His face pulled into a tear-stained frown. 'What do you mean?'

'They were working for someone. Someone who claimed to be Father's friend.'

Lucius's eyes widened again. 'Who?'

Vita hesitated. Should she tell him? But he was her

brother, and after all he'd been through, she owed him the truth.

So, taking a deep breath in, she let the whole story spill from her. Of fleeing with Festa, then going back to the house and finding Father's body. Of being kidnapped by one of the assassins and sold to Otho as a slave. Of sharing a cell with Brea and Col, making an enemy of the Skull-Crusher and being forced to feed the wild beasts. Then of her suspicions about Agrippa and how, with Leander's help, she'd had them confirmed at the banquet. Finally of Brea's discovery that Agrippa was responsible for her own father's death, and of what had followed . . .

When she'd finished, Lucius stared back at her open-mouthed.

'You fought on the same side as a Blue-face? In the arena?'

A spark of anger flared up inside her. 'She's not a Blue-face. She's called Brea and she's a friend.'

He put his head on one side as if weighing things up, then nodded. 'She sounds brave. Her wolf too.'

'Col. And yes, they are.'

'Will they be all right?'

'If the gods are on their side.' She bit down on her lip, willing it to be true, though she knew the odds were stacked against them.

'Will someone come to rescue us?'

'I hope so.' But her throat tightened again, because how was that possible? Brea had no idea she'd been recaptured. And as for Leander, the last time she'd seen him was at the parade before the games. He must be with Taran now, waiting to mount their attack. The only real hope was if the rebels struck before Agrippa got here. Or Brea found him first . . .

Lucius frowned. 'But I don't understand. Why did Agrippa send those men to kill Father?'

Vita heaved a sigh. 'I don't know.' It was still a mystery, but she doubted she'd ever get the chance to discover the truth now.

A door banged somewhere in the distance. It was followed shortly after by footsteps – two sets, and coming their way.

As she pulled Lucius to her, the footsteps crunched to a stop and a key rattled in the lock. The door swung open to reveal two figures – the burly slave from earlier and another slimmer man wearing a hooded cloak, dark breeches and leather boots.

The bigger man stepped inside and made a grab for Vita, but Lucius sprang in front of her, fists raised.

'Leave my sister alone!'

'Proper little hero, ain't yer?' The slave gave a mocking laugh and shoved Lucius back down.

His companion shouldered past him and seized hold of

Vita's wrist. 'Keep the brat locked up here. I'll deal with the girl.'

Her heart lurched at the rasped command. It was him! Agrippa's man.

'Murderer!' She tried to break free but he grabbed a fistful of her gown and reined her in tight, smothering her in a cloud of sour-smelling breath.

'Are you going to come nicely or do we have to make you?' He nodded to the slave, who jerked back his hand as if to strike Lucius across the face.

'No, please! Don't hurt him.' She let herself go limp.

'Good.' Whipping a length of rope and a piece of cloth from his belt, the man bound and gagged her. Then, hoisting her over his shoulder, he spun round and strode quickly back out through the door.

XXVIII

The assassin lugged Vita across the courtyard and away into the gloom-filled house. She struggled against him, but with each twist and kick his grip only tightened and in the end she was forced to give up. She peered about, desperately trying to get her bearings, but the passageway wasn't one she recognized.

A smell of incense pricked her nose, getting stronger and more cloying the further along they went. She closed her eyes, fighting a growing urge to be sick. And then suddenly they had stopped and she was being toppled to the ground and thrust, blinking, through an open door into a dimly lit room beyond.

As the door rattled shut behind her, she spun round and

shoved her shoulder against it. But it was no use. It wouldn't budge. With a stifled groan she turned back into the room, then froze. A tall figure wearing a white belted tunic and a scarlet gold-trimmed cloak stood before her, a flickering oil lamp in his right hand.

'So, my fair princess, we meet again.' Gaius Cassius Agrippa surveyed her with cold grey eyes.

Vita backed away from him, heart pounding. But, instead of approaching her, he turned and walked towards an alcove set into the wall opposite. As the lamp flame flared she caught sight of a small stone table; mounted on it was a painted frieze of a bull being wrestled to the ground at knifepoint by a man in a red cap and cloak. Setting the lamp down beside a smoking incense bowl, Agrippa bowed his head and muttered a few words of what sounded like a prayer before swinging round to face her again.

'If your poor, dear father could only see you now . . .' He shook his head and heaved a fake-sounding sigh.

A ball of hot fury tore through Vita. She'd convinced herself she might be happy to be his wife once, but now the very thought repelled her. If she could only get free of this gag, she'd tell him so too . . . She shook her head from side to side, grinding her teeth against the cloth.

'What a wild-cat you are. I can see I am going to have to tame you!' In a sudden flash of silver, Agrippa whipped a slim blade from beneath his cloak. As he advanced on her, Vita's stomach gripped. This was it – the end of her story. She'd done her best to unmask him and get justice for Father, but it hadn't been enough. It was down to Brea and her friends to stop him now. Drawing what strength she could from the thought, she closed her eyes and readied herself for the blow.

But it didn't come. Instead, she felt a sharp tug on the gag. She blinked in amazement as the ends sprang free and it dropped to the ground.

'There. That's better, isn't it?' Agrippa stood back, lowering the knife to his side.

Spitting the taste from her mouth, Vita sucked in a breath and forced herself to stand tall. 'Why did you kill him?'

Agrippa raised a pale eyebrow in mock surprise. 'Kill who?'

'My father.' She clenched her jaw, doing everything in her power to keep her tears at bay.

'But I didn't.' His lips curled in amusement.

He was playing with her – like a cat plays with an injured sparrow. Well, he may have the advantage, but if he thought he was going to get the better of her with his words . . .

'You sent those men to do it for you. It's the same thing.' She spoke through gritted teeth.

'Maybe. But you'll never prove it. Not now.' He folded

his arms across his chest and looked her up and down, then frowned. 'Still, for a dead girl you've caused me a deal of trouble.'

A cold band of fear gripped Vita's throat. 'What do you mean?'

'Those idiots were meant to kill you too. They claimed they had. That you'd run off but they'd caught you and tossed you into the river to drown. I believed them, more's the pity.' He snorted and shook his head again, then his eyes locked back on hers. 'So you can imagine my surprise when I discovered you were hiding out as a slave in that jumped-up thug Otho's gladiator-school.'

'I wasn't hiding. I told you. That man . . . *your* man, he sold me to Otho.'

Agrippa's mouth pinched with anger. 'Once I have no further use for his services, he will be punished for his treachery like his comrade, have no doubt of that!' He raised the knife and stroked a finger along the blade before sliding it back into the leather sheath at his belt.

Vita swallowed. 'You still haven't told me why you did it.'

Agrippa looked off into the distance for a moment, then focused his gaze back on her. 'Your father claimed I was like a brother to him. And I never had any reason to doubt him until . . .' His expression darkened. 'Until a few short days ago.'

Vita licked her lips. 'What do you mean?'

'That meeting I was hurrying to when I caught you sneaking out dressed like a common house-slave?'

Her face flushed at the memory.

'It was to receive the news – the most unexpected news – that he intended to cancel our betrothal. And that, if I did not agree to it, he would withdraw his support and do all he could to prevent me from being voted in as senior magistrate at the next elections.'

Vita's eyes widened. So that must have been it! The thing Father told Mother he wanted to keep from her until after her feast-day was over. That he'd cancelled the betrothal . . .

Agrippa's eyes narrowed. 'I was right in my guess that he had not told you then?'

She shook her head. But something was wrong. Very wrong. 'Father would never have done such a thing without good reason!'

'Oh, I think his reason is clear enough, don't you? He saw me as a threat. A younger man, seeking appointment to a position he would soon have to stand down from himself. And taking his beloved "Little Owl" away from him too.' His voice rang with contempt as he spoke her father's pet name for her. 'So you see, I had no choice but to do what I did, though it pains me now to think on it.' Agrippa gave a choked sob and, fingering the gold torc at his neck, looked away.

Vita's eyes pricked with hot, angry tears. 'I don't believe you! Father loved you! He gave his blessing to our union.'

Agrippa heaved another sigh and turned back to face her. 'So he said. But he was a man of two faces. Like his daughter.' He threw her a sharp, taunting look.

'Like you, you mean!'

His cheeks coloured as they'd done earlier in the arena. 'You're clever – for a girl. Too clever, perhaps . . .'

The urge to run at him and strike him down was overwhelming, but instead, she took a breath and fixed him with a hard stare. 'What . . . what have you done with my mother?'

'Your mother?' He waved a ringed hand in the air. 'Oh, you have no need to worry about her. She is safe under lock and key at my villa outside the town boundary. In a short while, I will have my men "discover" her and bring her to me. Of course she has no knowledge of my part in her husband's unfortunate end. So, when the time is right, I hope she will be persuaded, grief-stricken though she is, to marry me. And then of course your former home and the rest of your father's not inconsiderable wealth will be mine.' His face glowed with a sudden smug satisfaction.

'But . . . but what about Lucius?'

Agrippa touched a finger to his head as if suddenly remembering. 'Ah yes, your little brother. He was going to be what you might call my guarantee.'

'What do you mean?'

'I was planning to use his "rescue" as ammunition to help persuade your mother of my suitability as a husband. But on reflection, I think now it will be best to dispose of him too.' He shot her a blood-freezing smile.

'No! Please, he's only a little boy.'

'A little boy who will grow to be a man and perhaps one day decide to wrest everything back from me that I have worked so hard to get. As for you, by rights you should have perished in the arena. But, though it irks me to admit it, you and that Blue-face friend of yours fought a brave fight. Of course, her attempt on my life was an outrage. But she will be punished for it when the soldiers recapture her, as they surely will. Though, alas, the she-bear's escape means I will need to devise another method of execution.'

He tugged at his chin and gazed off into the distance for a moment, then shot another sly look at her. 'You have such a vivid imagination, my dear Little Owl. I wonder if you can guess at what I have planned for *you*?'

He reached out a hand as if to touch Vita's cheek. She shrank away from him, stomach clawing with revulsion.

His gaze hardened. 'No? Well, it is no matter. You will find out soon enough.' Pressing his lips into a grim smile, he turned to the table behind him and trailed a finger across the frieze of the man wrestling the bull. At the same moment, the stone in his ring caught in a sudden flare from the lamp, turning the tip of the man's dagger blood-red in the reflected glow.

Vita gulped in a breath and hugged her arms to her.

Agrippa swivelled round to face her again, his eyes glittering with fresh contempt. 'What a lucky escape I have had! You would have made the most *unsatisfactory* wife.'

As he took a step towards her, the door rattled open and a man's voice called, 'Come quickly, master. You're needed outside. It's urgent!'

A look of irritation flashed across Agrippa's face. He hesitated, then drawing his cloak about him, he strode towards the door. But at the last moment, he turned back and fixed Vita with another ice-filled gaze.

'I will return shortly. In the meantime I leave you with this final thought, though it is one you must surely know by now. Not all stories have the ending we might wish for.'

XXIX

The door banged shut. There was a rattle and chink of metal, then silence. Vita sank to the floor, head whirling. Agrippa was lying about Father's reasons for cancelling the betrothal, she was convinced of it. But she believed what he'd said about Mother still being alive. Although only while she was of use to him – Vita had no doubt of that. The thing that mattered most now though was to get out of here and rescue Lucius before it was too late. But how?

She tried to think what Brea would do in her position. But the only thing that kept echoing round inside her head were Agrippa's final words.

Not all stories have the ending we might wish for.

He'd done his best to make sure of that, for Father and

for all of them, and there was nothing she could do to change it. With a shuddering sigh, she buried her face in her filthy, crumpled gown and gave in to a fresh wave of tears.

She was crying so much she didn't hear the scrape of metal in the lock until it was too late. She tensed. Was this it? Had Agrippa come back to finish her too? If so, she would beg the gods for it to be over quickly and that Father's spirit would be there to greet her in the world beyond.

Closing her eyes she bowed her head in prayer. But as she muttered the words, she felt the brush of cool fingers against her arm. She jumped back with a cry, hands raised.

'Vita?'

She blinked. A pair of dark eyes gleamed back at her from beneath the shadow of a hood. Eyes she recognized.

Her heart gave a quick jolt. Leander!

'But how—'

Leander tugged the hood back from his face. 'With a little help from my sharp-tongued friend here.' He flashed the blade of a knife in front of her.

'How did you find me?'

'Oh, that! After we raided the weapons store at Otho's place, I came back to the arena to look for you and saw that soldier marching you away. I followed you here, then found a friend to take a message to Taran to let him know. And now I have returned to save you.' He threw her a pleased-looking smile, then, snatching up her wrists, used the knife to cut them free.

'What about Brea and Col?'

He shook his head. 'I do not know. But the revolt has started. And they have set fires too. Agrippa and the ones who work for him have gone to see. It is how I managed to get in.'

Vita's stomach clenched. 'Fires? Where?'

'The streets where the ones in power live. This one too. We must hurry. With all the dry weather, it will be spreading quickly.' He made to take her hand, but she pushed him off.

'Lucius!'

His eyes widened. 'What?'

'My brother. He's locked up in the storeroom outside!' She dashed to the door and flung it open. A faint smell of burning pricked her nose. And sounds echoed towards her too. Shouts and cries, coming in off the street.

Heart racing, she snatched up her skirts and sprinted out into the passage, Leander close on her heels.

'That way, I think!' He jabbed a finger at another passage which led off to the right. They hurtled down it until they came to a door at the far end.

Vita yanked up the latch, but as she made to dash through it, Leander held her back.

'Let me check first!' He drew his knife and pushed past her. It wasn't long before he was back, sleeve held against his mouth.

'There is no one. But the fire is close. Here.' He bent and made to rip a strip of fabric from the bottom of her gown.

'Wait!' Staying his hand she fumbled at the hem and slid the firestone free.

He frowned. 'What is it?'

'A gift. I promised to keep it safe for a friend.' She closed her fingers over the stone and pushed it inside the thin slip beneath her gown.

A few moments later, strips of dirty yellow cloth tied over the lower half of their faces, they were ready to go. As they linked hands and stepped out into the night, the air around them pulsed with a strange orange glow. The shouts and cries Vita had heard earlier were louder now; more panicked-sounding. And she could hear a sharp crackling noise too.

'There!' Leander pointed to the house opposite. The thatch had caught. Sparks were whirling up into the air and showering down all around.

There was no time to waste. Breaking free, Vita flew across the courtyard and hurled herself against the store-room door.

'It's locked!'

'Let me try.' Leander pulled alongside her and slid the

knife-blade into the keyhole.

She glanced about, chest heaving. The house with the burning roof was fully ablaze now and the one next to it had caught too. A waft of thick smoke blew towards them, enveloping them for a moment and stinging her eyes. She shielded her face in the crook of her elbow and clutched at Leander's sleeve. 'Hurry!'

'I am doing my best, but the smoke—' He choked out a cough and doubled over, gasping for breath.

Snatching the knife, Vita rammed it back in the lock and jiggled it up and down.

Please, Minerva! Please!

She was about to pull the blade out and try again when it snagged on something. Keeping it steady she forced it sideways until at last, the bolt slid free. Sucking in a breath, she barged the door open and leapt inside.

'Lucius!' She peered frantically about her, throat gripping. She'd almost given up hope, when a small dark figure stumbled towards her from out of the gloom.

'Vita?'

'Brother!' She threw the knife down on a nearby barrel-top and pulled him into a fierce hug.

A rattle of wood sounded behind her.

'It's all right, Leander. He's safe!'

A hand clamped her shoulder. 'I wouldn't be so sure of that!'

Vita froze. The assassin! Pushing Lucius behind her, she pulled the cloth from her mouth and swung about to face him.

'What have you done to my friend?'

The man's eyes glinted back at her from the shadows. 'I wouldn't waste your time worrying about him!' In one swift move, he slid his hand to his waist and drew a needle-sharp blade from his belt.

Vita raised her fists in a desperate bid to hold the man at bay.

He gave a mocking laugh. 'Quite the fighter! Your father would be proud of you! Well, you'll be joining him soon in the Underworld. Your little brother too.'

She stumbled backwards, doing her best to shield Lucius, but there was nowhere left to go. The assassin leapt forward, dagger raised. But as he prepared to strike, a snarling growl sounded behind him.

'What the—' He started and twisted round.

Seizing her chance, Vita snatched Leander's knife from the barrel-top and thrust the blade into the man's right shoulder. It was a shallow wound, but enough to wrong-foot him. He staggered backwards with a sharp cry and fell sprawling to the ground.

At the same instant, a four-legged shape bounded through the open door followed moments later by a tall snake-haired figure, shield in one hand, spear in the other.

Vita stood rooted to the spot, scarcely able to believe her eyes. A startled cry at her side jerked her back to life.

'It is all right, brother. They are friends.' Reaching for Lucius's hand, she murmured a prayer of thanks and stumbled towards Brea and Col.

The wolf-woman gripped her by the arm. 'Are you hurt?'

'No. But Leander—'

'He will live. Where is he?'

'Who?'

'The Eagle-man.'

Vita's stomach gave a quick somersault. 'I-I don't know.'

Brea snorted and threw a frowning look at the assassin, now lying motionless under the watchful eye of Col. 'Who is this?'

'The one who killed our father.'

Brea shot a quick glance at Lucius and nodded, then snatched up the knife and offered it to Vita.

'No.' She pushed it away and took a step backwards. 'I . . . I can't.'

Brea grunted and kicked the man's foot. 'Let his gods decide his fate then.' As she signalled for Col to stand down, a ragged cough sounded from somewhere behind them. Brea spun round, spear raised.

'It is only me!' A slim figure appeared in the doorway, hands raised.

'Leander! Are you all right?' Vita rushed up to him.

'Yes.' He gave a quick rub of his forehead. 'But we have to go now. The fire is all around us!'

Brea poked her head outside. 'He is right. Come! Our friend will take you both to the marshes.' She and Leander exchanged quick nods.

Vita frowned. 'But what about you?'

The wolf-woman's mouth pulled into a hard line. 'My work is not yet done.' She spun round and strode back out through the door, Col following at her heels.

Ripping more cloth from her gown, Vita tied it across Lucius's nose and mouth. Then, fixing her own back in place, she took his hand and with Leander beside them, stepped out into the courtyard – filled now with a fierce roaring sound and lit by a pulsating orange light. Blinking against fresh waves of acrid smoke, she startled at the sight of flames now ripping through the houses on either side. It was only a matter of time before Agrippa's caught too.

They'd almost reached the door leading into the house when it banged open. A figure in a soot-stained white tunic came striding through it, red cloak billowing out behind.

'Have you found her yet? I can't afford for her to— Lupa? What in Jupiter's name—' Agrippa ground to a sudden halt, a look of total astonishment on his face.

The wolf-woman pulled Vita and Lucius behind her.

'Not Lupa, Eagle-man, but Brea – daughter of a man whose life you took before it was his time.'

Agrippa's eyes grew wider still. 'What are you talking about?'

'Three frost-seasons ago, you and your other Eagle-men friends came to our village. We had done you no harm, but you burnt our homes and cut my father's life-spirit from him, those of many others too. And you stole my brother to make into one of your fighting men and forced me to become a hunter in your beast-shows. But now I have tracked you down, Eagle-man, and it is my turn to take what is most precious from you.' She tossed her shield to the ground and took a step forward, spear angled at Agrippa's chest. Col leapt alongside her, teeth bared.

Agrippa threw back his cloak and whipped the knife from his belt. 'You may have escaped death in the arena, you and your little friend.' He shot Vita a look of ice-cold scorn. 'But you will not be so lucky this time.'

As he prepared to lunge, a voice rang out behind him. 'If it is a fight you want, Eagle-man, then you have it!'

A tall broad-shouldered figure in a hooded cloak stepped out into the courtyard behind him, a long curved sword clutched in his fisted right hand.

Agrippa spun round, knife raised. 'And who are you?'

The man advanced slowly, forcing Agrippa back towards Brea and Col. 'Our paths have also crossed before.'

Vita's heart gave a quick jolt. That voice! She knew it from somewhere . . .

Agrippa leapt to one side, face greyer than the ash-flakes now drifting down around them. 'What do you mean?'

'You may have chosen to forget me – a so-called "Blue-face" forced into the service of the Roman army. But I have not forgotten you.' The man's eyes blazed angrily from beneath his hood. 'How, all those many years ago, when we fought in battle in the northlands against the ones you call barbarians, you hid out in a ditch until the fighting was over. Then, as I pulled the one who commanded us to safety, how you dealt me a blow and left me for dead so you could claim the glory.'

Vita's mouth gaped. He was talking about Father, he had to be!

But the man hadn't finished yet. 'As you can see—' He yanked off his hood to reveal a lean, tanned face marked by a scar that coursed down his left cheek and along the length of his jaw. 'I recovered in spite of my wounds. And now I and my friend' – he jerked his head at Brea – 'have come to claim the debt you owe us and all those whose lives you stole.'

Agrippa's eyes narrowed. 'So *you're* the one who told Verus the truth?'

'Not me but an old friend. Another whose life you took before it was his time to die. But here, to make the fight fairer, have this. The one I took it from won't be needing it any more.'

The man pulled a soldier's *gladius* from beneath his cloak. He dropped it clattering to the ground and slid it towards Agrippa with the toe of his boot. Agrippa hesitated, then bent and picked it up.

As he straightened and readied himself to fight, a firm hand gripped Vita by her shoulder. She started and turned to see the wolf-woman's eyes burning back at her with a gold-green fire.

'You should go, while you still can.'

A knot formed in Vita's throat. But she was right. This was no place for them. She needed to get Lucius to safety before the whole town burnt to the ground. She sucked in a breath and nodded. 'I will pray to your god for you.'

Brea's left cheek twitched and for a moment the wolf's head Vita had painted on it seemed to spring to life. 'Thank you.' She flashed her a tight smile then turned back to join her friend.

Vita threw a shivering glance at Agrippa. She despised him and all that he stood for, but she didn't want to watch him die. With a quick nod to Leander, she snatched up Lucius's hand and turned to go.

As they reached the door, a sharp whistle sounded and a silver wolf shape came bounding towards them from out of the smoke-filled air.

Vita caught a final glimpse of Agrippa advancing on the wolf-woman and her friend, his blade glinting red in the light. Then another thick billow of smoke blew in and hid everything from view.

XXX

Vita woke with cries for help and the groan of fire-ravaged timbers ringing in her ears. For a moment she thought she was back there in the crowd-clogged streets, fleeing past row upon row of burning buildings, the heat from the blaze scalding her face, the thick clouds of smoke and ash choking her breath.

She snapped her eyes open and jerked upright, gasping in a mouthful of peaty-smelling air. A low whine sounded close by and a pair of yellow-gold eyes blinked back at her from the half-light.

Col! She pressed her face into the wolf's soft fur then darted a look at the empty space beside them. 'Lucius?' Where was he? She scrambled on to her knees and threw back the deer-skin covering the shelter entrance. As she crawled through it, a low chuckle sounded and the slim figure of a boy stepped out in front of her, blocking the light.

'Good afternoon, sleepy-head!'

She peered around him, shielding her eyes against the sun's glare. 'Where's my brother?'

'Safe and with friends.' Leander reached out and hauled her to her feet.

Her heart leapt into her throat. 'You mean she's here?'

He shook his head, frowning. 'Brea has not returned yet.' Col's ears pricked at the mention of the wolf-woman's name. He gave a high-pitched whimper and nuzzled the back of Leander's hand.

'I know, my friend, but she will. Taran too.'

So it was Taran who'd challenged Agrippa last night! But how could Leander be so sure they'd survived?

As if reading her thoughts, he fixed her with a defiant stare. 'We owe it to them to hope it may be so.'

She nodded. He was right. They couldn't give up on them yet. She shut her eyes and with all her heart prayed to the Horned One and Minerva to bring them safely back.

A hand shook her arm. 'Are you all right?'

She blinked and looked up. 'Yes. Can you take me to him? My brother, I mean.'

Leander gave a small bow. 'Of course. But we will leave

Col here. He has been causing quite a stir since we arrived.' He gave the wolf's ears a quick ruffle, then, fishing some scraps of meat from the leather pouch at his waist, tempted him back inside.

As they wound their way through the scattering of makeshift shelters, the people sitting outside followed their progress with curious stares. Vita flushed and clutched her arms about her, suddenly aware of her soot-stained skin and the grime-covered betrothal gown ripped halfway to her knees.

But all traces of embarrassment disappeared as she caught sight of the small curly-haired boy in an equally dirty tunic, jabbing a stick at an invisible enemy while a pair of women dressed in hooded cloaks looked on.

He looked up as they drew closer and ran towards her, arms waving excitedly above his head. 'Vita! Here's Vita!'

As he flung himself against her, the smaller of the two women hurried to his side. 'Now, Master Lucius, do not smother your sister like that!'

Vita's breath caught in her throat. 'Festa? Is it really you?'

'Of course it is, young mistress.' Slipping back her hood, Festa seized hold of Vita's hands and drew her into a warm embrace.

'But how—'

The maid pulled back, eyes sparkling with secrets. 'Oh, that's a long story. Too long for the telling now. Besides,

there is someone else who wants to see you. Very much.'
She turned and gestured at her companion now hastening towards them, hood down and gold hair flying out around her, blue eyes brimming with tears.

Vita opened her mouth to speak, but the only sound that came out was a loud, strangled sob. Then suddenly, a pair of soft arms were circling about her and a voice was saying her name, over and over.

She gulped in a breath and tried again. And this time the word burst from her in all its joy and its pain.

'Mother!'

Once they had found somewhere more private to sit, Vita insisted her mother tell her story first. She had pieced together most of it already from what Lucius and Agrippa had said. But her eyes widened when she heard how, led by Leander, a small group of runaways had rescued her from Agrippa's villa at first light that morning. Vita half hoped she might escape recounting the worst parts of her own adventure in return. There was so much about it that was bound to horrify Mother; make her ashamed of her too.

But when finally the time came, the words poured from her unchecked, like a river in full flood. The dreadful discovery of Father's body; the humiliation of being forced to work as a slave at the training school; the sheer terror of feeding the beasts and then needing to find every last drop of courage to fight alongside Brea and Col in the arena. But though her mother was clearly shocked at first, the more Vita told her, the more her eyes filled with a mix of amazement and pride.

As Vita revealed her final conversation with Agrippa and the fate he had intended for them after Father's death, her mother gave a shuddering groan.

'Mother? Are you all right?'

She looked back at Vita, her eyes filling with fresh tears. 'Oh, Daughter! And to think you were destined to become that monster's wife.' She shook her head then drew in a breath. 'Truth be told, I found it hard to accept what Felix told your father, that Agrippa had lied about saving his life on the battlefield. But your father believed him – and it seems he was right to do so. Though neither of us could ever have guessed what reprisal that serpent would take when your father called the betrothal off.' She pressed a hand to her mouth, stifling another sob.

Vita's eyes widened. So it was Felix who'd told Father the truth about what had happened after the battle. Agrippa hadn't known it was him – that much was clear from his accusation of Taran last night. But he'd used what people thought about runaways to make Felix the chief suspect in Father's murder, linking him by name to the crime and having his bracelet planted at the scene. And from what Taran said it seemed clear now too that he'd had the steward murdered. She felt a fresh pang of guilt at her own willingness, like so many others, to believe the accusations against him, when all he'd done was to try and protect her and her family against Agrippa and his deceitful ways.

Afterwards, when Vita had shared what she now knew to be the truth of things, the pair of them shed more tears and sat for a long time, arms around each other, lost in their own thoughts.

To give them the time and space they needed, Leander had taken Lucius and Col off to hunt for frogs in a nearby pool, while Festa went to seek fresh clothes for Vita and prepare a meal. Now, as she called them to eat, Vita cleared her throat and spoke again.

'It is not right that Festa is our slave.'

What she really wanted to say was that it wasn't right for any person to be treated as another's possession. She understood the terrible truth now of what cruelty and hardship it could bring. The loss of family, friendships, a way of life. And freedom. The freedom to do what you wanted and be who you wanted to be – or at least to try. But she held her tongue, fearing that at this moment, it would be too much for her mother to hear.

She waited for her to object, but to her surprise her mother nodded instead.

'I have already told Festa she is free to lead her life as she wishes. She has accepted her freedom but says she wants to come with us.'

'Back to town?'

'No. To your uncle's house across the sea in Gaul. I cannot stay here, Vita. Not after all that has happened.' She shook her head and looked off into the distance again, blinking back fresh tears.

Vita's chest tightened. Gaul. It was so far away! She glanced at her mother's pale cheeks and line-etched eyes and let out a sigh. After everything that had happened, perhaps she was right...

A sudden shout went up behind them. As she twisted round, a group of weary-looking men and women in smoke-blackened clothes stumbled into the clearing, an assortment of weapons gripped in their hands – swords, spears, spike-covered clubs, even a trident or two.

Vita's mother clutched her arm. 'Who are they, Daughter?'

Vita stiffened. 'I...I don't know.'

But then, as the camp-dwellers flocked around them, embracing them and calling them by name, her doubt fell away. The rebels! Taking in a breath, Vita leapt to her feet and sped towards them. As she drew closer, she spotted Leander and Col weaving in between them and a huddle of other more nervous-looking folk – men, women, children too – who she guessed must be former slaves. She hurried over to join them.

'Is there any sign?'

Leander shook his head. 'Not yet. But there are more coming through.' As he pointed to the start of the secret path they had followed across the marsh last night, another group emerged from between the clumps of tall grasses, some nursing wounds, all looking dazed and exhausted. She scanned the dirty faces, but neither Brea nor Taran were among them. And as Leander went from person to person, it was clear from the shake of their heads they hadn't seen them either.

Gradually the flow of people reduced to a trickle then dried up completely. A knot formed in Vita's stomach. They weren't here, which meant they'd either been captured – or worse . . .

She drew in a long, juddering breath. But as she turned back towards the clearing, a sharp bark rang out behind her. She spun round to see Col haring off down the path.

She shot a puzzled look at Leander.

He lifted his shoulders and frowned. 'A deer?'

Raising a hand to her eyes, Vita peered after the wolf again.

But it wasn't a deer . . .

'It's them!'

Leander's eyes widened. 'What?'

'Look!' She pointed to where Col was now busy leaping

in circles around two approaching figures. A tall broad-shouldered man, one arm in a sling, and supporting him as best she was able, a blue-painted woman with dusty grey snakes for hair.

※※ XXXI ※※

Much later, after they had eaten and Vita had changed into the clean patched tunic Festa had found her, she and Leander made their way to Taran's shelter.

He hoisted himself up off the pile of marsh-grass he'd been lying on as they approached. 'Greetings, comrades. Brea is off with her wolf getting cleaned up. She'll be back soon enough. Come.' He beckoned for them to join him. And now, as his voice broke the late-afternoon stillness, Vita remembered where she'd heard it before. Of course! The leader of the actors – the one who'd asked Janus for the jug of wine . . .

They sat cross-legged facing him. As Taran slid his right arm, wincing, back into the sling, Vita's stomach knotted.

It was made from a strip of filthy woollen fabric, but she could see now in amongst the dirt what she hadn't noticed before. Patches of scarlet and the glint of gold embroidered thread.

Noticing her gaze, Taran lifted his arm and gave a bitter-sounding laugh. 'The Eagle-man fought bravely, I will give him that.' His face, still grimy from the fire, took on a distant look as if remembering.

Vita shivered and turned her head away. Justice had been done, but it was not the sort Father would have looked for. Still, at least Agrippa had had the chance to fight back.

She swallowed and turned to face him again.

'Did the rebels win?'

He frowned. 'We freed those who wanted to be freed. But there are too many who have let the ones in charge make slaves of their hearts as well as their bodies. As for dealing a blow to those who call themselves their masters, it is like scratching the face of a giant.' He shook his head and let out a sigh. 'Their power is too much now. I was foolish to think otherwise. Even in our great queen's day, her victories were only fleeting.' Pressing his lips into a hard, tight line, he yanked a piece of marsh-grass from the pile and set about shredding it between soot-stained fingers.

Vita's heart jolted. 'You mean the hare-queen?'

Taran flicked his gaze back on her and nodded. Then, before she could ask any more questions, he cleared his throat and spoke the words of a song.

'Fairer than swan.
Swifter than eagle.
Stronger than bear.
Braver than wolf . . .'

He shook his head again and glanced away grimacing.

Vita hesitated. Then, pulling back her shoulders, she drew in a breath and carried on.

'Friend of the downtrodden,
defender of right.
She let her hare guide her,
show her the way . . .'

Taran's eyes flashed with a sudden dark fire. 'How does the daughter of an Eagle-man know these words?'

She blinked and tucked a loose curl behind her ear. 'Brea taught me. She said the one who made them knew the queen. But . . .' She frowned. 'That can't have been you, you're too young.'

Taran gave a weary-sounding laugh. 'Why, thank you! Though I feel like an old man with all these cuts and bruises.' He shifted into a more comfortable position before going on. 'The words aren't mine, that's true. But

Brea learnt the song from me. I am of the queen's tribe – the Iceni – though most of them are slaves or farmers now, not the proud warriors they once were.' He puffed out a breath and tossed the piece of grass away, then fixed Vita with a fierce stare. 'But it is important for her to know it. To understand how brave her ancestors were.'

Vita frowned. The wolf-woman had said she was from north of the wall, not the flatlands in the east where the Iceni lived. She threw a questioning glance at Leander, but he returned it with a shrug.

Taran studied her thoughtfully for a moment then carried on. 'I can see you do not follow me yet. Well, let me tell you a story of my own. When I was little more than a boy – twenty summers ago now – the Eagle-men came to my village like they did later to Brea's, and forced me and others like me to join their army. Our commander treated us like slaves and I spent all the time in those first few years thinking of ways to escape. But then fortune smiled on us. He met with the sharp end of a warrior's spear and was replaced by a new commander – a brave man who led from the front and expected us to fight as hard as any Roman legionary, but who treated us fairly in return.' He shot her a knowing look. 'I think you have guessed his name already?'

Vita's chest gripped. 'Marcus Tullius Verus!'

Taran nodded. 'You know the truth now of what really took place that day on the battlefield. And why I too had cause to be avenged against the man who claimed to be your father's friend.'

Before Vita could reply, Leander cut in. 'But what happened after?'

'I was rescued by the local tribespeople and brought back to health by their wise man.' Taran touched a hand to the scar on his face as he spoke the words. 'I lived there with them for many years. Found a woman too. But when she and our child died of sickness, I had a longing to be with my own people again. So I took my leave and journeyed south.'

'And then?'

Taran's expression darkened again. 'A farmer who'd agreed to shelter me for the night betrayed me to the soldiers of a local fort. They sold me and another "runaway" they'd captured – the one you call Felix, though his real name was Cadoc – to the master of a band of travelling gladiators. It is where I met Brea too, though neither of us knew the Eagle-man in each of our stories was one and the same. Not until yesterday when she told me she had finally learnt his name.'

Vita shook her head. 'But I don't understand. How did Brea end up at Otho's training school?'

Taran heaved a sigh. 'My friend Cadoc and I made a plan to escape. We took Brea with us, but we lost her in the dark and she was recaptured and sold on again when the gladiator group arrived in Londinium. I am not sure she has quite forgiven me yet.' He threw them a rueful smile then went on. 'We tracked her to the training school and set up camp in the marshes with a new plan to free her and all the others sold into slavery too. Our army grew and . . . Well, you know the rest.' He gestured at the wounded being tended nearby. 'It was Cadoc who told me Agrippa was here in Londinium. He made the discovery after he took up his post as steward in your father's household.'

Vita's fingers balled into fists. 'You mean, to spy on us!'

Taran shot her a grim smile. 'To gather information, yes.'

'Would you have killed my father if he had found out?'

He put his head on one side and studied her for a moment. 'I can see his spirit shines on in you.'

Her eyes stung with fresh tears. But as she made to look away, a hand gripped her arm. 'It was never part of our plan to harm him. Verus was a good man. I knew that from my time serving with him. And Cadoc said the same. It was why, when he realized who your father's Eagle-man "brother" was, he wanted to share the truth with him – how he did not deserve that gold hero's trophy he wore round his neck. Though he could never have guessed what would follow. For your father, and himself as well.' Taran shook his head and let out another sigh.

Leander threw her an I-told-you-so look.

Vita's chest tightened. 'What happened to him? Felix – I mean, Cadoc?'

The muscles in Taran's cheek twitched. He shook his head slowly.

Vita shivered. 'I am sorry.'

'He was an honourable man. Your father too.'

She swallowed against the lump in her throat. He was right. And the complete opposite of Agrippa. A man so full of pride and so fearful of losing the name of hero he was prepared to go to any lengths to protect it, even though it had never rightly been his. She shivered and glanced back at Taran. Father would have been completely opposed to what this rebel leader and his followers had tried to do. But perhaps, if they'd had the chance to meet again, he might at least have understood his reasons for making a stand.

Taran adjusted his sling and lay back against the pile of marsh-grass with a groan.

Vita darted Leander a look. 'We should go. We can come back later when you and Brea have rested.'

'Wait!' Taran signalled for them to sit again. 'You have not yet heard the final part of my story. About Brea and her ancestors.'

Vita's breath caught in her throat. She leant forward, eager to hear more.

'You have seen the hare on her ankle?'

She nodded.

'It is well drawn, but when I first saw it two summers back, that is not the reason it caught my eye. I had seen it before, you see. On someone else.'

Vita's heart gave a quick flutter. 'Who?'

'An old woman who, by the time I met her, was already close to her life's end. She was of our people – the Iceni – but had spent most of her life away from her homeland. It was only after her spirit gave the sign it would soon be leaving her that she decided to bring her story home.'

Leander leant forward now too. 'What was it – her story?'

'She told how as a girl, she was there alongside our queen and her army at every great battle they fought, including the one here in Londinium when the queen burnt the Eagle-men's people from their homes.' Taran jerked his head in the direction of the town. 'And how after the last battle, the one where the Eagle-men finally beat back our tribe, she managed to escape when so many, including our brave queen, perished.'

Vita's skin prickled. 'What did she do after that?'

'She travelled north, sleeping in ditches and caves and scavenging for food, until at last she entered the lands of the Brigantes. A local chief's wife took pity on her and gave her shelter. She felt safe with them and after a while she married a man from the tribe and had a daughter of her own. The baby's father was Brigantes, but the woman wanted the child to have something to remember her and her own mother by. So, when she was nearly full grown, she arranged for them both to be marked with the sign of the hare.'

Vita's chest tightened. 'Who were they?'

Taran's eyes narrowed. 'The child was Brea's mother. The old woman, the one who came back to our tribe to die, she was Brea's grandmother.'

'Does Brea know?'

'Yes.' A pale-skinned figure in a grey tunic and breeches stepped out from behind the shelter, her long hair – freed from its plaits and freshly washed – the same silver-blonde colour now as the fur of the wolf at her side.

Taran rolled his eyes and gave a mock frown. 'Trust a hunter to steal up on her poor unsuspecting prey.'

Brea arched her eyebrows. 'You should not have let these two fool you into dropping your guard, comrade.'

He laughed. 'I have been telling them the story about your hare. Your friend here knew a little of it already. I have filled in more of the gaps, though not quite all.' He threw the wolf-woman a look that was hard to read.

She gave a clipped nod then turned her gaze on Vita. 'Taran has told you what end the spirit-stealer made?'

Vita drew in a breath and nodded.

'Good.' She reached down and stroked Col's head, then glanced back at Taran. 'When do we leave?'

'In the morning, as soon as we have packed up the camp. My spies tell me the Governor is set to be recalled from his wall-inspecting duties. His Eagle-men are busy clearing up the town, but it won't be long before they come after us. It is time for our comrades to seek a new home.'

Vita swallowed. 'Where will you go?'

The pair exchanged another quick look before Taran answered. 'We have a mission of our own across the sea.'

'What do you mean?'

Brea stared out across the marshes. 'To find Fyn.'

Vita jumped up and ran to her side. 'You know where he is?'

'Germania.'

'But how?'

Taran gave a small cough. 'One of Agrippa's men was persuaded to talk. He had served under the spirit-stealer at the time and offered to share what he knew in return for his life. A fair trade, you will agree.' He threw them a grim-faced smile, then sat up straight and sniffed at the air. 'Take me to where the smells of food are coming from, will you, boy? After so much talk I am hungrier than a bear fresh from a winter's sleep.' He thrust out his good arm and signalled for Leander to help him stand.

As the pair made their way slowly across the clearing, Vita turned back to face her friend. 'I . . . I thought I might never see you again.'

The wolf-woman fixed her with a steady green gaze. 'The Horned One must have heard your prayers.'

'I am glad.'

'I am too.'

Vita heaved out a breath. 'I'm sorry. For not telling you the truth before, about who I really was, I mean . . .'

Brea pressed her lips together then gave a quick nod. 'You had already proved yourself our friend and that is what counts. Is it not so, Col?'

The wolf gave a small yip of agreement. Vita bent to pat him, cheeks flushing. As she lifted up again, her eye snagged on the hare above Brea's left ankle. She frowned.

'What did Taran mean about not telling quite all of your hare's story?'

Brea's face took on a closed look. 'It is not for now. I will tell you some other day. Here, I have something for you.'

'What is it?'

'You will see.' Reaching inside the sleeve of her tunic, she fished out a small object and pressed it into Vita's hand.

Her heart lurched as she stared at the bronze owl-key nestled in her palm. She glanced up at Brea in wonder. 'But how—?'

'After I joined up with Taran and the others, we came back to the arena. Nine-Fingers tried to stop us. He is Eight-Fingers now.' She gave a snort. 'The one called Janus fled in fear, but not before I ripped the night-hunter from around his neck.'

Vita ran a fingertip over the bird's tiny jet-black eyes and pressed it to her chest. 'Thank you.'

The wolf-woman nodded. 'I know it is precious to you. The gifts from those we love and have lost always are.'

Vita gave a sudden start. 'Wait! I have something for you too.'

She dug down inside the neck of her own tunic until she found what she was looking for. 'To keep you and Col safe on your journey.' She pulled the firestone free and held it out to Brea.

The wolf-woman's eyes widened, then shone with sudden tears. Taking it from her, she held it to the light and murmured a word Vita didn't understand. Then whistling to Col, she looped her arm through Vita's and they set off together towards the distant chatter of voices and the welcoming glow of the fire.

❧ XXXII ❧

The next morning, Londinium was like a different city as Vita and her mother, accompanied by Leander, picked their way one final time towards their old home. Although the larger stone buildings – the temples and the Forum – were still standing, it was clear from the piles of blackened rubble and smoking timbers in the surrounding streets that the fires had done their worst.

But Vita's heart lifted when at the corner of their own street her mother called back to her. 'Daughter! It is still there! Look.' She pointed to a row of smoke-damaged houses up ahead. 'We may yet salvage something to take with us on our journey.'

As they neared the house, though, it became plain from

the mess of clothes and other belongings strewn across the street outside that thieves had got there before them. They waited anxiously at the door while Leander made a quick scout of the rooms. He returned a few moments later, his face pulled into a frown.

'There is no one, but much has been damaged or taken.'

Vita's mother gave a choked cry. 'Let me see.' She pushed past him and hurried off into the gloom.

He made to follow, but Vita held him back. 'I'll go.' She set off after her, but pulled up short as she reached the study door. If the thieves had been in here too, she couldn't bear it. Swallowing hard, she pushed it open.

Her stomach gripped at the sight that met her eyes: Father's desk and chair both overturned, his papers torn and trampled, and worst of all, countless precious scrolls scattered across the floor. But then, as she caught sight of the books sitting untouched on the higher shelves, her heart gave a small flutter of hope.

A soft pad of footsteps sounded behind her. Leander drew alongside, eyes widening as he gazed about the room.

'I have never been in such a place. What are these?' He gestured at the scrolls on the shelves.

'Books.'

'With stories inside?'

'Yes. And other things too. But the type with stories are my favourite.'

'Have you read them?'

'Not all, no.' Vita's throat squeezed at the sudden thought that now she never would.

Reaching up, Leander pulled one of the scrolls down and held it out to her. 'Will you teach me?'

She blinked and forced a smile. 'If you like.'

'I would like it very much. We are good friends, you and I.' He put his head on one side and looked at her, then nodded as though deciding something. 'I think it is time.'

'Time for what?'

'That I told you my real name.' He threw another look at the scroll, then drew in a breath and met her gaze. 'Hani. My name is Hani.'

'Hani.' She listened to the sound the letters made. 'It is a good name. A strong name.'

'It was my father's. And his before him. In our people's tongue it means "happy".' His eyes clouded suddenly. 'It is the only thing I have now from my land.'

'Your land?'

'The Romans call it Arabia. It is dry and hot and the sun shines there much more than it rains. Not like here.' He pulled a face and gave a pretend shiver.

This time when Vita smiled, it was for real. He offered her the scroll again. She took it and scanned the title. '*The Odyssey*. It is a good choice. The story of a brave man who went to war and then spent many years and many adventures finding his way back home.'

The boy's face filled with a look of wonder. 'Did he make it?'

'That would be telling.' Vita shot him a mischievous glance then slid the scroll into her sack, and gave a small bow. 'Thank you, Hani.'

He frowned. 'What for?'

'Rescuing us.'

'Helping is better. Like you said the first day we met, you didn't need rescuing. But you are welcome anyway. Perhaps you will pay me back with that story?' He tipped his head at the sack.

She laughed. 'Agreed! But now, would you mind seeing if Mother is all right? There is something I have to do on my own.'

After he had gone, she took a final look around her, then turned and stepped back out into the passage. As she approached the door to her room, her heart beat faster, fearful of what she might find. Sure enough, the thieves had done their worst here too – the bed stripped bare, the mattress slashed and spilling straw, and her clothes-chest thrown open, what remained of the contents flung across the floor. They weren't what she had come for though . . .

Darting over to the bed, she dropped to her knees and reached beneath it. At first her fingers found nothing except empty space. But then, reaching again . . . Yes . . . there!

With a heart-swoop of joy, she pulled the box from its hiding place and set it down on what was left of the mattress. She gazed at it for a moment, fingers stroking the smooth, polished surface. Then, pulling the owl-key from her tunic, she slotted it into the keyhole, turned it and lifted up the lid.

The contents were all there as she'd left them – the papyrus scroll; the glass bottle filled with thick black ink; the pens; the wax tablet and stylus too. A sudden memory of her feast-day bubbled up. The words Father had spoken as he'd given the box to her – his last precious gift . . .

You have a talent for words, Little Owl. You must be sure not to waste it . . .

She closed her eyes and pressed her hand to her chest.

I won't disappoint you, Father, I promise.

Taking the scroll from the box, she scored a piece from it with the stylus. Then, opening the bottle, she loaded her pen with ink and after a little while of thinking, began to write. When she'd finished, she slipped the square of papyrus up her sleeve and stowed the box safely inside the sack.

She was about to go and find the others when her eye caught on something poking from beneath a crumpled tunic on the floor. As she bent to pick it up, her chest tightened.

It was her poem. The one about the hare-queen. Uncurling it, she took a deep breath and began to read.

But the more she read, the more she knew in her heart that the old Vita might have been happy with such a story, but she wasn't that person any more. She had another to tell now – a truer and better one. She just needed to find the right words. And the right people to hear it . . .

By the time they arrived back at the camp the sun was already halfway to noon. But the clearing was empty now, the only sign people had been there a few scorched patches of earth and a scattering of dead marsh-grass.

Vita's stomach knotted. Where were they? Taran had promised they'd wait for them. But then, as she scanned about, fear mounting, a high-pitched laugh rang out from the far side of the clearing, followed by a loud yipping cry.

'There they are, look!' Hani pointed to where three figures sat on a log, a small boy and a silver-furred wolf playing tag in front of them.

As Festa hurried to Vita's mother's side, Taran and Brea rose too. The rebel leader surveyed them with a frown. 'It is late, friends. We must go now or we will not make the coast by nightfall.'

Vita's mother set down the sack she was carrying and took a step forward. 'We thank you for waiting and for all you have done to help us.'

Taran gave a clipped bow. 'It is a pleasure, Lady. Your husband was an honourable man, and though ours was not the Roman way of doing justice, the ones who took his life have paid for it.'

She gave a small shiver then nodded. 'When we arrive at my brother's house I will write to the Governor to tell him the truth of what Agrippa did. And I will be sure to mention your bravery and that of your friends too.' She nodded at Brea and Hani, then turned back to Taran. 'Tell me, might we pay our respects at my husband's burial place before we leave? It is not too far from here.'

'I am sorry. There is no time.'

She dipped her head. 'I understand.' She turned back to Vita and Lucius. 'Come, my children. We must gather our things for the journey ahead.'

'Wait, Mother! I have something I want to give you first.' Vita slid the piece of papyrus from her sleeve and pressed it into her hands.

Her mother gave a puzzled-looking frown. 'What is this, Daughter?'

'For a memorial stone, when we reach Uncle's house in Gaul.'

Vita's mother scanned the words. When she looked up again, her eyes were bright with tears.

Lucius tugged on her gown. 'What does it say, Mother? What has Vita put?'

She dabbed at her cheeks and drew in a breath. 'She has written that your father Marcus Tullius Verus was a just and honourable man. That his name will live on in our memories. And that his family loved him more than words can say . . .' She rolled the papyrus up and smiled at Vita. 'It is beautiful, Vita. Your father would have thought so too. You know how proud he was of you. Of your writing also. He was right to encourage you in it. You have real skill. We will make our offerings to his spirit before the stone carved with your words instead.'

She pulled her into a quick hug then turned away, lips trembling, and busied herself with fastening the ties on Lucius's cloak.

Vita picked up the sack containing her writing-box and walked over to where Brea stood apart, looking eastwards out across the flooded marshland, Col at her side.

As she drew near, the wolf-woman pulled an object from beneath her cloak. Vita ground to a halt. It was Agrippa's torc. She shuddered at the sight of the dirt-smeared gold band. But what would she do with it? As if in answer, Brea reached back her arm and flung it out across the water. For a moment, the torc seemed to hang in the air like a gold coiled snake preparing to strike, then it plunged beneath the peaty-black surface and was gone.

Brea turned at her approach. 'You saw?'

Vita nodded.

'It was my offering to the Horned One for the defeat of our enemy.'

They watched together as a grey heron, disturbed by the noise, lifted into the air and flew off in the direction of the river, then Vita gave a small cough. 'You must come back to my uncle's house when you have found Fyn. All of you, including Col, of course.' She bent down and ruffled the wolf's ears.

The wolf-woman flashed her a smile. 'Thank you, but we will go home to our people.' She jerked her head to where Hani stood deep in discussion with Taran. 'The boy says he will go with you though. Maybe stay a while if you would like it?'

As Vita glanced back at him, her chest filled with a warm glow. 'I would, very much.'

'As for Taran, once a warrior always a warrior.'

'Like your ancestor the hare-queen, you mean?'

Brea's eyes sparked with sudden fire. 'Who told you that?'

Vita met her gaze. 'No one exactly. But your grandmother is from her tribe. And Taran told me she had the mark of the hare made on herself and your mother also, in memory of her own. I remembered after how in the song, the queen let her hare show her the way . . . I didn't understand what that meant. I still don't now. But I know the hare was special to her too.'

Brea frowned. 'I always said you were quick-witted. But I cannot lie to you. What you guess at is true.'

Vita's heart quickened. 'But what about the hare?'

Brea stared out into the marsh again. 'The Romans said that the queen had a tame hare. That she kept it close to her and before a battle she would release it to see which way it would go. If it ran towards the enemy then it was a bad omen. But if it ran towards her own army then she knew they would win.' She gave a loud snort and shook her head. 'Another story they told about her to make her and her victories seem smaller. But that was not it. The hare-spirit *lived* in her. Guided her to do what was right in defence of her people.'

'I think the hare-spirit is strong in you too.'

The wolf-woman frowned again. 'Perhaps. My grand-mother was the queen's youngest daughter. Despite what the Eagle-men choose to believe, she escaped their death-blows. My mother may have told my father this. I do not know. But if she did, he kept her secret safe, even from me and Fyn. Though had he lived, perhaps one day he would have sung us the story.' She gave a sigh.

'So how did you find out?'

'From Taran, when he asked how I got this.' She tilted her ankle to show the hare. 'But he said it was best that no one else knew. If the Eagle-men found out, they would use it against me. March me through the streets as they have done to other enemies of noble blood, and mock our queen's name all over again. It is why, when you asked me what had happened to her daughters, I did not want to say.'

'That one of them had survived?'

The wolf-woman nodded. The pair of them stood in silence for a moment, then Brea turned to face her again.

'Thanks to the blessings of the Horned God and the courage of good friends' – she threw Vita a meaningful look – 'my tale is not yet over. Yours either. But what will you do next? Now that you have found your mother and brother?'

Vita pondered the question. She had been many things these past few days. Daughter, sister, slave, actor. Even a gladiator of sorts. And if the gods allowed it, she would be other things too – perhaps one day even a wife and mother. But above all she was Vita, spinner of stories. Including her own . . .

'I want to be a . . .' Vita searched for the word in Brea's tongue and failed. 'It is "writer" in Latin.'

Brea shrugged. 'I do not know that word.'

'A storyteller. It is what I have always dreamt of being. I can be me when I write. Do anything; go anywhere.'

Brea nodded. 'Perhaps you will sing our story one day? But if so, do not forget about your friend the bear.' She flashed Vita another smile. Then, with a quick whistle to

Col, she turned and strode back towards where the others were readying themselves to leave.

Vita looked after them for a bit. Then, reaching into the sack, she pulled out the writing-box and hugged it to her chest. When the time came, she would do justice to them – all of them. To Brea and Col. To Hani and Festa. To Taran, Cadoc and the rebels too. And one day she would take her words to the Emperor's court and tell them there as well, so that everyone would know the truth.

Putting the box back in the sack, she reached for the owl-key and pressed it to her lips.

But before that, Minerva, I will write of my father, Marcus Tullius Verus, and with your help, make him live again through my words.

A warm hand touched her arm. Vita turned to see Hani smiling back at her.

'Ready?'

Slipping the key inside her tunic, she pulled back her shoulders and nodded.

She was ready. Ready for the next part of their story, and the adventures that lay ahead of them across the shining sea.

HISTORICAL NOTES

I do love watching a good 'swords and sandals' epic on the big screen! Two of my favourites are the Hollywood classic *Spartacus*, and Ridley Scott's *Gladiator*.

Both feature plenty of bravery, heroism and sacrifice, plus the blood, sweat and brutality of gladiatorial combat in the Roman arena. However, the gladiator heroes in both films are men, with the women consigned to supporting roles as slaves, wives or girlfriends.

But women fought in the amphitheatres of the Roman Empire too, and when I saw a photograph of a carved stone relief in the British Museum of 'Achillia' and 'Amazon', two female gladiators (or *gladiatrices* as they are called now), my story whiskers began to twitch. Further research fanned the spark and led to the creation of my two young heroes, Vita and Brea.

Ancient Rome was the heart of the Empire, but when I learnt that Roman London (*Londinium*) had its own arena – the remains of which were discovered in the late 1980s – I knew this was where Vita and Brea's battle for truth and justice should take place. And what better time to set it than during the reign of the famous emperor Hadrian, the man responsible for the great wall stretching eighty miles across the far north of Britannia.

BRITANNIA, LONDINIUM AND ROME

My story is set in 125 CE, some 180 years after Julius Caesar's first invasion of Britain. As the Romans set about attempting its conquest, a number of the resident Celtic British tribal rulers made pacts with Rome and the greater part of southern Britain came under Roman influence. The revolt led by Boudicca, queen of the Iceni tribe, in 60 or 61 CE, during which her forces burnt Londinium to the ground, proved a shock to the Roman army. But after several notable successes, her eventual defeat and death heralded the consolidation of Roman power. By the time Hadrian became Emperor in 117 CE, much of the land was firmly under Roman control. But the tribes in the far north continued, successfully, to resist any attempt at occupation – echoed in the backstory of Vita's father and her future husband Agrippa, both of whom had campaigned with the famous Legio IX Hispana in the 'Northlands'.

Londinium, which Hadrian visited in 122 CE, was the provincial capital and home to the Governor, the Emperor's representative, appointed to rule Britannia on his behalf. With a population – in the early to mid second century CE – of around 45,000, combining Romanized Britons and people from provinces across the Empire, it was an exciting, cosmopolitan place to be. But the privileged and comfortable life Vita and her family enjoy at the start of my story was not typical of the majority, especially those outside the capital. Most, like Brea's people, would continue to live in the roundhouses of their ancestors until the end of the Roman period and beyond.

At the time *Vita and the Gladiator* is set, the city was home to many grand new public buildings, including a huge forum-basilica complex, where councillors and magistrates like Vita's father met to make decisions and enact justice.

Around the year 125 CE, a timber amphitheatre for gladiatorial games was rebuilt in a combination of wood and stone, with a capacity of somewhere between 5,000 to 7,000 people. It was a venue for wild animal fights, executions and, of course, gladiatorial combats. In recreating it, I have tried to be as faithful as possible to what is known of its structure and layout, making only minor modifications in the interests of the story. There is currently no archaeological evidence of a gladiatorial training school (*ludus*) in Londinium, but it is plausible one existed. I like to think it's only waiting to be uncovered!

SLAVES, GLADIATORS AND ACTORS

Roman society was class-based. The *Patrician* and *Senatorial* classes sat at the top, followed by the *Equestrian* classes and the *Plebeians*, which included people from a range of professions – from plumbers and farmers to teachers and architects. Members of these classes were all *citizens*, which entitled them to rights in relation to governance, law and property. But women's rights were more restricted than men's. For example, they couldn't vote.

Next were the *freedmen* and *freedwomen* – slaves who had managed to buy their own freedom or been freed by their former masters, as in the case of Festa, who is eventually freed by Vita's mother.

Finally, at the bottom, came the *slave class*. Slaves, like those working in Vita's household and in Otho's gladiator school, were the property of their masters and could be bought and sold at will. They couldn't hold citizenship and had no rights of their own. Though many were treated well, the less fortunate were often whipped and mistreated. As a result, some slaves made a bid for freedom, like Taran's marsh rebels in my story. If caught, such 'runaways' could expect a whipping at the very least, to be branded with a hot iron or, in the worst case, even killed.

The enslavement of people in the territories the Roman army conquered was a key contributor to the creation, expansion and long-lasting nature of the Roman Empire and slaves were used in every part of society and the economy. Prisoners-of-war might be forced to work in the mines as slaves or else sold to become *gladiators*. Outside the arena, gladiators themselves were considered the lowest of the low; besides enemy captives, others were criminals sentenced either to die by the sword (*damnati ad gladium*) – which meant, if lucky, they might be granted a limited stay of execution by fighting in the arena – or condemned to the games (*damnati ad ludos*). For these more fortunate ones, if they acquired the necessary skills and fought well, they could make a career of being a gladiator and might eventually win their freedom, like Otho. Others included slaves accused of being unruly, or debtors who sold themselves to the gladiator school to help pay off the money they owed. And then there were the volunteers (the *auctorati*), those who fought for financial reward or sought glory in the ring.

Though they existed, female gladiators were very rare. The thought of a woman fighting in the arena was a shocking reversal of the ideal of the Roman matron – decent, beautiful and devoted to her husband and family. Vita, like most other girls of her class, was destined to conform to this once she became Agrippa's wife. As a result, gladiatrices really drew the crowds. Some women, like their male counterparts, took up the role of a *venatrix*, or beast-hunter, a good fit for my native British character, Brea, used to hunting in the hills around her northern home.

All gladiators swore a solemn oath on entering the gladiator school. This was known as the *sacramentum gladiatorum*. Taking it meant that they agreed to being 'burnt by fire, bound in chains, beaten and killed by the sword' as their master (the manager of the school, or *lanista*) commanded.

There were different categories of gladiator, each with their own style of weapon and fighting gear. For example Otho, in his fighting days, was a Thracian (or *Thraex* – with a small shield and a curved dagger), while Cronos is a *provocator*, a 'heavy', fighting with a sword, large shield and a decent amount of armour. Though *provocatores* usually fought each other, most others were matched with another type of fighter, with different armour and equipment, to ensure a more exciting contest for spectators.

Despised outside the arena, inside it the gladiators were respected and often worshipped as heroes – the Roman equivalent of our modern-day celebrity sports stars, with stage names to match. Cronos the 'Skull-Crusher' and Brea's stage name of 'Lupa' are examples I had fun inventing for the story.

The games seem very barbaric to us today, but values were different in Roman times. The arena was the place where imperial justice was seen to be served and a sense of order reinforced – a reminder of the power of the Emperor in Rome and the meaning and worth of Roman citizenship.

Plays were another very popular form of entertainment. Like gladiators, *actors* were definitely third-class citizens, in their case both on stage and off. Vita is all too aware of this when the actor playing Theseus singles her out as his

Ariadne, but later on in the story, taking a part in her own play proves key, as readers will know.

REBELS AND WARRIORS

The Roman Empire owed its success to the discipline, organization and fighting skills of the Roman army: legionary soldiers like Vita's father and Agrippa (though – spoiler alert – he proves the opposite of a hero by the story's end); and members of the auxiliary forces which men like Taran and Brea's twin brother Fyn were conscripted into.

When they weren't engaged in military campaigns, soldiers built and manned forts, constructed roads and walls (including Hadrian's Wall) and kept the peace in the conquered territories. As previously mentioned, in Britannia, Boudicca and her army of what I have the Romans call 'Blue-faces' had been a notable adversary. And though the Roman army made several attempts to subdue and conquer the territories of the Caledonian tribes (now part of modern-day Scotland), in the end they resorted to wall-building to define the northernmost limit of their power.

They were fearful too of slave revolts, keen to avoid the repetition of a major rebellion like the one led by the famous gladiator-slave Spartacus in 73 BCE. Thanks to a piece of serendipity, I discovered that a significant part of Londinium had burnt down a second time at some point not long after Hadrian's visit, most likely between 125 CE and 130 CE. The exact cause of the 'Hadrianic Fires', as they're known, isn't clear. Some say they were the result of an accident, others of civil unrest, perhaps even a revolt of some kind. The roughly hacked-off head of a great bronze statue of the Emperor Hadrian, found in the River Thames near London Bridge in 1834, may support this idea. For me, the thought was storytelling gold and led to the exciting climax to the book.

GODS, MYTHS AND BEASTS

In addition to justice, storytelling is another important theme in the book – how stories are told, who gets to tell them and what their relationship is to the truth. Vita loves reading tales of heroes, gods and monsters. But during the course of the book, she learns from Brea, and in a more terrible way from Agrippa, that those who claim to give accounts of real-life events, whether written or spoken, are not always to be trusted.

It was common practice for people across the Empire to adopt the Roman gods, and to seek their favour and protection. Vita's personal favourite is Minerva, goddess of wisdom, justice and poetry, whose owl is the source of Vita's father's pet name for her. But she also prays to Fortuna, goddess of fate, fortune and luck, as gladiators would pray to her before heading out to fight. Meanwhile, there are several hints in the story that her intended husband, Agrippa, might be a follower of the mysterious Cult of Mithras, which revolved around the story of the god Mithras slaying a bull and was particularly popular with Roman soldiers and the aristocracy within the army.

Native British tribes such as Brea's would have had their own religion and mythology too; what we know of their beliefs mostly comes to us via the Romans, like the historian Tacitus. I have taken the lead of another author of stories set in Roman Britain – Rosemary Sutcliff – in imagining that one of the gods Brea's people worshipped was a god of the hunt – 'the Horned One' – a little bit of cheeky magpie thievery intended in homage to Sutcliff's brilliant story *The Eagle of the Ninth*.

Animals were significant for tribes like Brea's, not only as a means of survival, but also for their spiritual importance. In contrast, the Romans pitched beasts against each other and against people in the arena as a way of demonstrating their control over nature. In Rome, these included exotic beasts such as elephants, leopards, lions and rhinos; in Britannia, native beasts such as bears, bulls and wild boar were used. Beast-trappers, often soldiers, would be sent out to catch and deliver them straight to the arena. In my story, the boar and bear are delivered to Otho's gladiator school first, so both the reader and Vita can get better acquainted with the danger these creatures represented.

MORE INFORMATION

READ:

I can highly recommend *The Eagle of the Ninth* by Rosemary Sutcliff, the story of Marcus, a young soldier who goes in search of the fate of his father's legion, IX Hispana. More recent books set in the Roman world include the *Roman Mysteries* series by Caroline Lawrence, and *Circus Maximus: Race to the Death*, the first in a trilogy of books by Annelise Gray, about Dido, a young charioteer in Ancient Rome.

Books which helped with my own research and which adult readers might want to check out include:

Roman Britain by Guy de la Bédoyère (Thames and Hudson Ltd, 2013)

Gladiator: The Roman Fighter's (Unofficial) Manual by Philip Matyszak (Thames and Hudson Ltd, 2011)

Londinium: London in the Roman Empire by John Morris (Weidenfeld & Nicolson, 1998)

The World of the Gladiator by Susanna Shadrake (The History Press, 2005)

Agricola and *Germania* by Tacitus, translated by Harold Mattingly, edited by James Rives (Penguin Classics, 2010)

The Roman Amphitheatre in Britain by Tony Wilmott
(The History Press, 2008)

PLACES TO VISIT:
Roman Amphitheatre at the Guildhall Art Gallery, London
View the excavated ruins of the amphitheatre in a stunning, purpose-built underground gallery; this area was the heart of the original Roman town of Londinium.

cityoflondon.gov.uk/things-to-do/attractions-museums-entertainment/londons-roman-amphitheatre

The London Mithraeum
Nearby, visitors can view a collection of remarkable Roman finds before descending into the excavated ruins of the underground temple of Mithras.

londonmithraeum.com

British Museum and Museum of London
Exhibits in the Roman gallery at the British Museum include the stone relief of Achillia and Amazon, the two gladiatrices who helped inspire my story.

britishmuseum.org

The Roman galleries at the Museum of London give an

idea of what life was like in Londinium during the Roman occupation: re-creations of rooms from a Roman house, mosaics, coins, jewellery and tombstones to some of Londinium's citizens.

museumoflondon.org.uk

Hadrian's Wall World Heritage Site

Besides walking along the wall itself, there is a whole host of museums and archaeological sites linked to this remarkable structure, including the remains of the forts, milecastles and military settlements attached to it.

My personal favourites include:

Chesters – the most complete remains of a Roman cavalry fort in Britain

Housesteads Roman Fort and Museum – substantial remains of a Roman fort, including barrack blocks, a hospital and latrines, and fascinating finds which give a flavour of a Roman soldier's life on the wall.

Both in the care of www.english-heritage.org.uk/visit/places/hadrians-wall

Also:

Vindolanda Fort and Museum and the Roman Army Museum – an important construction and garrison base for the wall. Its museum is home to an amazing collection of artefacts including the famous Vindolanda Tablets, amongst the oldest surviving handwritten documents in Britain.

vindolanda.com

Other sites of interest

There are many other Roman sites up and down the UK which help bring to life what it was like to live in Britain during the Roman occupation. Here are some of the ones I enjoyed visiting while researching my story:

Bignor Roman Villa – bignorromanvilla.co.uk

Butser Ancient Farm – butserancientfarm.co.uk
Includes archaeologically accurate re-creations of a Roman villa together with ancient British roundhouses of the sort Brea would have lived in

Chysauster Ancient Romano-British Settlement –
www.english-heritage.org.uk/visit/places/
chysauster-ancient-village

Fishbourne Roman Palace and Gardens –
sussexpast.co.uk/attraction/fishbourne-roman-palace

Silchester Roman City Walls and Amphitheatre –
www.english-heritage.org.uk/visit/places/
silchester-roman-city-walls-and-amphitheatre

ACKNOWLEDGEMENTS

Writing a book can be an uplifting, even a joyous thing, but, like a gladiatorial combat, there is plenty of blood, sweat and sometimes even the occasional bout of tears involved too. I'm very fortunate to have had so many people on my side during this outing into the arena, all of them ready to provide the coaching, sparks of inspiration and moral support that every writer – and gladiator – needs.

I'd like to share any palm leaves and cheers that might come my way for writing Vita and Brea's tale with all of them.

Firstly, patron-in-chief Barry Cunningham and the brilliant team at Chicken House Books. In particular my editor Kesia Lupo for her wise advice, gentle steering and consummate blade-work to make the story the best and sharpest it could be, Rachel Leyshon for beta reading, and Esther Waller for her calm and collected focus on the detail and reassurance of all last-minute doubts. And to Sue Cook for helping give the sword additional polish at the copy-edit stage. Also to Rachel Hickman – warrior-queen of brilliant book covers and plenty more besides – and to Jazz Bartlett Love, Olivia Jeggo and Laura Smythe for all their support in bringing Vita to a wider audience.

A huge thank you too, to Nan Lawson and Steve Wells for a dream illustration and design pairing that has given the book a cover to die for, though not, thankfully, in the gladiatorial sense!

A giant *gratias* to Anthony Smart at York St John's University for kindly agreeing to review the historical notes at the back of the book for accuracy (and to Gráinne Cassidy at the Classical Association for putting us in touch, and Melanie Jones at the Historical Association for facilitating). Also to author Annelise Gray for providing very helpful clarification on a couple of key points relating to the world my story is set in. I am extremely grateful for the generosity of their time and advice and should stress at this point that any errors are entirely my own.

A resounding cheer to fellow authors Patricia Elliott, Miriam Halahmy, Cath Howe, Sarah Lean, Sue Reid and Jeannie Waudby; and writing group buddies Jill Atkins, Lizzie Bryant, Cath Jones and Sharon Wigley who, when I first broached the idea for my story with them, encouraged me to get my game face on and head into the arena without delay! Also to my fellow Time Tunnellers, Susan Brown-rigg, Barbara Henderson, Catherine Randall and Jeannie (again!) for being on my side throughout. And to dear non-writing friends and family who have always been there to urge me on with their love and support.

Plus a stadium-sized shout to all the booksellers,

librarians and teachers who have supported getting my books into the hands of young readers since the publication of my first novel, *Black Powder*, nearly seven years ago.

Last but in no way least, to my greatest supporter of all, my husband, Steve, who has been at my side, through thick and thin, putting up patiently with my training regime and supplying much-appreciated battle tips and tactics whenever I've found myself in a tight spot. I couldn't have done it without you!

This book is dedicated to my two lovely nephews, Brendan and Kieran Clark – gladiators both. And to you dear reader, for being brave and daring enough to follow Vita and Brea into the arena and let your imagination fly.